PENGUIN CANADA

THE PALE INDIAN

ROBERT ARTHUR ALEXIE was born and raised in Fort McPherson in Canada's Northwest Territories. He became the Chief of the Tetlit Gwich'in of Fort McPherson, served two terms as vice-president of the Gwich'in Tribal Council, and was instrumental in obtaining a land claim agreement for the Gwich'in of the Northwest Territories. He now lives in Inuvik.

Also by Robert Arthur Alexie

Porcupines and China Dolls

The Pale Indian

A NOVEL

ROBERT ARTHUR ALEXIE

PENGUIN
CANADA

PENGUIN CANADA

Published by the Penguin Group

Penguin Group (Canada), 10 Alcorn Avenue, Toronto, Ontario, Canada M4V 3B2
(a division of Pearson Penguin Canada Inc.)

Penguin Group (USA) Inc., 375 Hudson Street, New York, New York 10014, U.S.A.
Penguin Books Ltd, 80 Strand, London WC2R 0RL, England
Penguin Ireland, 25 St Stephen's Green, Dublin 2, Ireland (a division of Penguin Books Ltd)
Penguin Group (Australia), 250 Camberwell Road, Camberwell, Victoria 3124, Australia
(a division of Pearson Australia Group Pty Ltd)
Penguin Books India Pvt Ltd, 11 Community Centre, Panchsheel Park, New Delhi — 110 017,
India
Penguin Group (NZ), Cnr Airborne and Rosedale Roads, Albany, Auckland, New Zealand
(a division of Pearson New Zealand Ltd)
Penguin Books (South Africa) (Pty) Ltd, 24 Sturdee Avenue, Rosebank, Johannesburg 2196,
South Africa

Penguin Books Ltd, Registered Offices: 80 Strand, London WC2R 0RL, England

First published 2005

1 2 3 4 5 6 7 8 9 10 (WEB)

Copyright © Robert Arthur Alexie, 2005

Editor: Cynthia Good

Manufactured in Canada.

LIBRARY AND ARCHIVES CANADA CATALOGUING IN PUBLICATION

Alexie, Robert Arthur
The pale Indian : a novel / Robert Arthur Alexie.

ISBN 0-14-301553-2

I. Title.

PS8551.L4739P35   2004   C813'.6   C2004-906921-7

Visit the Penguin Group (Canada) website at **www.penguin.ca**

*For those who have supported and encouraged me
in my journey through this life*

PROLOGUE

✧

The Indian sat alone on the weathered bench atop the riverbank in front of the small northern community and stared at the river and the hills and mountains to the west. He could have been any age between forty and sixty: his hair was completely white; his face, devoid of wrinkles, was dark from the summer sun.

The river spewed forth from the dark and ominous mountains like the tongue of an ancient serpent about to devour everything in its path. Its clear, cold water surged silently past the community on its never-ending journey to the Arctic Ocean. Winter was coming and soon the river would freeze. Even then, the river would run under the ice; nothing could stop it. It provided his people with a means to travel and with the fish they ate during the summer. But it also took from them. How many had they lost? And why? Had they done something wrong?

The hills and mountains were ablaze with colour: reds, oranges and yellows. It was as if the Old People had set fire to the land in anger. Or was it sorrow? Maybe it was shame. Maybe they set fire to the land to hide the secrets and lies their People carried. He had carried one for so long it hurt his head whenever he thought about it. *Why did he give it to me? I didn't want it. Did I do something wrong?*

The Indian looked up and was surprised to see the sun had set and darkness now enveloped the hills and mountains. He wondered how long he had been sitting there. Hours? Days? Years? Forever? He shivered in the coolness of the evening, then took a few steps into the river. He dipped his hand and drank as the water soaked his shoes. He peered into the night, then stepped further into the river and was devoured by the darkness.

And still the river flowed as it had since the last ice age. It was alive, but it had no conscience. It was merciless, but never malicious. It was just a river on a never-ending journey.

Chapter One

The land is located in Canada's Northwest Territories to the west of the Mackenzie River, a few hundred miles south of Inuvik and a hundred years northwest of Yellowknife. It is a beautiful land with tall-standing trees, wide open valleys, low rolling hills and majestic mountains. It is also harsh and unforgiving; temperatures can rise to thirty-five degrees Celsius under the midnight sun and drop to forty-five below during the long, dark winter months.

The most prominent feature in this land is the Blue Mountains—tall, dark and foreboding. From deep within these fabled mountains the Teal River gushes, and then meanders through low rolling hills and boreal forest before merging with the mighty Mackenzie River.

This is the land of the Blue People, or Indians. Prior to European contact they were hunters and gatherers, and did not have an easy life. Theirs was a daily struggle for survival, and starvation was not uncommon. They fished along the rivers in the summer, then moved into the hills to harvest caribou in the fall. Theirs was a nomadic existence: moving from the mountains to the rivers, from where game was scarce to where it was plentiful. For thousands of years, the People lived in the Blue Mountains, usually undisturbed. But things were about to change; the future was unfolding as it should.

The future arrived in the form of intruders, or newcomers. The first of these arrived in the summer of 1789: a white explorer by the name of Alexander Mackenzie. There were other explorers, but they are not important to our story.

The fur traders arrived soon after and brought goods that made the lives of the People easier. This group set up a trading post on the Teal River that would later become the community of Aberdeen. The traders also brought something else to the People: the fiddle and dances called jigs, square dances and waltzes that the People would soon adopt as their own, and for good reason.

That reason arrived in 1850: the missionaries. This group would have the greatest impact on the People, but no one knew it at the time.

In 1903, another group of people arrived: the North West Mounted Police, now called the Royal Canadian Mounted Police. They established a post in Aberdeen, enforced the white man's law and have never left.

In 1921, the last of the newcomers arrived: the Treaty Party. There's a lot of controversy about what was or wasn't in the Treaty, but most of this is not important to our story. What *is* important is that the government and the People agreed that the Treaty contained a clause that states: "His Majesty will pay the salaries of teachers to instruct the children of the said Indians in a manner deemed advisable by His Majesty's government."

Even back then the People realized the value of the white man's education and didn't make a big fuss about it; they just didn't realize how it would be done. They put their faith and trust in His

Majesty and His Majesty's government and believed that their "said children" would be cared for; they had no reason to think otherwise.

It should be noted that the missionaries, who had gained the trust of the People, were influential in persuading them to sign the Treaty despite the fact that none of the People knew how to read or write. What the People didn't know was that the church would be given the responsibility of educating their "said children." It sounds like patronage and is now a contentious issue, but that's beside the point. The point is that the lives of the Blue People, like the lives of all indigenous peoples in the North, were about to take an ass-kicking not seen since Custer got his kicked at Little Bighorn. Some say it was retribution for Custer's demise. Some say it was Manifest Destiny. Others say it was just the way things were.

Soon after the People put their Xs on the Treaty, the first mission boat arrived in Aberdeen and thirty-five children were herded out of the Blue Mountains and dragged off to mission school. It had begun, but no one knew what *it* was. *It* was a time of mission schools, residential schools and hostels. *It* was a time of assimilation, integration and cultural genocide. *It* was a time of change and a new and emerging North.

In this new and emerging North, another community—Helena—was established in the 1930s on the Mackenzie River to the east of Aberdeen. By the mid-1950s, Helena had a population of fifteen hundred and boasted a new hospital, a radio station, two hotels, two bars and two retail stores. The government also built a high school and two hostels: one for Catholics and one for Anglicans. Hostels—that's what the government decided to call the residential schools, which used to be called mission schools.

By this time, Aberdeen had two stores, a nursing station, a small government office, a three-man RCMP detachment, a power-generating plant and not much else. Tugs and barges still plied the Mackenzie and Teal rivers each summer, bringing in the annual supply of goods. Air travel was still a novelty, and the mail took a few weeks to get to and from Edmonton. Some say it still does.

There were fifty white people living in Aberdeen, and more arrived every year. They lived in stick-built houses with running water, washing machines and electric lights. They associated with the People, but only if absolutely necessary.

There were between four and five hundred of the People living in the Blue Mountains, hunting, fishing and trapping. They stayed in extended family units and looked after their parents and grandparents, and only came to town during Christmas, Easter and for part of the summer. They lived in log houses with wood stoves and had no running water or electric lights. They didn't associate with the whites and were never invited to.

In 1959, the government built a school and a hostel in Aberdeen. The school was separated from the hostel and administered by the government, which brought in white teachers from the south. It would be another ten years before the first Blue Indian became a teacher, but in Indian Time that's a million years.

The hostel, despite having a new name, wasn't very different from the mission schools and residential schools in that it was funded by government and administered by the church, which still brought in white people from the south to supervise the boys and girls. No one thought about hiring one of the People to supervise; instead, they hired them to work in the kitchen and clean up: menial work.

The People still brought their "said children" to the hostel in September. The children, like their parents and grandparents before them, were still herded into dorms where their hair was sheared and cut so they looked like porcupines and china dolls. They were still deloused, given identical clothes to wear, forced to line up for meals, for school, for bed and for almost everything else. They were also still forced to pray and forget what their parents had taught them about the Old People and the Old Ways.

For the record, another thing remained unchanged: In the dark recesses of the hostels, some things still went bump in the night, but no one talked about it. Talking about it meant talking against the men and women of God, and that's something you never did.

Something else also happened in the early 1960s in Canada: The government bestowed upon its status Indians, and that included most of the Blue People, the honour of becoming Canadian citizens in their own land. This meant, among other things, that they had the right to vote, hold public office, own property, own a business, serve in the armed forces and consume alcohol without fear of losing their Indian status. The government was right: The newly acquired rights did not take away the Indians' status. They took away a whole lot more.

Chapter Two

In 1946, at the age of six, William Daniel, like all Blue Indians at that age, was taken from his parents and sent to mission school, where he was taught to read, write, pray, work and become a law-abiding Christian Indian. He was also beaten, hit, slapped, tweaked, strapped and abused in ways he'd never talk about.

Ten years later, in 1956, when Elvis was shaking his pelvis to "That's Alright, Mama," William, now sixteen, returned to Aberdeen to learn that he'd become an orphan. He did the only thing he could: He became angry with the Powers That Be and got on with life. Getting on with life meant becoming a hunter and a trapper, which is what he did. He later married another graduate of that infamous institution: Elizabeth Brian. They would have two children: John in September 1960 and Eva in December 1965.

William was a good hunter and trapper, but he wanted a change and was given that opportunity in the early 1960s when the oil companies moved north. William, like most young Aboriginal men of the day, took a job as a labourer since the hours were shorter than they were on the trapline and the money was better, and it was guaranteed. This change also meant that his children would be spared the experience of having to go to the hostel, or residential school, which may or may not have been a blessing.

In 1970, Aberdeen was your typical northern community with a population between six and seven hundred; most were Blue Indians. The community had almost one hundred houses, and except for a few that belonged to the government and were used to house white government employees, most were made from logs and had no running water, but they did have electricity. The community still had two small retail stores, a school that went up to grade eight and a hundred-bed hostel.

At the time, one of only two ways into the community was by airplanes that landed on the river with floats in the summer and with skis in the winter. The other was by river, using boats in the summer and dog teams, or these new machines called snowmobiles, in the winter.

Alcohol, prior to this time, was a new commodity, but it was now becoming a problem, and very few people, if any, saw it as such. There was a dramatic increase in public drunkenness, assaults, neglect and abuse of all sorts, but most took this as normal.

One person who thought this new way of life was normal was William Daniel. William was a good worker. That meant he did as he was told and never talked back, which is what he had done in mission school. He also made good money and partied hard during his time off. Time off meant booze, parties and fun; booze, parties and fun meant getting drunk, getting into fights and getting fucked. The last usually didn't occur with the one you loved, or were married to, but no one cared. It was normal, or becoming normal.

John and Eva were apprehensive when their dad returned from work. While it meant getting new clothes, gifts and money for candy, it also meant coming home from school to a party in progress, or a fight. Or worse, to find their dad in bed with another woman, or their mom in bed with another man ... but not sleeping. To make matters worse, their parents pretended that John and Eva weren't there.

John had taken on the responsibility of looking after Eva when his dad returned. He also grew increasingly quiet and his marks dropped in school. He wished they had grandparents like other children, but they didn't. They did have an aunt, but John didn't impose on her.

John was eleven in February 1972 when Chief James Thomas found him standing by the window in the empty house. The principal had called because John and Eva had not been to school for three days. Chief James knew what was happening; this wasn't the first time he'd been called to William and Elizabeth's house. He knocked on the door, and when there was no answer he opened it. The house was cold and dirty, and there were cups and dishes scattered everywhere. The power had been disconnected and the family had been using candles. Chief James spotted John standing by the window as if he were trying to blend in with his surroundings. "Where are your parents?" he asked in the language. John's expression didn't change. "Where's your parents?" he asked again, this time in English.

John trembled. "I don' know!" he said, almost crying.

The Chief put a hand on John's shoulder to comfort him. It was then that he noticed John's face and clothes were dirty and his moccasins had holes in them. He spotted an empty box of cereal on the counter and almost swore. "Get some clothes," he said. "Where's Eva?"

"Upstairs, sleepin'."

"Wake her up an' bring her."

The Chief took them to his home and they had their first good meal in weeks and their first bath in just as long. Bath was a galvanized tub next to the wood stove in the middle of the open living room and kitchen area.

As they bathed, Lucy, the Chief's wife, sat at the table and sewed patches over the holes in both the children's pairs of shoes. She and the Chief talked about John and Eva in the language, but John and Eva couldn't speak the language and only understood a few words.

After her bath, Eva stood in the middle of the room like an orphan. Lucy smiled and showed her the shoes. "There," she said. "Like new." Eva could only smile her thanks.

That evening, a couple came to visit Chief James and Lucy and they brought a girl whom John assumed was their daughter. The girl was younger than John but older than Eva, and at first she was shy, but then she began playing with Eva. They drew on some scrap paper with pencils and would occasionally laugh.

The Chief and Lucy talked to the couple in the language and were interrupted by a knock on the door. A young woman walked in holding a clipboard. She was the social worker, the first Blue Indian to hold that position in the community. She looked at John, and then at Eva, and then at the Chief. Her eyes were sad, almost hesitant. "What are you going to do with them this time?" she asked the Chief in the language.

John sensed they were talking about him and Eva.

"That's up to you," the Chief said.

"Lotsa families in 'a south lookin' for kids to adopt," she said, this time in English.

"They shouldn't be separated."

After a few awkward moments of silence, the social worker left, and Eva and the girl continued playing. Later that evening, the couple got up to leave. Only then did the girl look at John. She smiled, then disappeared out the door.

And so it was done: John and six-year-old Eva were made wards of the court and given up for adoption. Their parents never questioned the action of the Chief and the social worker. That is not to say they didn't cry, because they did. They cried long and hard and promised never to drink again ... but they did. They drank on the day they made that promise.

As John and Eva stood on the frozen river waiting to board the plane that would take them to the unknown, the Chief handed John an envelope. "That's my number," he said. "Call me if you have to. Call collect."

John wondered what "collect" meant, but didn't ask. The last thing he remembered the Chief saying would stay with him for the rest of his life: "You're young," Chief James said. "Get your education. Times are changing."

As the plane taxied onto the airstrip on the frozen river, John opened the envelope and found forty dollars. He looked at his sister and wondered why this was happening to them. What had they done wrong? Were they orphans? He knew they were going to Alberta, but Alberta was nothing more than a pink patch on a map of Canada where cowboys lived. He looked out the window at their house and wondered what his mom and dad were doing. Were they at home drinking and fighting? Maybe his dad had kicked their mom out again and brought another woman home. Maybe he had got her drunk and was now dragging her to the bed in the corner. Maybe he had taken off her pants and was between her legs, grunting. Or maybe it was another man between his mother's legs, sweating and grunting, while his dad lay passed out on the floor.

As the plane lifted off, he watched Aberdeen until it was swallowed up by the boreal forest. He watched the Teal River until it merged with the horizon. He watched the Blue Mountains until they disappeared into his memory. He promised never to return.

John and Eva were taken to Alberta and adopted by a white couple who lived just outside Calgary. Don and Katherine Olson were farmers and ranchers in their mid-thirties when John and Eva became part of their family. They had two daughters—Kendra, fifteen, and Jolene, thirteen—but cared for John and Eva as if they were their own children. Kendra and Jolene were quiet at first, but they soon referred to John as their brother and Eva as their little sister, and doted on her.

For the first time in their lives John and Eva experienced running water, telephones and television. They also knew that when they woke up their adopted parents would be there.

School wasn't easy at first, being the only Indians in an all-white school. There was teasing and name-calling, but it stopped in 1975 when John turned fifteen and grew to six feet. That year, he made the basketball team and lost his virginity to a cheerleader whose name he'd soon have to forget. She didn't tell him, but her father didn't take kindly to Indians, especially those who were doing his daughter.

John soon forgot about his hometown and looked forward to becoming a rancher and a cowboy, but not necessarily in that order. He also wanted to become a country singer, another Merle Haggard. He was fortunate that his adoptive father knew a few tunes on the guitar; the rest he learned from watching others or from listening to records and the radio. John won his first talent show in Calgary when he was sixteen, bought himself a good guitar with the prize money and looked forward to more contests and the big time. "I think I'm gonna become a country singer," he told his parents.

"What about college?" his mom asked.

"I've thought about it, but I'd like to try singing."

"It's not gonna be easy," his dad said. "Especially if you're not white."

"Yeah," his mom said. "You don't see too many Indian singers."

"There's Buffy Sainte-Marie."

"She's a woman."

"There's Charley Pride."

"Charley Pride's black," his dad said. "He's not Indian."

"I hear he's part Indian. So is Johnny Cash."

Don and Katherine realized his mind was made up. "Well, you're old enough to make up your mind," his dad said. "But you still have to find something else just in case."

"Well, if all else fails, I can become a rancher an' a farmer."

In June 1978, at the age of seventeen, John graduated from high school. He and Eva were standing in the yard outside the farmhouse. Eva, despite being only twelve, was mature for her age. "What are you going to do?" she asked. "Now, I mean."

"I have no idea," he said.

"You ever think of goin' home?"

John envisioned a small community with log houses, green grass, yellow dandelions and old people talking a language he never learned. He thought about the cold, the hunger and the loneliness. He thought about the drinking, the fighting, the strange men, the strange women and the shame. "I think about it once in a while, but I don't think so. You?" he asked. "You ever think about them?"

"Once in a while, but I can't remember them."

"I remember them, but all I remember is … drunk."

"Did they treat us bad?"

"No," he said. "They just didn't treat us at all."

"What's that mean?"

"They left us alone too many times." He remembered the last time he and Eva left the house with the Chief. He remembered the social worker and the couple with their daughter who smiled at him.

"I wonder if they're still alive," Eva said.

The thought had never crossed his mind, at least not until that moment. He wondered how old they were. They had been twenty when they had him, so that meant they were almost forty years old. *They*, he thought. *Not mom and dad; they*. "You?" he asked. "What you're gonna do when you finish school?"

"I'm going to be a nurse," Eva said without hesitation.

"What're you two doin'?" Kendra shouted from the steps. "Come on over here. We wanna get some pictures." Kendra was six months' pregnant and had driven in from Canmore, where she and her husband had a small ranch. Jolene had flown in from Vancouver, where she was working but not yet married.

For some strange reason, John thought about going home and it puzzled him. He had not thought about Aberdeen for years and he had never thought of it as "home."

"Speech," Jolene screamed in his ear, bringing him back to reality.

John smiled and remembered the day he and his sister had come to live with them. He looked at Eva and tears welled up in his eyes.

"It's okay, son," Katherine Olson said, putting an arm around his shoulders until the tears were gone.

"I just remembered the day we left Aberdeen and how alone we were," he said. "I just wanna say thank you for all you've done for us." He tried to remember the word for *thank you* in the language; he couldn't.

When John and Eva had first arrived, Don Olson questioned whether what they were doing was right. After a few months he never again questioned it. "Far as we're concerned," he said, "you're our children. Never forget that."

"I won't," John said.

John found work in the oil patch, and his size and strength made him ideal for the job. Being an Indian was, at first, a detriment, but he found a boss, Bill, who looked at his work and then at his colour and settled on the former and forgot the latter.

In 1983, Eva completed high school and enrolled in a nursing program in Calgary. There was no doubt in anyone's mind she'd finish it.

For the first few years after his graduation, John worked in Alberta and sang in any bar that would let him. However, in October 1984 his life would once again take a dramatic turn when the company he was working for took a contract on the Arctic coast and he and ten of his co-workers were sent north to Helena. Before leaving, he sent a dozen homemade demo tapes to a dozen record companies. He also did what Charley Pride had done, or hadn't done: He didn't tell them his ethnic background.

Helena, in 1984, had a population of thirty-five hundred. It also had three hotels, five bars, two retail stores, three convenience stores, three fast-food outlets and most of the amenities that any medium-sized northern community had. It also had money from the oil boom.

As he flew north on a Boeing 737, John wondered if his dad still worked for the oil companies and whether he would meet him. How would he look? He kept looking at the Indians on the plane and wondering if they were related to him. A couple of them looked at him and smiled, but said nothing. As he got off the mainliner in Helena, he was excited yet afraid, knowing that his hometown was only a hundred miles southwest. He was glad when he and his co-workers boarded a smaller plane that flew them even further north, where they got to work.

Chapter Three

Work was normal: long and hard. And the days were cold and
getting shorter. John remembered the winters up here were cold
and dark, while the summers were hot. This was the land of the
midnight sun, and he had returned home, almost.

It was during his first stint on the coast that John met one of
his people for the first time since he had left Aberdeen: David
Matthew was a few years older than John and worked for the
company that had subcontracted John's. He was quiet at first, but
became friendlier as the days went by. He knew John's first name
and that he was from Alberta, but that's all he knew. As they were
killing time in the dining room one night he asked, "John, what
kind 'a Indian you're?"

John shrugged. "Blue."

"They have Blue Indians down 'ere too?"

"I'm originally from Aberdeen."

This didn't faze David. He'd heard of more than one Blue
Indian child being sent south to be adopted. "What's your last
name?" he asked.

"Daniel."

"Yeah? Who's your parents?"

"William an' Elizabeth."

David mulled that over, and then said, "Oh."

John didn't like the sound of that. "What?" he asked.

"Nothin'."

John knew it was something, but didn't ask. It was none of his business.

That was two weeks ago and he had got to know David as well as he could and learned he was a nice guy. That night, he and David and Elmer Goodenough were sitting in their room at camp getting ready to leave the next day for a well-deserved two weeks off. The room contained three beds—one bunk, one single—and not much else. They slept and changed here, and that was about it.

"Hey, John," Elmer shouted. Elmer almost always shouted. "Whatcha think we should do with our time off?"

"Going home," John said.

"What? You're not gonna stick around an' try out some of the local stuff?"

"Too cold for me." He didn't mention that he was afraid he might run into his mom and dad.

"Nothin' a little poontang can't cure," Elmer said.

John and Elmer had worked together for the last few years and were as close as any two friends could be without being homos, or at least that's what Elmer told others. Elmer played the drums and promised to be John's drummer should he ever get a decent band together and take off for the bright lights of Nashville. Elmer was white, but swore he had some Indian blood; it wasn't noticeable.

"You guys comin' back?" David asked.

"Yeah," John said. "Still got lots to do. What're you gonna do with your time off?"

"Go home an' party 'til 'a next time."

"What's in Helena?"

"Bars, booze, broads an' bingo."

"In that order?"

"In whatever order you want."

"Any nice-lookin' broads?" Elmer asked.

"Lots, but then they all get better lookin' at closin' time."

"Ain't that 'a truth," Elmer said. "You game?" he asked John.

John was thinking about it, but he was still worried about running into his parents. They were the last people on earth he wanted to see.

"I'll pay your hotel room," Elmer continued. "Fuck, I'll even buy the first roun'!"

"Okay," John said.

The next day, Friday, John and Elmer checked into the Blue Mountain Hotel. It wasn't the best hotel they'd ever been in, but it appeared to be clean and relatively quiet. They checked out the hotel bar as they were registering, but it was more like a lounge.

"Hey," Elmer asked the desk clerk, a young white girl who looked like she wanted to be somewhere else. "Is there a bar with a little more kick to it?"

She laughed. "There's the LC at the Helena Hotel. It's not really a hotel, but the bar's good. Everyone goes there."

"What's the 'LC' stan' for?"

"Lonesome Caribou."

"Wanna check it out?" Elmer asked John.

"You go ahead. I'm gonna call Eva an' my parents."

Two hours later, John walked down the street to the Helena

Hotel. The sign on the building was worn and faded, but the vehicles parked out front and the people going in and out told him he had found it. The name of the bar wasn't the Lonesome Caribou; it was the Lone Caribou. Apparently someone had decided to make it more colourful.

As he opened the outside door to the bar, he could hear Creedence on the jukebox belting out "Lodi" from over a decade ago, when bell-bottoms had been the height of fashion. As he walked through the second set of doors, he could smell the smoke, the beer and the cheap perfume that was worn like it was going out of style.

Once his eyes adjusted to the light, he figured the LC could've been any second-rate country bar in the south. It had the same dingy western motif: rough-hewn lumber on the walls, a black ceiling and a small stage with an even smaller dance floor. If there had been a house band, they'd long since moved on to bigger and better things. As John would later learn, the jukebox contained nothing from the eighties. It contained mostly country songs from the fifties and sixties and a few tunes from the seventies, and it was loud.

"Hey, John!" Elmer shouted as he walked in. "Over here!"

Elmer was feeling no pain and sitting with David and a couple of locals.

"Who's 'at?" a woman at the table asked.

It was then John noticed Elmer was already in love, or going for it. She was a nice-looking Indian in her twenties and very high, or very drunk. "How's it goin'?" he asked Elmer.

"Fuckable."

"Looks it."

They laughed, but the woman didn't get it.

"Have a seat," David shouted.

John thought about asking David if his parents were here, but didn't. He decided to take it easy since he was in a strange place and among strange people. Besides, he was not into drinking to get drunk like his good friend Elmer and most of the people in there. He was surprised to see that the Indians outnumbered the whites. "Hey, Elmer!" he shouted. "We could surround you an' burn your wagon an' there's nothin' you can do about it!"

"Fuck 'at noise! I'm one 'a you—I mean—us!"

"Who's your friend?" the woman asked, or rather slurred.

"That's John," Elmer said. "An' that's all you need to know."

"John who?"

"Holmes," John said. "John Holmes."

David, Elmer and a few others got that one, but she didn't.

"Hey, Dave!" John shouted. "Are all 'ese people Blue Indians?"

"Most 'a them. Some are Slavey, Loucheux or Inuit."

"What 'a fuck are Slavey, Loose Shoe an' Inoot?" Elmer asked.

David laughed and gave a short history lesson. "Slavey Indians are from 'roun' the Wells an' Loucheux are from McPhoo an' Inuit are from Inuvik an' up north."

"What 'a fuck is a McPhoo?"

"Fort McPherson."

"Where's 'at?"

"Down 'roun' 'ere!"

"Oh," Elmer said, and then asked John, "Any your kin?"

"No idea," he said, then looked at David.

David read his mind and shrugged. "We're all related one way or 'nother!"

"What'll it be?" the waitress shouted in John's ear.

He turned and saw her for the first time and decided she belonged on a poster. Her shoulder-length hair was black and her skin was brown; she was beautiful. Her sweatshirt said Tuk-U on the front and, despite it being too large for her, she looked sexy. "Blue," he said.

"Roun' for everyone!" Elmer shouted.

John watched her leave and then turned to David, who read his mind. "Tina Joseph," he shouted. "Blue, no relation, but then who knows?"

"Where's she from?"

"Aberdeen, but lives here."

"Attached?"

"No idea. Don't think so."

Tina came back and Elmer gave her forty dollars. "Keep the change!" he shouted.

"Hey, Tina!" David shouted. "You attached?"

"Who wants to know?"

"My bud right here," he said, and nodded to John.

John looked for a way to disappear, but Tina was already looking him up and down. She smiled. "Only if he ain't queer, married or kinky."

"Straight, single an' just a little."

John hoped he'd shut up.

"Where you from?" she asked John.

"Alberta."

"Whatcha doin' up here?"

"Workin'."

"Where you live?"

"Alberta."

"What band?"

"No idea," he lied. "Was adopted."

David heard, but it was none of his business. He had one aim and that was to get home to his old lady who'd promised to work him over and good.

Tina left and began waiting on other tables. Unbeknownst to John, she checked him out more than once during the next hour. He drank very little and gave no indication he was weird or crazy. She liked that.

The next morning, Saturday, at nine o'clock, John was in the hotel restaurant sitting at a table near the window. The red neon sign in another window said "open" and ten people sat at various tables. Tina walked in, spotted him, then smiled and walked over. "Hi," he said and stood.

"Mornin'," she said as she sat across from him.

"Glad you could make it."

One of the restaurant owners, an elderly Chinese, came to their table. "Coffee?" he asked Tina.

"Please."

"You?" he asked John. "More coffee?"

"Please."

After he'd left, Tina asked, "So, where you from? Originally, I mean."

"Aberdeen," John said and watched her expression.

"You're kiddin'."

"Nope."

"Who's your parents?"

"William an' Elizabeth."

It took her a few seconds, but she put John Daniel together with William and Elizabeth and came up with William and Elizabeth Daniel. "Oh."

John wondered what it was with all this "oh" shit. Were they still the town drunks? Were they mass murderers? Were they dead? "What?" he asked.

"Nothin'," she said. "So, how long you been gone?"

"Lef' in seventy-two."

"First time back?"

"Yeah."

"You goin' up?"

"To Aberdeen? Not likely. What's up there?"

"Not much," she said. "How old are you?"

"Twenty-four. You?"

"Twenty-two. How long you here for?"

"Heading south tomorrow. Be back in two weeks." She smiled. "You work full time at the bar?" he asked.

"Nights an' weekends. Weekdays I work for the government. Savin' up for college next fall."

"Where?"

"Calgary."

"Whatcha takin'?"

"Nursing or legal secretary. Don't know yet."

"My sister's in nursing college," he said. "University of Calgary."

"What's her name?"

"Eva."

"How old?"

"Eighteen going on nineteen."

"How many sisters do you have?"

"Three: Eva, Kendra an' Jolene."

"Were they all adopted?"

"Just me an' Eva."

"Brothers?"

"None."

"What's your mom an' dad do?"

"They own a ranch near Calgary," he said and figured she had the most beautiful eyes he had ever seen. She smiled and he got shy, but not uncomfortable. "What's to do in town?" he asked to change the subject.

"Diddly," she said and then laughed, knowing she was in control. "Jam session this afternoon an' talent show tonight."

"Yeah? What's the prize?"

"Three hundred."

"Should try it out."

"You sing?"

"Now an' then."

"Come aroun', buy a roun', as they say."

"I will."

As they talked, he noticed she always seemed to be smiling and didn't appear uncomfortable with him. Twice she let out a loud laugh that made everyone in the restaurant turn and look, but she wasn't embarrassed. Sometime later, Elmer walked in looking like something the cat dragged in. He picked up a cup of coffee and joined them.

"Hey, El."

"Hey, an' please don't shout."

John laughed. "This is Tina," he said, and then to Tina, "this is Elmer."

"As in Fudd," Elmer added. "As in wabbit hunter."

Tina laughed. "You look hungover."

"I am."

"Well, have a seat," she said. "I've gotta go. See you later?" she asked John.

"Sure. When's it start?"

"Jam starts around three or four. Talent show at seven."

After she left, John asked Elmer, "Leavin' today?"

Elmer shrugged. "Think I'll stay for a day or two. Nice town. My kind 'a peeps."

"Me too."

"She's nice."

"That an' there's a talent show tonight. Might make some extra bucks."

"When you leavin'?"

"Monday, Tuesday. Who knows? Don't wanna grow roots."

"Me neither."

That afternoon, John and Elmer went to the Lonesome Caribou to take in the jam session and check out the competition. John sat at the bar and talked with Tina when he had the chance and she introduced him to Clint, the hotel's owner.

Clint had come from the old country in the late thirties when he was in his teens. In his younger days, he wanted to be a cowboy and shoot Indians like he'd seen them do in the movies, but those days, alas, were long gone. He changed his name and floated around western Canada looking for work as a cowboy, but he finally had to admit that he was allergic to horses. He came north in the early fifties and later began working at the Helena Hotel.

He had purchased it about ten years ago and let the hotel section go to pot, but kept his bread and butter going: namely, the LC. He was now biding his time until he could sell, travel the world, check out the babes and live the good life. He had a wife, but got rid of her about five years ago after he found out she was screwing her ass off in the rooms with the customers while he was downstairs working his off. Clint turned sixty this year, but claimed he was sixty-five since most people told him he didn't look a day over eighty.

Later that afternoon John entered the talent show. "What's your name?" Clint asked.

He almost said John Daniel. "John Williams."

He decided to go with Williams since it was Hank's last name and, minus the s, his own middle name. It was also the name of the man who had spawned him in some primordial hellhole called Aberdeen.

"You related to the Williams in Aberdeen?" the bartender asked.

"Nope, I'm from Calgary."

There were eighteen people entered in the talent show and John was number sixteen on the list. When his turn finally came, he did a Merle Haggard song that had a little kick to it. The competition was good and he needed something that would turn the judges' heads since his tall good looks weren't going to do diddly for the two men and two women, all of whom came in together. He cruised through "Swinging Doors" and had the crowd up and hollering, and that must have counted for something because he won three hundred bucks.

"Nice," Tina said as she brought a round to John's table.

"Thanks," John said as he paid. "Sound better in the shower."
She grinned. "I'd like to hear that."

He smiled and watched her walk away. He was glad he'd stayed; he had won three hundred bucks and was going to get laid, or at least he hoped so. He watched her serve the customers and she seemed to get along with everyone.

As the night wore on, John watched some of the locals get up on stage and sing. Some were good, others weren't, but the audience didn't seem to mind so long as the singer could half-ass carry a tune. They danced to everything except the singers who were booed off stage. Even they didn't seem to mind, since they were almost always pissed to the gills.

At ten-thirty, Tina brought them a round. "You gonna get up?" she asked John and nodded toward the stage.

"Whatcha wanna hear?"

"Anything by Hank, Lefty or Merle."

"My kind 'a woman. Who I see 'bout gettin' up?"

"Me, an' your up nex'."

"Good. What's the catch?"

She smiled and left little doubt in his mind that *she* was the catch.

The next morning John watched as Tina came out of her bathroom wearing nothing but a towel and a smile. "That smells great," she said. "Whatcha cook?"

John grinned and handed her a cup of coffee. "Ham an' cheese omelette with toast."

"Wow!" she said as she sat at the table. "Where'd you learn to cook?"

"From my mom an' sisters."

She was about to tell him he'd make some woman a great husband, but didn't. "When's your plane?" she asked as she ate.

"Three bells."

"When you comin' back?"

"Ten days."

"You ever think about returning for good?"

"Never."

"No good memories?"

"None that I can remember," he said, and then thought about the Chief. "Except the old Chief."

"Chief James?"

"Yeah. He took us in when we were alone. Is he still living?"

She stared at him for a few seconds. "Yeah," she said. "He's only 'bout fifty-something."

"Really? I thought he'd be older. He gave me forty dollars an' his phone number when we left. He told me to call, but I never did."

"You should call him."

"Would he remember me?"

"I think so."

"Does he have a phone?"

She picked up the phone book and handed it to him. "We've come outta the bush an' gotten civilized," she said. "We've even got television an' a highway up there. Want me to call him for you?"

"Sure."

She picked up the phone and dialled the number from memory. "Hello, Chief. This is Tina Joseph. Good, an' you?" She laughed. "How's Lucy?" Again she laughed, and then she got serious. "Chief, you remember William an' 'Lizabeth's son?" She smiled at John. "Yeah, that's him. He's working on the coast for a couple months. Lives in Alberta. He's sitting with me right now." She kept looking at John, and then she handed him the phone.

"Hello?"

"Hello, John. How are you?" the Chief asked.

"Fine. An' you?"

"Doin' good. How old are you anyways?"

"Twenty-four."

"Young." John smiled. "How's your sister?" the Chief asked.

"She's in college in Calgary, takin' nursing."

John remembered trying to find something for Eva to eat in a cold and empty house. The smell came back to him. The house smelled like death and forgotten promises. He remembered his mom and dad fighting, or rather his dad fighting his mom. He remembered strange women in bed with his dad and strange men in bed with his mom … but not sleeping. They were grunting. He remembered the loneliness, and the shame of walking to school in dirty clothes.

"You comin' home?" the Chief asked.

"I don't know. I don't think so."

The Chief was silent for a few seconds. "They put you with a good family?" he asked.

"They did."

"Good. You finish school?"

"Yes."

"That's good. Was hopin' for that." The Chief was waiting for John to ask about his parents, but he didn't. *Maybe it's just as well,* Chief James thought. "You ever come up, let me know. You can stay with us."

John remembered the Chief's house. It was made from logs and had a wood stove. It had no running water, yet it was comfortable and there was always something to eat. "I'll do that," he said. "I always wanted to call to say thanks, but I never did. I'm sorry."

"Don't be," the Chief said. "That's the way it was in those days."

"Anyhow, thanks to you an' your wife."

"You're welcome. When you're goin' home?"

"Today."

"You say hello to Eva from me an' my wife."

"I'll do that. Thanks again."

"Okay. Goodbye, John."

"Bye." John hung up, and then realized he had not asked about his parents. Tina also noticed. "What's his address?" John asked her.

"General delivery."

Up in Aberdeen, Chief James called his son, Alfred. Alfred's wife, Eunice, answered the phone. Eunice's maiden name was Daniel. "I heard from him," the Chief said in the language.

"From who?"

"William an' Elizabeth's son."

"John?"

"Yes."

A few hours later, John was in his hotel room getting ready to leave. He picked up some hotel stationery and wrote a note. It was simple and to the point: Chief James. Thanks. John Daniel.

He put three hundred dollars in the envelope and gave the letter to the desk clerk when he checked out. Then he met Tina in the parking lot. "Tell me about your family," he asked as she drove him to the airport.

"Nothing to tell. My mom died when I was young. She drowned, an' I was raised by my grandparents."

"What's their names?"

"Abraham an' Sarah. My mom was Margaret."

"Dad?"

"My mom never told my grandparents."

"Sorry."

"Don't be. I've no idea who he is an' if he came back into my life I wouldn't care. What about you? Why don't you ask about them?" She turned to find him staring blankly into space.

"It's just my memories aren't that good." he said. "Can't remember anything but drinkin' an' fightin'."

"I'm sorry."

"Don't be."

"In a way, you're lucky," she said. "At least you got out an' did well for yourself."

"Lots of changes?"

"Lots."

"Like?"

"More drinking, more violence, more suicides, more killings, more of everything."

"How many?" he asked. "Suicides, I mean." He could tell she was trying to figure out a number.

"Too many," she said.

"Why?"

"Don't know. Most of them do it when they're drunk." The conversation was getting dismal, so she decided to change the subject. "What about you?" she asked. "What're you gonna do with your life?"

"I'd like to get into country music an' see if I can make a living at it." he said. "Just don't know if the world is ready for an Indian singer. Still a lotta racism down south."

"Lots up here too."

"So I've heard."

The airport terminal was small and did not have a restaurant. It did have a concession stand and John and Tina stood by the large windows overlooking the parking lot and drank coffee. "Can I tell you something?" she asked.

"Sure."

"I've never done this before. Spend the night with anyone after so little time."

He smiled. "I'll take that as a compliment."

"It is. Can I ask you something else?"

"Sure."

"Do you have a girl?"

"No," he said, and then grinned. "Not yet. What about you? Anyone special in your life?"

"No," she said, and then she too grinned. "Not yet." She touched his hand. "I had a good time."

"So did I."

"Hey, John!" Elmer shouted from the door leading to the airport ramp. "Time to go!"

John turned to Tina. "Can I see you again?" he asked. "When I get back?"

"I was hoping you would."

"I'll be back in about ten days."

"Call me when you get to town."

They stood there for a few awkward seconds, and then they hugged. As John boarded the 737, Tina wondered why she hadn't told him she recognized him. It wasn't until he had mentioned Chief James that she remembered he was the young boy in the Chief's house, and Eva must have been the young girl. She remembered he was quiet, but Eva was always smiling.

As the 737 lifted off and slowly gained altitude, the Blue Mountains appeared in the distance. John tried to see if he could spot Aberdeen, but he couldn't. He wondered what his mom and dad were doing. Did they live in the same house? Were they still drunks? Did he still beat her up? Did they still sleep with other people? He thought about Tina and wondered where that would lead. She was everything he was looking for in a woman: beautiful and intelligent with a good personality.

Later that night, as soon as he arrived in Calgary, John called Eva from the airport. "How was it?" she asked.

"Uneventful," he lied.

"See any kin?"

"None." She didn't ask, but he knew what she was thinking. "I didn't see them either," he said.

"You comin' over?"

"Yep, see you in a bit."

An hour later, he was telling her of the cold, Helena, David Matthew and Tina Joseph. "Sounds like a nice girl," she said.

"She is."

"You gonna see her again?"

"I'd like to," he said, then changed the subject. "You remember the Chief?" he asked.

"Chief of what?"

"Chief of Aberdeen. He took us in when they left us alone." Eva said nothing. "I talked to him today," John continued. "Nice man."

"Don't remember him."

"Gave me forty dollars when we left."

"Yeah?"

"Sent it back to him with interest."

"Good," she said. "They got phones up there?"

"Yeah."

"Call her."

He did, and Eva talked to one of her own for the first time in years although she had no idea who "her own" were. She was an Indian and that's all she knew.

Tina tried to picture Eva, but couldn't. She had been only nine when she'd played with Eva on the floor of the Chief's house. She wanted to tell Eva, but didn't think she'd remember. How old had she been at the time? Five? Six?

"Well," John was saying. "I should let you go. It's gettin' late."

Eva waved at him. "Don't hang up yet. I wanna say good night."

"Eva wants to say good night," he told Tina.

"Good night, John. Miss you."

"Me too." He handed the phone to Eva and went into the kitchen.

"It's nice to talk to you," he heard Eva say. "You made quite an impression on my brother 'cause you're all he's talked about since he came back."

"Thanks," Tina said.

"Anyhow, it's gettin' late. Good night, Tina."

"Good night, Eva."

Eva held up the phone to John, who was standing in the kitchen doorway. "Say good night, John-boy."

"Good night, John-boy," he shouted.

"Good night," he heard Tina say, and then she hung up.

"You look like you're in love," Eva told him. He could only grin. "How old is she?" she asked.

"Two years younger 'an me."

"Any woman'd be lucky to get you."

"I know."

"We are modest tonight, aren't we?" Once again, he could only grin. "Wonder what they're doin'?" she asked.

John pictured the old house with no lights, no water and no food. "Never asked an' nobody told me."

Back in Helena, Tina prepared for bed and another week in the trenches of bureaucracy. She pressed her nose into the pillow where John's head had been less than twelve hours ago and wondered if this was what love felt like. She wondered why he had not asked about his parents. Did he know?

A few days later, Chief James came home from the post office smiling. "What?" his wife asked in the language.

"I got a letter from my girlfriend," he said in English.

"Hah! You're too old to have a girlfriend," she responded in the language.

"I got you, don' I?"

She smiled, and then he showed her the three hundred dollars. "From where?"

"John Daniel."

"For what?"

"I gave him forty dollars when they left," he said, and then gave her the money.

She noticed the worried look on his face. "What?"

Chief James then asked a question that had plagued him for years. "I wonder if what I did was right."

"It was the only way."

He shrugged. "It was." Still, he wondered if he should have asked a relative to take them.

❖

The building appeared to be an institution, like an old hospital. From the outside, the lights within appeared to be a sickly yellow. Inside was a long hall with doors on either side. The doors, like the ceiling and the floor, were white, or what used to be white. Over the years they had lost their brightness and were now a dingy white, almost yellow. Behind each door was a room that contained two night tables and two beds.

In one of the rooms, the two beds contained two men in white smocks. At first glance, they both appeared to be white; they weren't. One was an Indian: a pale Indian. His was a paleness that could come only from a prolonged lack of exposure to the sun. He appeared to be in his fifties, but the lack of light, his benign expression and the paleness of his skin made it difficult to tell. His arms were folded across his chest and his hands were tucked under his arms as if he were cold. He was looking at the city lights through the wire mesh that covered the windows, and appeared puzzled. He saw the reflection of the room in the window. Everything was distorted: bent and twisted out of shape.

Chapter Four

On Wednesday, November 14, John and Elmer were on a plane heading north and looking forward to returning, despite the cold. Actually, John was looking forward to seeing Tina and had called her every night since he'd left. He'd never had this much fun with anyone, nor had he ever been in love before … at least other than a few times that could be chalked up to hormonal activity raging out of control.

Tina took some time off work and met him at the Helena airport, where they hugged, and then kissed. "Geez, you smell nice," he said. He wished he could've taken her right there, or in her car. "Can't stay too long," he said. "Gotta plane waitin' for us. Be back in five weeks."

"That'll be Christmas."

"Yeah. I might even stay."

"I always go home for Christmas," she said.

"Need company?"

"You mean it?"

He really didn't want to go to Aberdeen, but he was in love. "Why not," he said. "Gotta do it sometime. How bad can it be?"

"Hey, Elmer! John! Over here!" It was their boss, Bill.

"Gotta go," John said, and gave Tina another hug. "God, you really smell nice."

"Thanks."

As John walked away, Tina smiled at the two Indians standing next to Bill. "Hi, Ken. Hi, Richard."

"Hey, Tina!" they shouted in unison.

"That's Ken an' Richard," she hollered to John, "keep away from them!" She laughed, and then left.

John turned and looked at the two big Indians, then introduced himself. "John Daniel," he said, shaking their hands.

"Any relation to Jack?" Ken asked.

It took John a few seconds to get that one. He smiled. "Not that I know of."

"Where you from?" Richard asked.

"Alberta, by way of Aberdeen." John could see the question so he answered it. "Was adopted."

"Who's your parents?"

"William an' Elizabeth."

It took them a few seconds, and then they both said, "Oh."

Over the next few weeks, John got to know Ken and Richard better than he did David. They were not afraid of work, but they were also, in the words of the medical profession, fucking nuts. However, it was an Indian kind of nuttiness: crazy and funny.

Five weeks later, on Friday, December 21, John was at the Helena airport on the phone with Eva, who was at their parents' home. "I'm gonna stay for the holidays," he said.

"With Tina? In Helena?"

"Yeah. Might go up to Aberdeen."

"Really? You think you'll see them?"

"Small town."

"Yeah, I guess. Let me know an' take some pictures. She there with you?"

"She's on her way out."

"El stayin' up there too?"

"Nope, he's already gone."

Tina arrived as he was saying goodbye.

"Hey, Tina. Wanna give us a ride to town?" Ken asked.

"Sure," she said. "Car's outside." And then she walked into John's arms. "I missed you."

He held her tight. "I missed you too."

"Love ..." Ken said.

"... Sucks," Richard finished.

"You workin' tonight?" John asked Tina on their way into town.

"Yeah. Start at six 'til closin' time. Hey," she said to Ken and Richard, who were sitting in the back, "where you wanna go?"

"Take us to the candy store,"

"What're you gonna do there?" John asked.

"Pick up the essentials an' head home," Ken said.

"How?"

"Hop a cab."

Tina dropped them off at the liquor store and Ken looked at the building and smiled. "If I die, stuff me an' put me in here," he told Richard.

"You *are* stuffed."

"Fuckin' A!"

Tina and John then drove to her apartment and spent the afternoon making love. Afterwards, she laid her head on his chest and listened to his heart while he stroked her hair. "John?"

"Yeah?"

"I'm so glad I met you."

"So am I."

"Can I tell you something?"

"Sure."

"You remember the last time you were at the Chief's house, back before you were sent away?"

"Yeah, I remember."

"Remember that girl that played with Eva there?"

"Yeah," he said, and then rolled over and looked at her. "Was 'at you?"

She smiled. "That was me."

"You smiled at me."

"I know."

He kept looking at her. "You smiled, and then got shy."

"I know that too."

"Wow."

"You know, I've never felt like this about anyone."

"Like what?"

"You know," she said.

"Know what? Tell me."

"I think I love you."

"Think?"

"I love you."

"That's better," he said. "I love you too."

That afternoon, John had his first taste of caribou meat in years and liked it. He did not tell Tina he had all but forgotten how it tasted, but she didn't need to know that. He remembered his mom going out and returning with caribou meat, which she cooked for them and then that was all they ate; that and cereal with no milk, just water. He couldn't remember his dad going hunting, and wondered where his mom got the meat. Did she buy it? Beg for it? He remembered seeing young boys his age going into the hills with their dads to hunt. They came back and talked endlessly about their trips; some of them had even shot their first caribou. Their parents would put on a feast for them and talk about a young boy's first hunt and tradition. John and Eva usually went with their mom, who would hoard meat and bannock, which she brought home and fed to them for a few days. He used to wish that his dad would take him hunting, and then put on a feast for him, but it never happened.

"Want some drymeat?" Tina asked.

He took it. "You make this?"

"Me? I can barely cook let alone make drymeat. My grandmother made this."

"How old is she?"

"Early sixties."

"When you goin' up?" he asked. "To Aberdeen, I mean."

"Sunday. Still wanna come?"

He shrugged. "Don't know," he said.

"You don't have to. You can stay here. I'll be back Thursday."

"Want me to come?"

"That's up to you."

"I don't wanna see my parents," he said.

"What?" she asked, surprised.

"I don't wanna see them."

At first, she wondered what he was talking about, and then it dawned on her: He didn't know. She stared at him and wondered what to say next.

"What?" he asked.

"They never told you?"

"Who? Told me what?" In his mind, he already knew what she was going to say.

"John, I don't know how to tell you. They're dead."

Even though he had known what she was going to say, it didn't register for a few seconds. "What," he said, more statement than question.

"They died."

"When?"

"Eight or nine years ago. John, I thought you knew."

"No one told us."

"I'm sorry. Are you okay?"

"Yeah," he said. "It just comes as a shock." He tried to remember how they looked, but that image was buried with the others he'd tried to forget over the years. "How?"

"They froze. At their cabin."

"Didn' know they had a cabin."

"All I know is Edward found them."

"Edward who?"

"Edward," she said. "Geez, how much do you know about your family? Edward Brian; your uncle; your mother's brother."

This was the first John had heard of his uncle. He knew he had an aunt, but she lived down south somewhere. "She had a sister too."

"Olive; Olive Rowe. Lives in Whitehorse. Married with kids. Comes back once in a while."

"What about him? He have any brothers or sisters?"

"Who?"

"My father."

"He's got a sister in Aberdeen."

He remembered. "Eunice."

"Yeah. She's married to Chief Alfred."

"My uncle still there?"

She wondered why he didn't know this. Didn't he keep in touch? Of course not.

"What now?" he asked.

"John, he's in an institution in Edmonton. I thought you knew all this."

"No one told us. What happened to him?"

"Went quiet after he found your parents."

"Quiet?"

"Yeah. He never talked an' couldn't look after himself, so they sent him south."

"Anything else I should know about? They have any more kids?"

"Who? Your mom an' dad?"

"Yeah."

"No. You okay?" she asked.

"I'm jus' wonderin' what I should tell my sister."

"Geez, I thought you knew all this."

After a few seconds, he came up with an answer to his own question. "I don't think I'll tell her 'til after Christmas," he said. "That'll give me time to think about what to say, an' I don't need to spoil her Christmas."

Tina looked at the time. "I've gotta be at work in a few minutes. Wanna drop by later?"

"Sure."

"You'll be okay?"

"Yeah. Jus' so much to take in all at once. I got any cousins I should know about?"

"Edward wasn't married, Olive's got some kids an' Eunice an' Alfred have three." She looked at the time again. "I've gotta go."

"Can I use your phone?"

She didn't ask, but he told her nonetheless. "Gonna call my aunt in Aberdeen."

"Good."

"Don't remember too much of her."

"Nice woman. You'll like her. I'm gonna be late," she said, and then left.

John sat around for a few minutes, then picked up the phone and called Chief Alfred Thomas in Aberdeen. A woman answered. "Hello?"

"Hello. Is this Eunice?"

"Yes, it is. Who's this?"

"John. John Daniel."

Tina was right. She was a nice woman and already knew he was in Helena. They talked for about a half an hour and she told him of his mom, but never spoke of his dad. She also told him of his other aunt in Whitehorse. "She's in town for Christmas. Stayin' at Edward's house," Eunice said. "You comin' up?"

"Yeah. I'll be up with Tina tomorrow nex' day."

"It's gonna be good to see you again. How's your sister?"

"She's doin' good."

"I heard she's takin' nursin'."

"Yes, she is."

"That's good."

"I haven't told her yet."

"Tol' her what?"

"We didn' know about our parents," he said. "Nobody told us."

"Nobody knew where you were."

"I know. Well," he said, looking at the time, "I should go."

"It's good to talk to you."

"Yeah, same here."

"We'll see you tomorrow nex' day then?"

"Yeah."

"Goodbye, John.'"

"Bye," he said, and then hung up and sat around for a few minutes wondering what was going on with his life. He felt almost relieved and suddenly looked forward to going to Aberdeen, and he knew why: They were not there. He picked up his jacket and walked out the door.

As he climbed the steps to the LC, he could hear the Righteous Brothers on the jukebox: "Unchained Melody." When he entered, he saw about ten couples slow dancing, looking as hungry as diners at an all-you-can-eat buffet. He spotted Tina at the bar and walked across the floor and sat on a wobbly stool. "How did it go?" she asked.

"Okay. She's nice."

"Told you. Wanna beer?"

"Sure."

"Hey, John!" someone shouted.

He turned and saw David Matthew sitting in the corner with three girls. "Sit with them," Tina said. "I'll be over later."

"How's it goin'?" John asked David as he sat at their table.

"It's goin'. You?"

"Not bad."

"This is my ol' lady, Verna," David said, nodding to the girl on his right.

"Hi, Verna."

"Hi, John. How're you?"

"So far, so good."

"Whatcha doin' in town?" John asked David.

"Jus' down for the day. Might stay the night. We'll see."

Sometime around nine, when the LC was picking up steam, Tina came to their table. "You should sing a few," she said to John.

"Whatcha wanna hear?"

"'Sing Me Back Home.'"

"You wanna hear that dismal song?"

"People'll dance to gospel music if it has a good beat," David said. "Whatever you sing, don't sing 'Blue Christmas.'"

"Or 'Little Drummer Boy,'" Verna added.

He did the Merle Haggard song, and then a couple by Hank. He even threw in one of his own and they liked it, but then again they were all pretty hammered. He wished he'd brought his guitar. Maybe next time. He was certain there would be a next time. He was certain there would be a lot of next times.

Later that night, after closing time and after Tina had got off work, she and John walked back to her apartment hand in hand. Despite the cold and the dark, he was glad he had gone to the LC; it had kept him from thinking too much about his family and the shit that life had put them through. He was wondering what would have happened if he and Eva had stayed. Would they have gotten their education? Not likely. Would he still have met Tina? More than likely. Would they have gotten together? Who knows.

"So," Tina asked, "you make up your mind about coming home with me?"

"I'll go if you got the room."

"Got room, but you're gonna have to sleep in the spare bedroom. My grandparents don't take kindly to premarital sex."

"I meant in your car."

She laughed. "Only if you pay for gas."

"Sure."

"I told my grandparents about you," she said. "They wanna meet you."

"They know about my parents?"

"Yeah."

"An'?"

"An' what? You were sent 'way long ago, an' now you're back."

"Sounds simple."

"What did you expect?"

"Oh, I don't know. I kept expecting to see them. Was even afraid of going up."

"Now?"

"Now it's different." And he knew why: They weren't there.

She had nothing to say. She hadn't known his parents and she hadn't really known him when he was younger. She'd only known him as a little boy standing next to a wood stove looking lost.

✦

The pale Indian heard voices and was glad he couldn't see the people talking. When he *did* see them, they were white: white people. When he saw them, he tucked his hands further into his body until he could feel his heart beating. He wanted to ask what they were doing, but didn't. He didn't want them to know he was slow and stupid. When they took him by his arms he ran into the fog and they didn't follow. He'd rather go into the fog than have them cut off and bury his arms. He wondered why he thought they'd do that.

They got him up in the morning and told him to dress, and then to shave and wash, and then to eat. Sometimes they gave him needles, and then searched for his soul, but they never found it. Sometimes, during the summer, they took him outside. He liked the sun, the wind and the smell of the grass when it was just cut. It smelled like the hills and mountains in the spring. He could see the hills and the mountains, and he could see people, but they were far away. Maybe they knew he was slow and stupid.

He looked out through the wire mesh and saw snow, but it was dirty, not white like the mountain snow. Then he began moving. He kept his eyes on the floor. The man in green was pushing him again. They were going to eat, and then they were going to watch hockey, and then they were going to wash, brush and go to bed. It was like being in mission school, or like being in the army, except everything was white. Maybe he was dead and this was heaven. His head hurt and he wished they'd poke him again. He usually fell asleep after they poked him, and did not dream.

It was then he smelled the smoke. He was back in the room again; his room. He wondered if the white man was in the bathroom sucking in flames and belching out smoke again. But this smoke was different: This smoke came from a fire made from wood. How did he know that? Had he made a fire to keep warm?

He turned toward the window and looked at the darkness, then cocked his head and listened. He thought he heard screams and shouts, like they were coming from a great distance. From where? He saw the fog flowing under the door. It sounded like it was being pumped into the room by a small engine. He took a deep breath and closed his eyes.

He opened his eyes and was surprised to see he was on the river. How long had he been here, and where was he going? It seemed strangely familiar, like he'd been here before.

The sun was shining and the snow on the river and on the hills was a blinding white. He looked down at his snowmobile; it was yellow, like the sun. His mitts were made of moose skin trimmed with beaver fur and they were beaded: bright red flowers with green leaves. He smiled. In those mitts were his hands: warm and cozy.

From a distance, he could see the smoke rising from the trees straight up into the sky. What was it? Who was it? Then he remembered, and for a brief instant he was frightened. But that sense of fear was lost when he saw the fog coming downriver. He took a deep breath and resigned himself to its inevitability.

After a few moments, or maybe it was a few days or a few years, he heard the sound of a small engine and emerged from the fog. He was still on the river and the sound was that of his snowmobile, or Ski-Doo.

He could smell the smoke as he approached the cabin. Even from this distance he could see that the door was open. He drove up the bank, slowed, and then shut the engine off. It was quiet for a second, and then he heard them shouting. They were drinking again. He could also smell the homebrew.

He hated homebrew; he hated all homebrews. He had watched them make it once. They mixed malt and sugar and added yeast, and for a while it smelled like bread. Later, it smelled like … homebrew.

"Shut 'a fuck up!" the man shouted.

"Not for you!"

He walked up to the door just as the man hit the woman. She fell back, hit her head against the wooden table and then crumbled to the floor. The man, his already dark face made darker by the sun and the wind, turned and sneered. "What 'a fuck you lookin' at?"

The pale Indian was about to say something, but the dark man suddenly turned white. "What?" he asked.

The pale Indian was confused. He was about to say something, but someone else answered. "I ask what 'a fuck you lookin' at?" said the voice in the dark.

"Nothin'," the dark man turned white said. "I thought this ol' man was up." He looked at the name on the bed. "Brian Edward."

"That's Edward Brian. An' he ain't been up since he got here."

"How long ago was that?"

"Eight years now."

"What happen to him?"

"No idea. What I look like, a doctor?"

"You look like the janitor!"

They laughed.

"Come on! Let's get on with our rounds."

"He don't look like a white man."

"He's an Indian."

"An Indian? Like Geronimo?"

"Yeah, like Geronimo."

"Where's he from?"

"Up north."

"Where?"

"The NWT."

"Where's 'at?"

"The Northwest Territories."

"They have Indians up there?"

"I guess so."

"I thought only Eskimos live up there."

Chapter Five

It was Saturday morning and John and Tina were in her apartment having coffee and toast. "I wanna get some gifts for my aunts," he said. "Don't know what to get."

"Kitchen stuff, blankets, something useful."

"What about your grandparents?"

"Leave that to me. Better yet, why don't you get a bottle of rye for my grandfather."

"What kind?"

"Canadian Club. Gave him one last year. He's prob'ly still got it."

"Doesn't drink much?"

"Has a drink now an' then. That's about it."

"Your grandmother?"

"Only drinks wine at communion. What about you?"

"Never felt the need to. Got more important things to do."

"Me too. You ever feel outta place in the bars?"

"Not if I got a guitar in my hand an' a song in my heart." He took out a notebook and wrote something.

"What's that?" she asked.

"Song ideas."

"You write anything?"

"Actually, I've written quite a few, but they're mostly all garbage. Couple are good."

"Lemme hear one."

"Did one last night. Called 'Looking for You.'"

"What's it about?"

"It's about you."

"Really? You wrote a song about me?"

"Wrote it on the way back to Calgary. Took all of ten minutes."

"Yeah?"

"Best songs are written in less 'an ten minutes. At least that's what they tell me."

"I'm flattered."

"Thanks."

"I gotta work at nine-thirty. Takin' a break from two to six, an' then I'm on 'til closin' time."

"You're really putting in the hours."

"Gotta save up for college."

"When we leaving?"

"Tomorrow noon."

Soon after she went to work, John went shopping for a few hours, and then returned to her apartment and looked at her photo albums. He saw photos of her grandparents and her mom, but none of her dad. He wondered who he was. Did he up and leave her mom? Had they been married? He then realized she had the same last name as her grandparents; her mom had never married. One photo caught his eye, and for a brief moment he thought it was of Eva. It wasn't. It was of Tina. He pictured them, as children, playing on the floor in the Chief's house, and then decided to call Eva.

"So, how's it goin'?" she asked.

"Not too bad," he said.

"Where's Tina?"

"Workin'."

"When you goin' up?"

"Tomorrow," he answered. "Hey, do you remember the last time we were in Aberdeen? Before we were sent out?"

"No. Why?"

"I remember the Chief an' his wife talking to another couple. They had a young girl with them. She was on the floor playing with you. She was older than you, but younger than me."

"Yeah?"

"That was Tina."

It took Eva a few seconds to digest this bit of information. "So, me an' Tina have met before, but I can't remember it."

"She does."

"She does? Wow. This is like kismet."

"Could be," he answered, and then to avoid answering any more questions, said, "Well, I gotta go. I was supposed to meet Tina an' I'm late."

"Okay. Don't forget to call from Aberdeen."

"Will do."

"We've had some people come home an' it wasn't a good experience," Tina said as they drove to Aberdeen two days before Christmas.

"What do you mean?"

"I mean adopted children come home expecting to find their parents living the good life on the land an' sober, but they don't an' they aren't."

"I didn' expect that."

"I'm not saying you did. All I'm saying is we've had children who came home with high expectations only to be disappointed. We've also had birth mothers who thought their adopted children would have had a better life in the south. Some have, but a lot haven't."

"Meaning?"

"Meaning they've come home with more problems than they left with."

"Like?"

"We had a young man come home not too long ago with a drug problem an' he expected our band to provide him with a living. It doesn't work like that. There are no reserves up here an' there is no real band government, at least not yet."

"What happened to him?"

"He started gettin' into trouble, so the Chief paid his way back south an' that was it. There's the mountains," she said.

He saw them in the distance. The sun had set, but the clouds were still red and the mountains appeared pink. They weren't as large as he had pictured them, but they were still far away. Soon the lights of the community became visible through the trees. "That Aberdeen?" he asked, and then felt foolish.

"Yes!" Tina said excitedly. "It's good to be back home again."

"Somebody wrote a song about that already."

"One of my favourites."

"Mine too."

They drove down the main street of Aberdeen and he could remember nothing of it. It was new to him what with the newer houses, the snowmobiles, the trucks and the lights. He couldn't remember this many lights; everyone had Christmas lights on their houses. They passed a large, nondescript building he didn't recognize. "What's that?"

"The Saloon."

"They got a bar in town? How's it doin'?"

"Business is good, but people are divided on whether it's good for the community or not."

"Should check it out."

"It should be open tomorrow."

They pulled up to a simple house with a large living room window and he could see people he assumed were her grandparents. She waved at them and they waved back. The first thing he noticed as he stepped into the house was the smell of caribou meat and bannock cooking. He took off his cowboy boots and followed her in. Her grandparents hugged her, and then all three turned to him. "John," Tina said, "this is my grandfather, Abraham, an' my grandmother, Sarah." She turned to her grandparents and spoke the language. "Grandfather, Grandmother, this is John Daniel."

John was surprised that Tina spoke the language. He was even more surprised that her grandparents didn't look a day over fifty, yet they were both in their early sixties. They looked more like her parents.

Abraham and Sarah both remembered the day John and his sister were sent away. They also remembered the day his uncle, Edward Brian, brought his mom and dad to town. "Welcome home, John," Abraham said, holding out his hand. "It's nice to see you again."

John shook Abraham's hand. "Do you remember me?"

"Of course," Sarah said. "You were a small boy then. Now you're a big man. Come in an' eat."

As they ate, they asked John about where he had been sent and about his life on the farm and about Eva. "How you make your living?" Abraham asked.

"Working on the oil rigs an' singing."

"Ahem!" Tina coughed loudly.

"Singin'?" Abraham asked.

"Slingin'," John lied. "Slingin' bales of hay on my dad's ranch. Gonna take over one of these days."

"Hard work, farming?"

"Long hours, hard work."

"Same as trappin'."

John shrugged. "I suppose."

A few minutes later, the door opened and in came two men, two women and six children. Tina introduced John to her uncle, Robert, and his wife, Jessie, and to her aunt, Caroline, and her husband, George. She also introduced her six cousins, but he couldn't remember their names. They made themselves at home and kept smiling at him. Tina saw this as a good time to get out of the house for a few minutes. "Grandfather, John and I are going to see his aunts and Chief James," she said in the language.

As they left the house, John said, "They're nice."

Tina smiled and held his hand. "Where do you wanna go first?"

"Let's go see the Chief."

"Alfred an' Eunice are probably there too."

Alfred and Eunice *were* at Chief James's house, and so was his Aunt Olive. When he walked in with Tina, they couldn't believe how tall he was. They hugged him and told him how glad they were to see him. Eunice and Olive were in tears. They almost told him how much he looked like his dad, but didn't. He did notice that Eunice looked a lot like an older version of Tina: a little heavy, but the same smiling eyes and the same grin, almost the same laugh.

A young girl, around fourteen or fifteen, came out of one of the bedrooms and looked around, and then at John. When she spotted Tina, she let out a scream. "Tina!"

They hugged each other and another young girl came out of the bedroom. "Hey, Tina."

"Hey, Liz."

"Sarah, Liz," Tina said, and then turned to John, "this is John. John, this is Sarah an' Liz. Sarah is Alfred an' Eunice's, an' Liz is Bertha an' Isaac Moses's daughter."

Sarah and Liz looked up at John, and then looked at Tina and giggled. "Is he your boyfriend?" Liz whispered.

"Yeah," Tina whispered back. "Awesome, eh?"

"Totally," Sarah whispered.

"He's your cousin."

"What?"

"His name's John Daniel; he's your mom's nephew." Both girls looked confused. "He's your Aunt Elizabeth's son," Tina added.

Sarah thought for a few seconds, then said, "That's before my time, I think."

"Yeah," Tina said. "You were still in Pampers, suckin' on a bottle."

"I *wish* they had Pampers back then," Eunice said, and everyone laughed.

That evening, they asked John about his life, his adoptive family and Eva in between feeding him caribou meat, drymeat and bannock. "Where is she now?" Eunice asked.

"At my parents' ranch."

"We should call her."

John was in such a good mood he almost said yes. "I'd rather not," he said. "She doesn't know about our parents. I'll tell her after Christmas."

"We understand," Eunice said.

John and Tina left around eleven. "You glad you came?" she asked as they walked up the main street.

"I'm glad now," he said, then stopped as if he'd seen a ghost.

It could have been any abandoned house on the prairies: the windows and the door were boarded up, the logs were old and weathered, and the roof was sagging. It was his old house.

"You okay?" Tina asked.

"Yeah," he said. "Didn' think it was still standing."

"Nobody's lived there since a long time ago."

They arrived at her grandparents' house to find them already in bed. "You okay?" she asked again.

"Yeah, not a prob," he said, and then gave her a kiss on the cheek. "Good night."

She watched him walk into the spare bedroom, and then she heard her grandmother calling her. She opened the door to her grandparents' bedroom. "What?" she asked in the language.

"Are you going to marry him?" her grandmother asked.

"Yes."

"Did he stay with you in Helena?"

"Yes."

"Then it's okay. As long as you're going to marry him."

"I am."

"Has he asked you?"

"Not yet, but he will."

She closed the door, went into her room and changed into her nightgown and then walked into John's room. He was already under the covers and she crawled in next to him. "What're they gonna say?" he asked.

"They're okay with it," she said. "They already know you stayed with me in Helena." She kissed him and he rose to the occasion. Afterwards, she told him, "I'm so in love with you."

"I love you too," he answered, and stroked her hair. "Tina?"

"Yeah?"

"I've never felt like this before."

"Like what?"

"In love."

"Me too," she answered. "Can I tell you something?"

"Sure."

"I knew the moment I saw you."

"Knew what?"

"That I wanted you. That I wanted to get to know you better."

He rolled over on his stomach and looked at her. "Tina?"

"Yeah?"

"Will you marry me?"

She looked at him. "Are you serious?"

"Yes."

"Are you sure?"

"Yes, I am."

She didn't answer him right away, but the tears in her eyes told him what all the words in the world couldn't. "Yes," she said after a few moments. "I'll agree to marry you, for now. But we don't have to do it right away. We can wait."

"For what?" he asked.

"For me to get my education an' you to follow your dream."

"Okay."

"Just wait here," she said, getting up.

"I ain't goin' nowhere."

She laughed. "You'd better not," she said, and then went and knocked on her grandparents' door.

"Yes?" her grandmother asked in the language.

Tina opened the door. "He asked me," she said.

"What did you say?" her grandfather asked.

"I said I'd think about it."

"What?" her grandmother said.

"I'm teasing. I said yes."

"When?"

"We'll talk about that later."

The next morning, John dressed and then walked into the living room to find Tina and her grandparents sitting at the kitchen table. Tina smiled. "They wanna know when."

"Right after I have a shave," he said.

They laughed as he walked into the bathroom and Tina came in a few seconds later and watched him shave. "You're not gonna change your mind, are you?"

"Not likely. Been thinkin' about you an' me for the last month."

She hugged him. "Coffee is on."

"Be right in."

She left and he looked at himself in the mirror and wondered if he was doing the right thing. He could leave and never come back and they'd never meet again in this lifetime. But he didn't want to; he wanted her, and badly. He smiled, then walked into the kitchen to face his soon-to-be in-laws. They both looked happy. "What's to do in Aberdeen?" he asked as he poured himself some coffee.

"Nothin' much. Most people are just gettin' ready for tomorrow."

He tried to remember his last Christmas in Aberdeen, but it came to him in bits and pieces. The homebrew, the drinking, the fighting, the cold, the loneliness, the tears of his sister because once again they had woken up to no tree, no presents and no parents. He lowered his head and shook off tears.

Tina knew something was bothering him. "What's wrong?"

"I just remembered my last Christmas here."

"Was it that bad?"

"Worse."

He wondered if she'd understand. She'd grown up in a home full of love and caring; he hadn't. "We woke up an' my parents were gone, again. There was no tree, no presents an' it was cold an' we had nothing to eat."

She pictured a little boy and a little girl standing in the middle of a cold and empty house on Christmas Day. She wondered what she had been doing at the time. She would've been nine and she had always had good Christmases. Meanwhile, John and Eva had been just down the street. "I'm sorry," she said.

"It's over with," he said, and then remembered he was supposed to call his sister the next day. He'd have to tell her the truth. "I'm suppose to call home tomorrow," he said. "I've gotta tell my sister."

"What does she remember?"

"Nothing, or so she tells me."

"It'll be easier on her."

"I hope so."

"What about you?" she asked. "What you wanna do today?"

"What do your grandparents do on Christmas Eve?"

"Go to church an' visit."

Abraham had been listening to the conversation. "You hunt?" he asked John.

"I've hunted deer an' elk."

"Caribou?"

"No, no caribou." The memory of watching other boys go off on their first hunt returned.

"You ever drive a Ski-Doo?"

"Yeah, drove just about everything you can think of."

"Ever drive dogs?"

John smiled. "Not that."

Abraham looked at John's feet. "I think one of my shoes will fit him," he told his wife in the language.

"They might be too small," she said.

"Caribou are ten miles from here," he said to John. "Wanna go?"

John looked at Tina, who was smiling. "Go," she said. "Do you good an' he's gonna make sure you know how to hunt."

"If I'd known I was gonna go, I'd 'ave brought my gun."

"He's gonna lend you a pair of shoes."

"I wonder if Chief Alfred would lend me his snowmobile."

Tina called the Chief. "Chief, John is going hunting with my grandfather an' needs a Ski-Doo." She looked at John and smiled. "Okay ... an' hey, you can tell Eunice an' Olive we're gettin' married, but it's a secret." She burst out laughing and hung up.

"What he say?" John asked.

"He said there's no such thing as secrets with them two. Everyone's gonna know by the time you get back."

"You don't have any jealous boyfriends, do you?"

"Never went out with anyone from Aberdeen, before you."

He was about to tell her he was not from here, but he was. This was his hometown.

Sarah brought him a pair of moccasins and he recalled the day Chief James had walked into their house. He remembered the smell, the loneliness and the cold. He had told Eva to go back to sleep, since she was cold and hungry and he had nothing to feed her. He pulled on the moccasins, then went into his room and got his down-filled parka. He came out looking like he meant business.

"Now you look like a hunter," Abraham said.

A few minutes later, while on his way to the Chief's house to pick up the snowmobile, he walked by the old house. He was surprised to see very few log houses in the community. Most were like Abraham and Sarah's: three-bedroom prefabricated bungalows with furnaces and no outhouses. He remembered hauling water, cutting wood and running to the outhouse. No one did that any more in Aberdeen. Progress had come north.

As he approached the Chief's house, he could see Alfred outside getting the snowmobile ready. "Hi, Chief," he said.

"Hello, John. So you're gettin' married?"

"Yes."

"She's a nice girl, but you know that."

"I do."

"Remember them words," he said, and laughed. "Here's my gun. Shoots good."

"Thanks."

"First time?"

"First time for caribou."

Chief Alfred looked at the sky. "One hour up, four hours huntin', one hour back. Be back 'roun' four or five," he said.

"Think we'll get some?"

"Abraham is always lucky when it comes to huntin'."

Two hours later, they were in the hills. John was following Abraham when they spotted a small herd of about twenty cows and yearlings. He shut off his machine, took out his gun and walked up to Abraham. "They're cows an' calves," he said.

Abraham turned. "Yeah?"

"Do you take cows an' calves?"

"We have to. Bulls are poor this time of year. Your dad ever take you hunting?"

"Yeah, but only for deer an' elk, an' only bulls."

"I mean your real dad."

"No."

"So this is your first caribou hunt."

"Yes, it is."

"See that cow on the right? Shoot that one first, the rest will run left. You hit it, they won't run far."

John took a deep breath, kneeled, took another deep breath, aimed and fired. The cow dropped and, just like Abraham had said, the others ran to the left but stopped a short distance away. A few minutes later, seven caribou lay in the snow, motionless. John and Abraham started their snowmobiles and drove to the caribou. Then Abraham said something in the language, but John didn't ask what. He knew Abraham was giving thanks to whoever put this caribou there for them.

"You ever skin caribou?" Abraham asked.

"No, but if it's anything like deer an' elk, I shouldn't have a problem."

One hour later, they had skinned and cut up the caribou, and had put them in the sleds. Abraham had made a fire to brew tea and keep warm. He filled two cups, gave one to John, and then sat on his snowmobile. John joined him and looked at the hills and the mountains in the distance. It was cold, but beautiful, almost surreal, like they were the last persons on earth. "I was there when they sent you out," Abraham said.

John kept looking at the hills, sipping his tea. "I know. Tina told me."

"She remember that?"

"She remembered playing with Eva on the floor. I remembered that too."

"Chief James, he worried about it for a long time. He wondered if he did the right thing."

"They sent us to a good family. They treated us like their own."

"That's good." After a few seconds, he said, "I've been married forty-two years. In all that time, I've never hit my wife or been with another woman."

John thought about his mom and dad, and then looked once again at the hills and the mountains. "I understand," he said.

"Your uncle, Edward, he was sweet on Tina's mom."

"He was?"

"Yes, he thought of her as his girlfriend."

He wondered if Edward was Tina's dad. If he was, then …

Abraham noticed John was thinking. "But," he said, "he's not her dad."

They returned to Aberdeen around five o'clock, just after the sun had set, and put two of the caribou in Abraham's shed. "Take the res' to the Chief for feast," he told John, and then went in the house just as Tina walked out. "He did good," he said to her in the language.

Tina smiled. "You did good," she said to John.

He grinned. "Wanna ride?"

She smiled with a hint of wickedness. "Later. Right now we should take this down to the Chief."

"I get it."

"I know. An' you will," she said, and then stood on the sleigh as he drove the snowmobile down to Chief Alfred.

"I'll give it out tomorrow or nex' day," he told John as they put the meat in his shed. "Come in for tea an' somethin' to eat."

They walked in and made themselves at home. Loud disco music was coming from one of the rooms, so Eunice knocked on the door and Sarah stuck her head out. "Turn that music down," Eunice said. "It's too loud."

"That's disco, man. That's good stuff!"

"I'm not a man, man!"

They laughed.

"Hey, Tina," Sarah shouted. "I hear you're gettin' married."

"Yep."

"Really? Why?"

Tina turned to John and said, with pride, "Look at him!"

Sarah giggled and closed the door.

"Kids an' disco," Alfred said. "Gimme fiddle music any day."

"You're jus' gettin' old," Eunice said.

You could tell he was about to say something, but didn't. "So, lotsa caribou?" he asked John.

"About twenty," John said. "Lots of tracks."

"What you hunt down south?"

"Deer an' elk."

"Enough about hunting," Eunice said. "When you're gettin' married?"

"We haven't set a date yet," Tina said. "We just got engaged. Give us time."

"I haven't even told my family," John said. "I'll tell 'em tomorrow."

"Are you gonna move back?" Olive asked.

"No, my job is in Alberta," he said, then looked at Tina.

"An' I'm gonna be goin' to college nex' fall," she said. "We'll worry about where we live later."

"So when are you gonna get married?" Eunice asked again.

Tina looked at John and he shrugged. "Up to you."

"John's gotta go back to work an' so do I," she said. "Maybe this spring sometime. Hey, we'd better get goin'. I have to get ready for church."

John remembered that most of the community attended church on Christmas Eve, and afterwards they shook everyone's hand and wished them a Merry Christmas.

As they walked back to her grandparents' house, she asked, "Wanna go?"

"Sure."

"You don't have to if you don't wanna."

"Is that your way of asking if I'm into religion?"

"Yeah."

"Not really. My parents encouraged us, but didn't force us."

The church was full, and Tina had been right: Most of the community knew they were going to be married and offered their congratulations. After church, John listened to Christmas carols on the radio as he drove Tina and her grandparents home. As they passed the old house, he thought about burning it to the ground.

※

The music was coming from the hall. It sounded like Christmas music. He liked Christmas: the decorations, the school concerts, the church services, the smell of new moose skin moccasins, the candies, the Japanese oranges, the dancing. He didn't like the partying, the fighting, the yelling, the shouting, the curses … and he didn't like the alcohol. He hated the smell of homebrew and it still lingered. It was as if it had permeated his skin.

He opened his eyes and looked at the dark man and the woman. They were in the cabin and it was a mess: clothes, dishes, pots and pans were strewn everywhere. It smelled like smoke, dried meat, rotting meat and homebrew. He wondered how they could live like this and drink that stuff.

The woman was dressed in a blouse and slacks. Her long, black, messy hair covered her face. He remembered she was beautiful when she was young and when she wasn't drinking. She was looking at the man whose back was turned to him and the look was one of fear and hatred. Then she looked at him and almost smiled, but the man hit her and she fell back as if in slow motion. Her head hit the corner of the table and there was a dull thud.

The man turned. He was wearing a pair of dirty, stained coveralls. He was drunk and angry; his eyes were bloodshot and spittle hung from his mouth. "What 'a fuck you lookin' at?" he sneered.

"Don't hit her."

"Why? What you're gonna do about it?"

He wanted to say something, but his head was pounding. It was as if they were driving nails into his brain.

"You think you're smart just 'cause you were in 'a fuckin' army!" the dark man shouted.

"Don't hit her."

"She's my fuckin' wife! I'll do what I want!"

"She's my sister."

"So?" the dark man sneered, and then turned and kicked the woman on the floor. She did not move.

"I said don't hit her."

"Why? What you're gonna do about it?"

He was getting a headache again. The pain was excruciating. He wanted to hit his head with his fists. He closed his eyes and tried to scream, but he had not screamed since ... How long had it been? Forever?

"What you gonna do about it!" the dark man screamed.

"She's my sister."

"So what?"

"I love her."

"You love her?" the dark man said sarcastically, and then looked at the woman on the floor. "Humph," he grunted. "She tol' me you loved ..." The sound of the fog pouring in through the broken window and the door drowned out whatever the dark man said next. He sneered as the fog swallowed him.

"What?" he asked. "Who?" He wanted to run in after him, but the fog was gone. It had turned into a very bright light. It was the sun. He was looking at the sun.

"Who what?" a voice said, coming from the sun.

He wanted to answer, but he didn't know what to say. Maybe this was God. What do you say to God?

The attendant shone his flashlight on the pale Indian. "Who what?" he asked again.

The pale Indian said nothing.

"Who what?" the other attendant asked.

"What?"

"Who what?"

"Who what who?"

"Never mind."

He heard it from a great distance: the roar of the fog getting louder and louder. The woman was still lying motionless on the floor and the dark man was still there, spittle drooling from his mouth. He turned, looked at the woman, and then kicked her.

The pale Indian's breathing was coming in gasps. He was hyperventilating, getting angry. Why couldn't he hear the dark man? Had they cut his ears off? "What?" he asked.

The dark man looked at him. "What?"

"What you said?"

"I said she had my kid!"

The pale Indian looked at his sister lying on the floor. "I know."

"So how can you love her?"

"She's my sister."

"What? What 'a fuck you talkin' about, you stupid bastard?"

"Don't call me stupid. I'm not stupid."

The bright light was back again. He wondered what it was. And why was it so bright? Maybe it was aliens from another world. Maybe they were lost too. Then he heard them speak, but they were too far away to understand. Maybe they were speaking alien.

"Hey, Steve."

"What?"

"He spoke!"

"Who?"

"Ol' Ed."

"What he say?"

"I don't know. He just mumbled."

"He mumbled?"

"Yeah."

"So he mumbled. Let's get goin'. There's a good movie I don' wanna miss."

The light was gone and darkness took its place. He wondered which was real. Was the cabin on the river with the man and the woman real? Or was this real? He wished this place were real. He didn't want to go back to the cabin.

Chapter Six

John and Tina woke early on Christmas Day and gave Abraham and Sarah their gifts. There was another church service at eleven that morning, which Sarah and Tina attended; John and Abraham didn't. John was trying to think of what to say to Eva about their parents. He also had to tell his family that he was engaged. He looked at photos while Abraham told him of his family history and how most of them were related in one way or another. John realized that he and Tina might be related on her mother's and his father's side of the family. They may be fourth or fifth cousins, once or twice removed. It was so far removed, though, he was sure their kids wouldn't be sitting on a porch swing picking on a banjo. "What happened to my parents?" he asked Abraham.

Abraham wondered if John knew. He had been young when he'd left. "What do you know?" he asked.

"Tina told me they died up the river and my uncle found them."

"That's about it. Nothin' much I can add. They were drinkin' an' must 'a passed out an' froze. That's when Edward found them."

"What can you tell me about my uncle?"

"What you know about him?"

"Nothing. I didn' even know I had an uncle."

"Don' know when he was born, but he join the army when he was young."

"When?"

"Sixty-one. He wasn't even twenty."

"When did he come back?"

"After you lef'. Seventy-three, I think. Yeah, seventy-three, 'cause he found your parents the year after."

"What happened to him? Up at the cabin, I mean."

"He said he found them. Never said much after that. He brought them back to town all dressed up, ready to bury."

"Why'd he go quiet?"

"Nobody knows. He was always quiet, slow."

"Slow?"

"Yeah, he wasn' retarded, jus' slow. He use to take care of himself, but after he foun' your parents, he just seem to go inside. Know what I mean?"

"Yeah, I think so. Anyone go see him?"

"Eunice an' Olive went out once, but they said he just sat there an' didn' say a thing. He didn' even know them."

John wondered what made his uncle go silent. And how could his parents freeze? They were Indians. But they were drunken Indians. Drunken Indians and the cold do not mix.

Later that afternoon, Sarah and Tina began preparing Christmas dinner. "You call your sister?" Tina asked.

"Not yet."

"Will you?"

"Have to."

"They're gonna wonder why you haven't called yet."

"Yeah, guess you're right," he said, and then took the phone into the bedroom. Eva answered. "Merry Christmas," he said.

"Merry Christmas to you. Why didn't you call earlier? We were worried."

"Busy morning."

"Whatcha do?"

"Went visiting an' talked with her grandfather."

"They nice?"

"Yeah."

And then she asked. "You see them?"

"No," he said. "I've got some bad news."

Somehow he wasn't surprised when she said, "They're dead." It wasn't a question; it was more of a statement.

"Yeah, they died ten years ago."

"How?"

"They froze upriver at their cabin, according to what I've heard."

"That's too bad."

"You don't feel bad?"

"I don't remember them," she said. "Anything else I should know about?"

"We have two aunts, one uncle an' a few relatives."

"Yeah?"

"Remember I told you about Chief James? His son is now the Chief an' his wife is our aunt. Her name's Eunice."

"She's our mom's sister?"

"No, our father's."

"She nice?"

"Yes. We also have another aunt who lives in Whitehorse, but she's here for the holidays. Her name's Olive."

"What about the uncle?"

He's nuts, he thought. "He's in Edmonton. In an institution or someplace like that."

"What? Why?"

"No idea."

"Is he nuts?"

"Tina's grandfather told me he was quiet and couldn't take care of himself, so they sent him there."

"Wow. Anything else?"

"That's it."

"How are you?" she asked.

"Okay. You?"

"Great! How many people there?"

"Six or seven hundred."

"Really?"

"Yeah, lots of changes. Not the same as I remember. Different an' not all good."

"Why?"

"Drugs, alcohol, violence, same ol', same ol'."

They talked for a few more minutes, and then he talked to his parents and his other sisters and wished them all a Merry Christmas. "You got a number we can reach you at?" his mom asked.

He gave it to her, then hung up and took the phone back into the living room. "What they say?" Tina asked.

"Nothing. They jus' asked a few questions."

"Maybe they don't want you to marry someone from here."

He grinned sheepishly. "I forgot to tell them."

He redialled the number and Eva answered again.

"I'm gettin' married," he said, then hung up and handed the phone to Tina.

A few seconds later, it rang. "You answer it," she said.

He only grinned, so she picked up the phone. "Hello."

"Tina?" Eva asked.

"Yeah?"

"Is it true?"

"Yes, it's true, but I'm having second thoughts," she said, and then laughed.

"Congratulations!"

"Thanks, but it's all happening so fast."

"When's the big day?"

"Haven't set it yet, but sometime in the spring, or nex' fall."

"Why so long?"

"He's gotta get back to work an' so do I. And I have to save up for college nex' fall."

"Where are you going?"

"Calgary, I hope."

They talked for a few minutes, and Tina met his parents on the phone. "They're nice," she said as she hung up.

"They are. You'll like them."

"I'm sure I will."

The next day, for whatever reason, John found himself standing in the cemetery that was next to the church and covered with at least two feet of snow. There was a large spruce tree, probably a few hundred years old, decorated with Christmas lights. At least a hundred granite, marble and wooden crosses poked through the snow. He checked the graves near the church and eventually found his parents. Their wooden crosses were painted white and had their names on them. They'd died in February 1974, two years after he and Eva had left. They'd been in their early thirties; they'd been young. He looked at the hills and the mountains and wondered why he felt no anger or sympathy. Over the last decade, he'd thought about returning to kill his dad for all the abuse he'd put them and his mom through. But now, today, the day after Christmas, he felt absolutely nothing. He turned and walked away, and wondered what his uncle, Edward Brian, had seen. He shook off the thought and tried to get into the holiday spirit.

He returned to Abraham and Sarah's and helped them cut up caribou meat for the feast, then decided to take a nap. A few hours later, Tina woke him and they took the meat down to the community hall where the feast and dance was to be held. John was surprised to see so many people. One of the elders said an opening prayer in the language and the feast began. It was traditional and there was a lot to eat. He had caribou soup, boiled meat and bannock. After everyone had eaten, the local minister said a prayer, and then Chief Alfred spoke in the language and John had no idea what he was talking about. "What's he sayin'?" he asked Tina.

"He's thanking the people an' hopes they had a good Christmas."

After Chief Alfred finished, his father, Chief James, spoke in the language and looked at John, and then mentioned his name.

"He's telling them about you," Tina said. "Stand up."

He did and everyone applauded, and then he sat back down and Chief James continued speaking.

"He's telling them about your hunt with my grandfather. He's saying you left when you were young, so you never had the chance to go hunting, to get your first caribou. But now, you've returned an' you've got your first caribou an' you're sharing it with the people."

The people looked at him, nodded their approval and applauded.

Chief Alfred spoke again and this time they applauded louder. Tina looked as if she wished she could disappear. He assumed correctly that Chief Alfred had told them about their upcoming marriage. "An' don't forget dance tonight!" Chief Alfred said in English. "Start at nine!"

As they walked back to the house, John recalled the dances. He remembered the fiddle and guitars, and the square dances, waltzes and jigging. "We gonna go to the dance?" he asked.

"You wanna?"

"Not really. I'm tired."

"Me too," she said, and then whispered, "We'll be home alone."

"I'm not that tired."

"Good," she said, smiling.

That night, after they had made love, Tina asked, "You wanna head back tomorrow?"

"Yeah," he said. "This is a little too much too fast for me."

And then John had a thought, a flashback if you will. He remembered the tradition of walking around on New Year's Day. This meant meeting at the Chief's house early in the morning and walking from house to house wishing everyone a Happy New Year. "Do they still walk around on New Year's Day?" he asked.

"Yeah, they still do that."

He remembered the last time they'd come to his house and found his parents both passed out. The Chief said nothing and led the men out while John and Eva watched through one of the many holes in the attic floor. They had been cold, hungry and dirty. He shook the memory off and tried to think of better times; warmer times; summer. But even in the summer, they had still been hungry and dirty.

✧

The leaves were green, almost luminescent. It had been a long time since he'd seen them this green. He looked at the hills and the mountains and wondered why they were blue. The last time he went up into the hills, they were green and grey, not blue. He wondered why the river was silver, and not brown. Things were not what they seemed.

"Hi, Edward."

He grinned. "Hi."

She was a beautiful girl, barely twenty, with long, black hair and an infectious smile. She was dressed in a pair of black slacks with black running shoes and a pale yellow blouse over which she wore a blue cardigan. She sat beside him on the bench. "Whatcha doin'?"

"Nothin'," he said. "Jus' lookin'."

He remembered she liked walking along the shore, picking up stones and throwing them into the river. He wanted to take her in his arms and tell her he loved her like he seen them do in the movies. He'd told Elizabeth he was in love with Margaret and wanted to marry her. He wanted to live in one of those towns in the south where nobody knew who he was. He wanted to go to a place where they didn't call him stupid or slow. He wondered if she'd marry him, even if he was stupid. They were almost the same age, but he dropped out of grade nine when it became too difficult for him. He didn't like being called slow and he hated being called stupid. He did like the hostel, though. At least there they made rules he could follow and not get into trouble.

"Did you really join the army?" she asked.

"Yeah." He had joined a few days earlier when the soldier had come to town. Floyd asked him to join. He said he'd take care of him. *They'll make men out of us,* he'd said. *We'll make good money too.* It was then he thought maybe she'd marry him if he became a man and made money.

"When you're leavin'?" she asked.

"Couple 'a weeks."

"Me too. Back to school."

A week later he was outside their house talking to her father, Abraham. Over the last few years he'd helped Abraham and Sarah by cutting wood and getting water from the creek, or ice from the river. He was trying to show them he was a good man and a hard worker. He also did that to get close to her, but something was wrong. Over the last few days he'd hardly seen her. He'd gone to her house a few times, but she stayed inside and never came out. Maybe she was mad at him. Maybe she didn't like him because he was slow. Maybe they were right; maybe he *was* stupid.

"When are you leaving?" Abraham asked in the language.

"Tomorrow," he answered in the language, then switched to English. "Me an' Floyd."

"How long?"

"Don' know. Two, three months."

"And then?"

"Don' know."

Abraham smiled and put an arm on his shoulder. "You'll be okay."

She came out carrying a galvanized tub full of clothes, walked by without looking at him and began hanging clothes on the clothesline.

"Margaret, you forgot this," Sarah said in the language, holding up a bag of clothespins.

Margaret walked to her mom, her arms folded across her as if she had a stomach ache, took the bag of clothespins and then walked back to the clothesline, her gaze never once leaving the ground.

"She's going back to Helena for school," Abraham said.

"Oh."

Being in the army was like being in mission school: He lined up, they shaved off his hair, they gave him the same clothes as everyone else, he slept in a big dorm, he ate in a dining room and he did what they told him to do and he did it without asking. Whatever he couldn't understand, Floyd helped him with. He wondered if Margaret was still mad at him. He wondered what he had done to make her mad. He wished he could write to her, but he didn't know what street she lived on and his letter might get lost. He wished he were smart, like Floyd and the rest.

"You comin'?" Floyd asked.

"Where you goin'?"

"Edmonton for the weekend. Gonna have some fun."

"Okay," he said, even though he didn't like to go to the bars. Maybe he could go to the place they have those rides. He had fun there. Everyone acted like kids there.

Later that night, or early the next morning, they tried to get a taxi to take them back to the base but Floyd was drunk and had no money. He had some, but even so, each time they tried the driver would look at them and drive off.

"Fuck it!" Floyd said. "Let's walk. It's only thirty miles. We can do 'at in our sleep."

Three hours later, they were on the highway walking back to base when he heard the big truck and stepped off to the side of the highway. He turned just in time to see Floyd put his arms up in a futile effort to stop the big truck. It was futility, but it was instinctive.

And just like that, Floyd was gone, and so was the truck. He couldn't remember how far he had to run before he finally found Floyd. It had to be Floyd. He was wearing Floyd's clothes, but his face was gone and his arms and legs were twisted and bent out of shape. He tried to fix them, but they were broken. He tried to wake him, but he knew Floyd had disappeared into the night and had gone back to the Old People up in the Blue Mountains. He didn't know how long he waited, but after a long, long time, he saw the lights. They were far away, but they grew brighter, and then blinded him.

After a long while, the lights disappeared and someone asked, "Private Brian, are you okay?"

"Yes, sir."

"What happened to Private Chinke?"

"Truck, sir. Big truck."

"Where is it?"

"It's gone, sir."

"Did you get the licence number?"

"No, sir."

They kept him in the hospital for a long time and a doctor came in each day and checked his heart, then looked for his soul with a bright light. They had another doctor come in and ask him questions, and they even made him write some tests. He kept looking for Floyd to help him, but Floyd was AWOL again.

After what seemed like forever, the sergeant told him he was going home. "Private Brian?"

"Yes, sir."

"We're sending you home."

"Home, sir?"

"Yes, you're being discharged for medical reasons."

He didn't know what that meant, so he just said, "Yes, sir."

The doctor tried one last time to look for his soul, but he couldn't find it. "I don't know how he made it this far without anyone noticing," he said to the sergeant.

"Me neither, but he was a good soldier."

Chapter Seven

It was Tuesday, February 26, and John was on the Boeing 737 heading north from Calgary to Helena. He'd put in over a month of work on the coast, and then spent a few days with Tina in Helena before going to Calgary to visit Eva and his parents. He was a week early for work, but this time he returned with his rifle and guitar hoping to use one or the other in the short time he had with Tina before going out for his final shift. While in Calgary, he'd sent another demo to a small record company that was interested in him.

Tina met him at the airport, and on their way into town she showed her the engagement ring he'd picked out for her. She got so excited she almost drove off the road. She pulled over, took the ring, put it on her finger and cried. And even when she cried, she still looked beautiful. As they kissed, he teasingly unbuttoned her pants, and when she did not object, he put his hand further down. Not surprisingly, she was wet. "Geez," she moaned, "you really get me excited."

"I've noticed, an' I'm glad."

"Me too, but we'd better get outta here before we cause an accident."

"Want me to drive?" he asked.

"Sure, but I should warn you, I'm gonna touch you too."

"Good."

"Jus' make sure you don't go off the road."

He grinned. "I might go off, but never off the road."

An hour later, Tina was naked and talking to her grandparents on the phone in the language, telling them it was official. "So," he said, after she hung up and got back into bed. "What they say?"

"They're jus' about as excited as I am."

He touched her pussy, which was soaking wet. "Somehow I don't think so."

"John!"

"What? Am I gettin' too graphic?"

She pulled the blanket over her head. "No. You can never get too graphic. It's jus' I'm not used to it ... but I love it, an' I'll get used to it."

"Good," he said, removing the blanket and looking at her. "My family is anxious to meet you."

"Think they'll like me?"

"Of course."

"When?"

"When's a good time for you?"

"When do you come back?"

"Middle of April."

"Wanna go down?" she asked, and he kissed her breasts, and then her stomach. "Not there," she said. "I meant Calgary."

"I know," he said and moved further down her body. "Jus' wanted to see if you'd get it."

"Of course I got it," she gasped as he kissed her pussy. "You an' I think ... ahh ... alike, you know. Do you?"

"Do I what?" he asked and came up for air.

"Wanna take me home in April."

"Sure," he said, and then got back to business "You workin' tonight?"

"No," she moaned. "Took the night off."

"Wanna go an' sit?"

"Sure, but let's finish what we started."

Later, after they'd finished what they'd started, John and Tina walked into the LC and sat with David Matthew and his girl-friend, Verna. Tina and Verna began chatting it up about jobs, college and weddings.

"Cousins," David said to John. "So, whatcha up to these days?"

"Time off 'til next week."

"Me too."

"Where you working now?"

"Norman Wells, full time an' permanent."

"Is that good?"

"I think so."

"Hey, John!"

He turned to see Ken and Richard and wondered if they were joined at the hip. "Hey, boys. What's up?"

"Price 'a beer an' my pecker," Ken said as he and Richard sat down.

"Fuckin' A!" Richard said.

"Leas' Don Fuckin' Ho put some real shit-kickin' music on 'a juke," Ken said. "Guess his disco days are over. Tol' him not to go to no more fuckin' discos in 'a south. Next thing you know, he'll be glowin' in 'a dark."

In late January, Clint had decided to go disco and had put all the latest hits on the jukebox and had even installed some disco lights and a disco ball. He'd also ordered a disco shirt that looked more Hawaiian than Studio 54, and had some platforms that were supposed to be the rage, but obviously not in Helena or anywhere civilized. Ken and Richard took to calling him Don Ho, but Clint had no idea who the fuck Don Fuckin' Ho was. Disco in the LC had lasted for all of one week. In the end, Clint should've listened to Tina, who'd said, "I told you a hundred times, this is a country crowd."

Don Ho was sitting on his usual stool at the end of the bar and had gone country. He was sporting a red western shirt, stonewashed jeans two sizes too small for his already skinny frame and new cowboy boots made from imitation snakeskin that had cost him thirty dollars at the Army and Navy in Edmonton. "Hey, John!" he shouted.

"Yeah?"

"Sing us some tunes."

"Where's your deadly shirt?" John asked.

"Burned 'a fuckin' thing."

"You look like Butch Cassidy," Richard hollered at him.

"Really? You think so?" Clint asked, remembering that Paul Newman played Butch in that movie. He puffed out his chest, showing off his brand new red satin cowboy shirt with white fringes.

"Yeah!" Ken said. "You look like Butch Cassidy on Sunset Boulevard during gay pride week!"

Clint's chest deflated. He promised to burn this fucking shirt and bar Ken the next chance he got.

"Hey, Butch!" Richard shouted. "Ain't Butch a pansy name?"

Clint was going to bar that fucker, too.

John got up on stage and sang some Ricky Skaggs, then did one by Kristofferson and kicked ass with Waylon. He finished with a couple by Hank and Lefty, and one by Merle.

Clint took the time to run upstairs to his apartment and change his shirt. He chose a dark blue flannel that made him look like he'd just stepped off the cover of an Eddie Bauer catalogue. He checked himself out in the mirror. Satisfied, he went back downstairs, blended in with the crowd and promised to get himself some real shit kickers the next time he was in Edmonton.

"Hey, Butch!" Richard shouted to him. "I hear the outdoors look is the lates' rage."

"It is?"

"Yeah," Ken said. "In gay Par-ee!"

In early March, John, Elmer, Ken and Richard were on the coast working their last shift of the season. According to Bill, their supervisor, they'd be done by mid-April.

On their second night at camp, John brought his guitar to the dining trailer and was surprised when Richard walked in with a fiddle. "Didn' know you could play," he said.

"Shee-it," Richard said as he tuned up. "Can play almos' anything with strings. Give your guitar to Ken an' me an' him will show you how it's done in Aberdeen."

John handed over his guitar and Ken and Richard played music he hadn't heard for a long time. He remembered one of the last dances he attended in Aberdeen before he and Eva had been sent south. Everyone had been having a good time until his parents came into the community hall. They were drunk, again.

✦

The fiddle player was moving from side to side and he was sweating. His rubber slippers were pounding a hole in the floor. The guitar player was strumming to beat hell. He had on a pair of sunglasses and his baseball cap was cocked to one side.

About sixty people were on the dance floor in their new moose skin moccasins or slippers, and the Chief was calling out a square dance. The tree in the corner swayed back and forth and the ornaments danced in the light. Someone popped one of the hundreds of balloons stuck to the walls and everyone jumped. They were having a good time and everyone was smiling and laughing.

He wished he could join in, but he'd never danced in his life. But he liked watching and he loved the smell of tanned moose skin. They never had dances like this in the army and they didn't have any feasts, at least none with caribou meat, caribou soup, bannock, tea, oranges and tons and tons of candies.

He had been glad when the Chief had come to his house and welcomed him home and asked if he was going to the feast and dance. He said he was and hoped Margaret would be there. On the day of the feast and dance, he dressed in his uniform and sat with the Chief and his wife. After the feast, the Chief spoke and wished everyone a Merry Christmas, and then welcomed him home in front of everyone. He stood and they all clapped for him. All during the feast, he kept looking for Margaret, but he never saw her. Maybe she was home in her room. Abraham and Sarah came over to say hello and they had a girl with them. She looked like she was ten or eleven. Maybe they had another baby while he was gone.

"Yahoo!"

"Weee-hooo!"

Everyone looked toward the door and stopped smiling, then tried to ignore the new arrivals. He didn't have to look up to know William and Elizabeth were here, and to know they were drunk again. He wished they'd go home and leave the people alone. Despite the intrusion, the fiddle player still fiddled, the guitar player still guitared and the dancers still danced, but they didn't *woo-hoo* any longer, or at least not as loud.

William's eyes were glassy and his hair was a mess; spittle hung from his lower lip. He was wearing his dirty coveralls again, as if he was going to work, and his rubber boots were hard and frozen. Elizabeth was wearing a dirty nylon jacket and a dress; her stockings were bunched up around her ankles. She too had glassy eyes and spittle on her lip. Her hair was braided, but it was still a mess. Even from across the floor, he could tell she had a black eye, again. They were drunk, but they didn't know it. They thought they were having a good time, but they were embarrassing.

He hung his head, picked up his paper bag and walked across the floor, hoping they wouldn't see him. He still didn't like beer, and he hated homebrew and those who drank it. It made them slow and stupid. *Maybe that's what's wrong with me. Maybe I'm full of brew.*

The next day he went to visit Abraham and Sarah, but they'd moved to a new house that had an indoor toilet, running water and a furnace. They didn't need anyone to cut wood or haul water for them. He wore his uniform and kept waiting for Margaret to come out of the bedroom, but she never did. The little girl he'd seen at the feast was there with them.

"This is Margaret's daughter," Sarah said in the language.

He looked at her and smiled. She smiled, and then got shy. It took him a few seconds to translate what they'd said in his head, and then it dawned on him: If she had a daughter, she was married. "She's married?" he asked.

They laughed, and then looked at each other, confused. "Who?" Abraham asked.

"Margaret."

They sat silent for a few seconds, and then Sarah put a hand on Abraham. "Don't you know?" Abraham asked in the language.

Know what? He shook his head. "Know?"

"Edward," Sarah said, "she died."

He sat frozen in time. He didn't know what to say.

"We thought you knew," Abraham said in English.

"Where she is?"

"We buried her, long ago."

The gravestone was simple: *Margaret, Beloved Daughter of Abraham and Sarah. Born 1944. Died 1963.* He tried to remember where he had been in 1963. He had been in the army with Floyd. He looked for Floyd's grave and found it. A wooden cross and plastic flowers adorned the grave. He looked around at the snow-covered cemetery. So much snow. They didn't get this much snow in the army.

On his way home he passed his sister's house, but it was empty. They were up the river. William had lost his job again, so they had to trap to make money. He wished they'd make some. The last time he'd seen them, he'd had to give them money so they could buy food. He'd seen them that night and they were drunk, again. And Elizabeth had a black eye, again. He wondered where his nephew was. What was his name? William? Abraham? John? He was just a baby. He was still in diapers.

He got to the house that once belonged to his parents and looked at the yellow machine and smiled. This one didn't need dog food as fuel and it went forever without getting tired. He walked into the house, turned on the lights and then sat. He did not remember how long he sat, but when he looked outside it was dark. He undressed, folded his clothes, kneeled, said his prayers in the language in his head and then went to bed. He had not eaten, nor had he washed. "Good night, Floyd." He held his breath and waited for an answer, but none came. He thought about Margaret and the little girl with no name.

Chapter Eight

It was the third week in April and they were in Tina's bed. Tina's head was on John's chest and she was touching him. "I was accepted into the program," she said.

"That's good," he said. "You sure that's what you want?"

"Thought about it lots, an' yes."

"It's your choice," he said, stroking her hair. He remembered he had done that to Eva when they slept in the same small bed in their attic while their parents were out or, worse, drinking and fighting downstairs. She'd lay her head on his chest and he'd stroke her hair and tell her not to cry.

"I've been talkin' to Eva," Tina said, "an' asking her about the program. She's really smart."

"She's got the brains. I'm stuck with the looks."

"Yeah, right."

"You set on a date?"

"Not really. What about you?"

"Your choice."

"I don't care when, I just want …"

"Want what?"

"Can we do it in Aberdeen?" she asked.

"We can do it wherever you want."

"I don't know why I worry. We've got time to plan it."

"All the time you want."

"Can I say something?"

"Sure."

"I don't want any children, at least not right away."

The thought hadn't crossed his mind. He wanted a career in music, and if that didn't work, he wanted to take over the family farm.

"Does that bother you?" she asked.

"Not at all."

"You sure? And don't say fuckin' A."

"Darn tootin'."

She laughed, and then got up to prepare for another Friday night in the trenches. "Told Clint I was gonna take next week off, maybe longer," she said.

When they walked into the LC, the smoke was thick and the perfume and aftershave were thicker. John didn't know if they put it on or drank it.

He joined Elmer, Ken and Richard at a table while Tina went to work. Clint was sitting on his usual stool at the end of the bar in a blue denim shirt, stonewashed jeans and brand new cowboy boots. He'd also bought a black Stetson like the one John Travolta wore in *Urban Cowboy* and was thinking of getting a mechanical bull and holding a wet T-shirt contest.

"Hey, Clint!" Ken shouted. "You look like one 'a the Village People!"

Clint wished the fucker would shut the fuck up. He was constipated and hadn't had a hard-on in the last couple of years, but there was always hope. He'd bought an Inuit carving made from caribou antlers and was grinding this down and mixing it with his morning coffee to see if the Japanese and Chinese were telling the truth about its magical and uplifting powers. There were billions of them, so he figured they must be telling the God's honest truth, even though they were commies and atheists.

Tina came over to the table. "What'll it be?"

"Give us a roun' an' get your ol' man on stage," Ken said. "An' get him to sing some Hank."

"Hey, John!" Richard shouted. "Should sing something from *Eddie an' 'a Cruisers.*"

Tina leaned over. "Sing one of yours," she whispered in John's ear, and then touched his thigh and gave him a woody.

The next day, John and Elmer went hunting with Tina's grandfather. They got a couple of caribou and returned to Helena after dropping off Abraham. Tina fried some caribou meat, and then she and John sat in the living room and ate.

"Whatcha lookin' at?" she asked.

"You," he said. "Jus' wonderin' how I got so lucky."

"I'm the lucky one."

"I still can't believe you're the little girl I saw in the Chief's house."

"That was a long time ago."

"I know, but like I said, I can't remember too much of that time, except the fightin' an' the drinkin', an' being alone with Eva."

"Must've been hard."

"It was. I didn't care about me, but I didn't like seeing Eva cold an' hungry an' wearing dirty clothes." Tears welled up in his eyes.

"You did good," Tina said. "You do know that, don't you?"

"I tried, but I was just a kid myself."

"Seen your mom an' dad a few times, but only from far. At least I think it was them. I never thought about them or Edward until you showed up."

"I tried to remember him, but I can't. No one talked about him."

"He never called?"

"We never had a phone."

"Maybe he wrote."

"Wouldn't know. Your grandfather said Eunice an' Olive went to see him once, and he didn't know them."

She looked at him. "You ever think of seeing him?"

"No, not until now. But why bother? If he didn't recognize them, how will he know me?"

"Yeah, you're right," she said. "Anyways, I'm excited about meeting your family."

He tried to remember his uncle, but couldn't. All he could remember was his dad, but he too was a stranger: an angry, quiet stranger, almost dangerous. The only time he had been happy was when he was drunk, and then he wasn't happy for long. His happiness turned to anger, and then to rage. John tried to picture his mom, but the only thing he could see was a quiet woman, scared and distant, with a dark face and darker eyes … and black eyes. How old had he been when his uncle left? If Edward had left in sixty-one, that meant he had been about a year old. Of course he didn't remember him: He had been just a baby.

✦

The baby had on a striped shirt and denim coveralls and was crawling toward the stairs that led to the attic.

"John!"

He jumped, looked at his sister, then walked over and picked up the baby and tickled him. The baby laughed.

"So, when's your plane?" his sister asked.

"After," he said, and then looked around for his brother-in-law. "Where's William?"

"He went to work."

He lifted the baby over his head. "Hey, John." The baby laughed and flailed its arms and legs. Spittle hung from its mouth. He was about to wipe it away, but his headache was back again. Maybe it was from the bright light. Every time he got a headache, the bright light came around. He closed his eyes and tried to squeeze the pain back into the light. He took a deep breath and smelled the smoke and the … what was that? He opened his eyes and looked through the wire mesh. It was dark outside. It was always dark. He wondered why the sun never stayed up all night like it did in … where was that place? There were hills, mountains and a river: a blue river. It flowed right by … Then it came to him in a flash of light. "Aberdeen," he said very slowly.

The attendant had his light on the pale Indian. "Aber-what?" he asked.

The pale Indian looked up at the attendant dressed in green. He looked like a tree: a tree with a white head. He was about to tell him again, but he was interrupted.

"What?" the other attendant asked.

"He said something."

"Who?"

"Ol' Ed."

"What he say this time? Mumble?"

"He said Aber-something."

"Aber-what?"

"I don't know."

"Aberdeen," the pale Indian said.

The two attendants looked at him. "Say again?" one of them asked.

The pale Indian wondered why he should say it again. Who were these people? What did they want? And why were they dressed like twins? Were they nuts or crazy? Why didn't they take their light somewhere else?

"What did you say, Ed?"

Who's Ed? Were they calling him Ed? His name was Edward, not Ed. "My name is Edward."

"Oh, okay, Edward. What did you say?"

He was confused. They must be crazy. They were driving him nuts. And now they both had their lights on him. He closed his eyes and took a deep breath.

"Think we should put it in the report?"

"What?"

"What he said."

"For what?"

"Didn't you say he never spoke since he got here?"

"Yeah, but that's just what I heard."

"Think I should put it in?"

"Whatever."

Chapter Nine

Calgary at the end of April was like Helena in June: The snow was gone and spring had arrived. John's parents and Eva met John and Tina at the airport on Sunday and each gave Tina a big hug. "Congratulations!" Eva said.

"Thanks," said Tina. She remembered the small girl on the floor of the Chief's house. She also knew, from talking to John, that Eva didn't remember that moment.

They all went out for supper that night and Eva asked about the People and the community. It was as if she and Tina were long-lost sisters catching up on the latest gossip from home.

On Monday, John and Tina went shopping, and then to his parents' ranch, where Tina and her soon-to-be father-in-law barbecued some caribou meat. Tina got to see first-hand the life of a farmer and rancher, and she liked it.

They drove back to Calgary that afternoon and stayed with Eva, and then went out for supper with her and Elmer. They spent the evening bar-hopping and listening to bands from all over looking for their big break.

"How many people trying to make it as singers?" Tina asked John as they were having a beer in one of the more popular bars.

"Don't know. Thousands."

"Really? What's your chances?"

"As good as the next guy."

"Whatcha gotta do?"

"Put together a band, hire a manager, write some songs, get some gigs, get a following, cut a record an' then pray."

"Is that all?" she asked, almost sarcastically.

"Kiss a lot of butt too."

"I can be your manager," Elmer offered. "Groupies turn me on."

"Groupies?" Tina asked John.

"Gonna hire some of them too," he said.

She laughed. "Is it a lot of work? The singing, I mean."

"Town to town, bar to bar. Lot of work for a few minutes of fame, and maybe fortune, if you're lucky. One in a million chance, or so it's been said."

"What if you don't make it?"

"Gotta think about that too. Figured I can work on the rigs, or look for a ranch, or even take over from my dad one of these days. Might even look at goin' to college and gettin' a trade or a profession."

On Wednesday, John and Tina went for lunch with Eva, and then toured the college and looked at places they'd like to live. That evening, Tina cooked some caribou meat and Eva finally ate drymeat for the first time in a long time and liked it. "This is great," she said to Tina.

"It is, isn't it?" Tina responded, and then asked, "You ever going back?"

"Not likely, but you never know where the jobs in nursing are going to be in the future. What about you? Where you goin' after you finish?"

"Always thought about going back home an' making a difference. But I've been having second thoughts."

"Is it that bad? The alcohol an' violence, I mean."

"It's bad all over, but you seem to notice it more in your own community."

"I don't remember anything about my parents or the community," Eva said with no hint of regret.

"Typical northern community."

"When are you going back? To Helena, I mean."

"We're going back on Sunday. John has to return to work in a week or two."

The next day, John and Tina walked, shopped and took in the sights. By six, they were tired and looking for some time alone, so they checked into a small hotel on the outskirts of town with a view of the Rocky Mountains. "Ah, peace an' quiet," John said as he flopped on the bed.

Tina joined him and let out a big sigh.

"I love you sooo much."

"I love you too," he said, and then ran his hand over her stomach and down to her groin.

"Oooh," she moaned. "If you only knew what you do to me."

Later, as they lay naked on the bed, she asked, "How long is your next shift?"

"Month an' a bit."

"End of June?"

"Yeah."

"You comin' up after?"

"Drivin'."

"And then?"

"Gonna get Clint to pay me if he hasn't gone completely redneck. I could spend a couple weeks there this summer, an' then we could drive down an' look for a place to live an' get you ready for college."

"Be August by then," she said. "Think I can find a part-time job here?"

"You could, no problem."

"Got that part of our life planned, anyways."

"Got our whole life to plan, but got lots of time to do it."

"I'm never gonna let you go," she said. "You know that, eh?"

"I can't think of anyone I'd rather spend the rest of my life with."

"I was thinking about a date."

"We're not even married an' you're looking for a date. What are you using me for: sex?"

"I meant a date for our wedding. And yes, I *am* using you for sex. At least for the time being."

"Oh," he said. "Okay by me."

She laughed. "I was thinking about next spring in Aberdeen."

"That's a long way off."

"I don't wanna rush into it. I wanna plan it good."

"Whatever you want," he said. "I'm just gonna pay for it, show up, say I do an' then jump you."

"Thank you. You're easy."

"Only for you."

She said, "You do know you're gonna have to jig, eh?"

"Sorta figured."

"Do you know how?"

He laughed. "Never jigged in my life. Only waltzed an' square danced a few times. What about you? You ever jig?"

"Are you kidding? Never!"

"Well," he said as he stood in front of the mirror. "Guess we'll just have to practise an' learn."

✧

The Indian in the mirror was pale, almost white. His unkempt hair was black, but showed traces of grey, and he needed a comb. He wanted to ask how long he'd been here, but he was tired and weak. How long had he slept? He was tired of sleeping. He felt sore all over and he hated the smell of the place. It smelled like disinfectant and urine. It smelled like slow death and forgotten people. He wished he were somewhere else. He remembered them coming in last week, the men and women in white. "Do you know where you are?" they asked.

He was in a city, but he didn't know which one.

"Do you know who you are?" they asked.

He wondered if they were slow or stupid. "Brian, sir. Private Brian." His voice was hoarse, almost squeaky.

They all smiled. "This is not the army, Edward," one of them said. "You don't have to call me *sir*. I'm a doctor."

He knew that. He just didn't want to believe it.

"Do you know where you're from?" they asked.

He looked out the window for the mountains, but they were not there.

"Do you know where you're from?" they asked again.

"Blue Mountains," he said. His mouth was dry.

"Here, have some water."

He drank the water, but it was different from the water in the Teal River.

"Do you know where you are?" they asked again.

He looked at the wire mesh and nothingness.

"Do you know why you're here?"

He looked for the dark man and the woman, but they didn't appear. He knew they were William and Elizabeth. He even knew Elizabeth was his sister ... but he was scared. Of what? Did they know what William had done to Elizabeth? Did they know what he had done to William? And did they know why?

"Edward, what are you doing out of bed?"

He looked at the black man dressed in green, then down at his bare feet on the cold floor. The black man in green led him from the bathroom to his bed, and then tucked him in. He closed his eyes and that's when he heard the dark man: "She had my kid, you stupid bastard!"

"I know."

"What do you know, Edward?"

He looked up at the attendant. He liked this one. He was black, as if he had passed spring in the Blue Mountains: sunburned and windburned. "She had his kid."

"Who?"

"William."

"William who?"

Chapter Ten

It was Saturday, June 29, and John had been driving for three days, taking short naps here and there. He was tired and needed a shower. He was glad when the Blue Mountains came into view. Even from fifty miles out, he could tell it was the Blue Mountains. He enjoyed the drive from Calgary and the scenery, but he couldn't get used to the mosquitoes that came out of nowhere. He also couldn't get used to the sun being up most of the night. He remembered, as a child, playing with other children late into the night during the summer when it was always light out. He also remembered why he had stayed out late: He didn't want to go home to another party or another fight, or to find one of his parents in bed with a stranger or, worse, someone he knew.

He arrived in Aberdeen at six o'clock that evening and drove to Abraham and Sarah's house, where Tina clung to him as if she was never going to let go. It was a feeling he wished would last for the rest of his life. She cried and buried her face into his neck, and she smelled so nice. "Miss me?" he asked.

"You bet," she answered. "Can't wait to get you alone."

Her grandparents were also glad to see him, and they roasted some fish for him outside and he loved it.

Later, he and Tina visited Chief Alfred and Eunice. "I'm glad you're back," Eunice said. "I've got something for you." She took him out to an old shed and removed a small paper bag from an old suitcase. "This is all we took out of the house. It's not much, just some pictures." She didn't tell him that his parents' house had been a mess when they'd cleaned it up. She didn't tell him there were no windows, no lights, and the furniture was old and broken.

When they went back into the house, John looked at the pictures. He'd seen them before, but that was a long time ago. There was a photo of his grandparents, photos of his mom and dad when they were young and an aged and blurry photo of their wedding day. "Who's this behind them?" he asked Eunice.

"That's your uncle Edward." His uncle was nothing but a blur. "Oh, before I forget," she said. "Olive heard from the hospital."

"Yeah?" Tina asked.

"They said he's talking."

"Talking?"

"Yeah. He hasn't said much since he left. Must be ten years now."

"What did he say?" John asked.

"Nothin' much. He knows who he is an' where he comes from. They say he's gettin' around on his own an' makin' progress."

"I wonder if he'll ever get better?" Tina asked.

"I don't know. He was always slow, you know."

"How did he get in the army?" John asked.

"He had a friend: Floyd Chinke. He helped Edward."

"What happened to him?"

"Who? Floyd? He died in the army. That's when they found out Edward was slow an' sent him home. He was good for a while, an' 'en he found your parents an' was sent south."

"Why?"

"He couldn't take care of himself an' he never said a word. Jus' sat there an' looked at nothin'. They figure seein' your mom an' dad did that to him."

"You think he'll ever come home?"

"I don't know. But Olive said they're going on holidays an' they might stop in an' see him."

Later, as John and Tina cruised around town, he asked, "Hey, where's Richard an' Ken?"

"They just got back from work," she said. "Probably at the Saloon."

"What about David?"

"I think he's in the Wells. Verna said they might move."

"What's to do on a Saturday night?"

"Nothin' much. The kids usually get together a game of scrub."

He'd forgotten about scrub: a never-ending game of baseball played by almost every kid in the community that usually went on all night.

"Wanna see the Saloon?" she asked as they came up to it.

It was nine and the sun was still high in the west. He needed a shower, a good night's sleep and some tender loving, but decided what the hell. "Sure."

He was not prepared for the darkness and the smell, but then he had not stepped into a bar quite like this for a long time. It took a few seconds for his eyes to adjust to the light, and then he realized that everyone was looking at him. He had the urge to check to see if his fly was open, but everyone soon returned to whatever it was they were doing.

There were fifteen tables scattered around the bar, a pool table and a new jukebox that was belting out some Kenny Rogers. There were no decorations, photos or ornaments of any kind on the walls that were already turning yellow from the smoke and wasted dreams. It was a typical Indian bar: dark, smoky, loud and country with the smell of cheap perfume.

"Hey, John!" someone shouted.

He peered into the darkness and spotted Ken sitting at a table in the corner with Richard.

"Come join us!" Richard shouted.

"They're still joined at the hip," John said to Tina.

She laughed. "You go ahead. I'm gonna sit with the girls at the bar."

John got a beer and then made his way through the crowd. Most people stared at him as if he were an intruder, but a couple of females looked at him, and then at his crotch.

"Hey, John. How fuck you doin'!" Richard shouted. "When you get in?"

No one *said* anything in this bar; they yelled, shouted or screamed it.

"Couple hours ago," he answered. "What you two been up to?"

"Same ol'."

"Hey," Ken said. "We're gonna party later. Wanna come?"

"Not tonight," John said. "Too tired."

"Well, if you fin' 'a time, come down to our apartment."

"You guys share an apartment?"

"Fuck no!" Richard said. "We're not 'at queer."

"We live nex' to each other in 'a sex-plex," Ken said.

"Where's that?"

"Jus' down 'a road. Look for 'a loudes' place an' you foun' it."

"They're gonna declare my apartment a historical site one 'a these days," Richard said. "More broads been screwed 'ere 'an in the Legislative Assembly an' House 'a Commons put together."

"You forgot the Senate," Ken said.

"Senators are dickless, which makes 'em useless fucks."

"Can't argue with that," Ken said. "So, how long you here for?" he asked John.

"Month."

"What then?"

"Head south an' try for the big time while Tina goes to college." While they talked, John looked around and wondered how many of the people in the Saloon that night had children at home who were going hungry. How many of them were going to have their children taken away in the next few days, weeks or months? He was glad when Tina joined them. "Hey, Ken! Hey, Richard!" she shouted.

"Hey, Tina!" they both shouted back.

Tina squeezed John's thigh. "Wanna go?"

"Sure," he said, and pushed out his chair. "Gotta go."

"Yeah," Ken said. "See you 'round."

As they stepped outside, John had to shield his eyes from the sun. "You ever get use to that?" he asked.

"What?"

"The sun."

"Don't bother me none."

"Gotta get use to it, I guess."

They drove to her grandparents' and he was very quiet when they went inside. He took off his boots and tiptoed into the kitchen for a glass of water.

"John!" Tina screamed.

He jumped. "What are you doin'?" he whispered.

"They're not here," she whispered back.

"Where are they?" he whispered.

"They got a camp about five miles upriver. They stay there in the summer."

"Oh," he said, then thought about the possibilities and smiled.

John heard the shower running and opened his eyes. It was eight o'clock but still dark. He pulled open the blinds to find the window covered with tinfoil to block the sunlight. *Nice idea,* he thought. He pictured Tina in the shower, wet and naked, and then joined her.

An hour later, he was sitting on the sofa wearing a T-shirt and jeans and sipping on coffee while Tina sat on the armchair drying her hair. She had on a bathrobe, her legs showing. He was watching an old boxing match between Ali and Liston on television.

"Thanks," she said.

"For what?"

"For doing my back. And for doing me."

"It was my pleasure. Or didn't you notice?"

"I noticed, but thanks anyways."

He grinned. "You've got a nice pair of legs."

"Thanks."

"Course they look better wrapped around me."

"I know."

"I can do you again, if you want."

She laughed. "I know you can, but I've got things to do. Besides, my legs are still sore." She looked down. "Look," she said,

"I still can't close 'em." Then she let out a loud laugh. "Geez, I can't believe I said that."

He smiled, and then stood, raised his arms and did the Ali shuffle. "I am the greatest," he said in his best Ali voice.

"You are."

"Thank you. We *are* getting comfortable with each other."

"I know. I've never had this much fun in my life."

"What do you mean?"

"I mean the sex, the conversation, no conversation, everything. It's so perfect. *You're* so perfect."

"I'm not, but you'll find out."

"I love you so much."

"I love you too," he said, and then got her up and held her.

Her hand went to his cock. "Geez!" she said. "Don't you ever get tired?"

"Not with you."

She laughed and kissed him and continued holding his cock. "Geez," she said, "I've really got to get dressed, or I'll never get out of bed."

"We don't have to use the bed."

"Kinky," she said and pulled on her jeans.

"What do you have to do today?"

"I've gotta pick up my grandparents. They want to go to church."

"How do you get there?"

"We can get there from the highway. There's a road to the fish camp. They stay there with four or five families."

They finished their coffee, then drove on the highway until they came to a clearing in the willows. The camp consisted of six tents, four smokehouses, three boats with outboards and four canoes. They went into her grandparents' tent to find them getting ready. Sarah handed John a brown paper bag, and from the smell he knew it was donuts—Indian style. He remembered his mom cooking donuts and the happy times they'd had when his dad was at work. His mom only drank when his dad returned, and then it wasn't happy: it was dismal, lonely and frightening.

They drove into town and went to church with Tina's grandparents. Only about thirty people showed up, mostly women and the elderly. John remembered sitting in the back of the church while Eva rested her head on his lap and slept. This was one of the places they came to get away from the drinking and the fighting. If they were lucky, some kid would take them home and they'd have something to eat.

After church, they took her grandparents home, and then back to the fish camp where John helped Abraham look at nets. Later, they had roast fish and bannock, and then drove back to town. "That was nice," John said.

"It was."

"Do they stay up there all summer?"

"Yes, ever since I can remember they've been up there."

His parents had never taken him out, at least not that he could remember.

"Let's drive around," Tina said.

They drove to the baseball diamond and watched about fifteen children playing ball. He noticed a few with dirty clothes and dirty faces, and wondered if they were here to get away from parties and fights at home. Were they hungry?

"Whatcha thinkin' about?" Tina asked.

"Bad ol' days," he said. "Jus' wonderin' how many of these

kids are here because their parents are drinking, or worse."

"What's worse?"

"Fighting, being hungry."

Later, at her grandparents', Tina did some laundry while John took out his guitar and began strumming. A few minutes later, he was trying to write or compose.

I was twelve years old, on my own
When I left the old hometown
Discarded by the ones that ...

He stopped and went brain-dead for a few seconds, then wrote in his notebook and continued.

I was twelve years old, on my own
When I left the old hometown
Discarded by the ones I loved
And cast into the wind
She was just a kid ...

Tina sat at the kitchen table and wondered what was going on in John's mind. What memories spawned those words?

I was twelve years old, on my own
When I left the old hometown
Discarded by the ones I loved
And cast into the wind
She was just a kid, but she was mine
And all the dad she knew ...

He wrote this down and continued.

She was just a kid, but she was mine
And all the dad she knew
She looked into my eyes and said …

He looked at Tina and wondered what Eva was doing right now. She was probably at their parents' house getting ready for the first of July celebrations like most people all over Canada. She's smiling, laughing and has not a care in the world. She's young, intelligent and beautiful.

"Finished?" Tina asked.

"Not really. Still got lots to do. Call it a work in progress."

"Sounds good."

"Sounds dismal. But country is dismal, or so it's been said." He looked outside and the community appeared deserted. "Where's all the people?"

"It's Sunday," she said. "Probably taking it easy, hungover, whatever."

"What's gonna happen tomorrow?"

"Games, races, feast an' dance."

He grinned. "Maybe we should practise."

She smiled and looked around as if someone was watching. "Wanna?" she whispered.

"Got any music?"

"We can call Ken an' Richard."

He laughed. "No, I don't need to practise. I'm gonna wing it all the way."

"You know, I've never felt like this," she said.

"Like what?"

"I mean I'm so happy. I just love being with you, holding you, looking at you, feeling you."

"I'm happy too. I enjoy everything about you. Can I tell you something?"

"Sure."

"I enjoy going down on you," he said. "You smell so nice."

She diverted her gaze, shyly. "Thanks."

"And taste even better."

"You're making me shy an' you're gonna make me cry."

"I'm sorry."

"Don't be. It's a happy cry."

The first of July in Aberdeen was something he'd enjoyed as a child and it hadn't changed very much since then. There were foot races, bicycle races, egg throwing and many other games. But seeing so many children brought back memories of his childhood, so he stood in the background while Tina joined in and enjoyed herself. She also enjoyed teasing the elders in the language or being teased by them.

There were five stoves by the open area near the church, each containing two large pots of caribou meat or caribou soup. There were also two open fires where fish was being roasted and tea was being made. This was for the feast.

"Hey, John," Richard called.

John turned to see Richard and Ken, who both looked like they'd seen better days. "What's up?" he asked.

"Diddly," Richard said.

"You two look like you just woke up."

"We did," Ken said. "In 'a drunk tank."

John smiled. "When you goin' back to work?"

"Nex' week," Ken said.

"Damn, I wish the Saloon was open," Richard said.

"It is," Ken said.

"What? Ain't nothin' sacred no more?"

"What you mean?"

"It's Sunday."

"It's Monday."

"What?" Richard asked. "It's Monday?"

"All day."

"Where 'a hell did Sunday go?"

"Same place Saturday went: oblivion."

"Wanna go for a few?"

"Dumb question."

"You?" Richard asked John.

"Not yet, maybe later."

"Hey," Richard said to Ken. "If it's Monday, we have to play at the dance tonight."

"Yeah, you're right," Ken said. "You're ugly an' stupid, but you're right."

"Up yours."

"You wish."

They left and John turned his attention back to the games. Tina and about thirty others were blindfolded and feeding each other pudding, or at least they were trying to. Most of it was on their faces. He smiled and took a few photographs.

The feast began at seven and it was almost the same as the one he'd attended in December, except this one was held outdoors on the grass field next to the community hall. It was livelier; people were laughing, joking and telling stories.

That night, Ken and Richard showed up looking and feeling better. They tuned up and began the dance. John and Tina joined in a few square dances and waltzed twice before Ken and Richard took a break. No sooner had they put down the fiddle and guitar than two other people picked them up and the dance began again.

"Fuck, I need a beer!" Richard said as stepped outside and wiped the sweat from his forehead. "Should distill 'is," he said, meaning his sweat.

"Drink it straight," Ken said.

"Might kill me."

The dance lasted until three o'clock, and then everyone began leaving. John and Tina drove her grandparents and two other couples and their seven grandchildren up to the camp on the highway, then returned home. Despite it being three-thirty in the morning, the sun was still high above the horizon to the north, and the house was stifling hot. They were both sweating and could feel dust in their hair and on their skin. They took a shower together, made love and then fell asleep soon after, tired but feeling good.

✧

He was tired but feeling good, almost excited. Today, for the first time since he could remember, they had gone out of the city. They'd got into a van and driven west, and for the first time in a long time he'd seen mountains. They were bigger than the Blue Mountains. They were the largest mountains he'd ever seen.

When he and Floyd were in the army, they'd look at the mountains and he'd get homesick. They never went home all that time they were in the army. Floyd told him there was nothing to go home for. He had no family. That's why he joined the army, he said. To get away from Aberdeen and to have a full-time job.

They drove for a long time before they came to the mountains, which swallowed them. They stopped to look at them three times. On the last stop, they had burgers, fries and Cokes. He liked that. He was sad when they turned around in the mountains.

"We gotta get back before it gets dark," Jim said.

"How come the sun don't stay up all night?" he asked.

Jim looked at him funny. "What?"

"How come the sun don't stay up all night?"

"Because it can't."

"The sun stays up all night in Aberdeen, in the summer."

"Is that so," Jim said.

He didn't know if Jim was asking him a question, or if he was telling him something, so he shut up. He looked at the mountains. They were grey, but the farther they drove, the bluer they got. He fell asleep and woke up when they arrived back in the city. He felt good. Maybe that was why he couldn't sleep now?

He looked through the wire mesh at the city lights that seemed so far away. He was taking walks in the yard and was not as pale as he used to be. He remembered when he used to get darker. That was when he went hunting in the spring with his parents up in the hills. They were dead. That much he knew. They had died when he was in mission school. They had been old. When they'd died, the school had sent him home. When Floyd'd died, the army had sent him home. He looked at the empty bed. The man they'd called Eli had died last week. They'd wheeled him out in his bed. He had been old. He wondered when they were going to send him home.

"Edward?"

He turned and looked at the black man dressed in green. It was Jim. He knew a Jim in Aberdeen. He was old. Did he die, too? And what about Chief James? He was not old. He was young, like him. But he was old now. He grew old in here. Maybe this was the place they sent the Old People. He knew it wasn't.

"Edward?"

"Yes, sir."

"Are you okay?"

"Yes, sir," he said, and then wished he hadn't. He had called the men in the mission school *sir*. He had called the men in the hostel *sir*. He had called the men in the army *sir*. He had called every man he had met since *sir*. The women were different. If they talked to him, he called them *ma'am*. That was what they taught him in the mission school and in the hostel.

Jim smiled. "I keep telling you, Edward. You don't have to call me *sir*."

"I'm sorry."

"And you don't have to be sorry."

"I'm sorry."

Jim smiled again. "You really should be in bed."

He was about to say he was sorry, but he smiled sheepishly instead and then climbed into bed. He wondered if the dark man, his brother-in-law, and his sister were going to visit him tonight. He had not seen them for a long time. Maybe the doctors were right. Maybe they were not real. Maybe they were just in his mind and in his dreams.

The doctors had told him he might remember new things each day, and he did. Some, like long-lost friends, he embraced; others, like strangers, he avoided. Today, for some reason or another, he thought about his mom and dad, and his two sisters who had always looked after him. That is until they got married. And he remembered their names: Elizabeth and Olive.

Elizabeth got married before he was in the army and she was still in Aberdeen. Or was she? Maybe she was in his dreams with her husband. But he knew she wasn't. They had buried her and her husband before he'd left. How did he know that? He could see the frozen river and their cabin. It really wasn't their cabin. It had belonged to his parents before they died. William and Elizabeth just took it over. They had to stay somewhere to trap. When he was young, it used to smell like drymeat, bannock, tanned moose skin and tobacco. His father used to smell like tobacco, sweet tobacco. He and Olive liked the smell.

Olive got married and moved away while he was in the army. They say she came to see him once, but he couldn't remember it. He liked Olive. She never married William and she didn't drink.

Chapter Eleven

It was Wednesday morning and Tina and John were in Helena, having arrived the night before. Tina had left her car in Aberdeen with Ken and Richard, who had promised to drive it to Helena on Sunday. "I'm handing in my resignation to the government tomorrow," Tina said as she came out of the shower.

"For when?"

"I'll give them a month's notice."

John handed her a cup of coffee. "Good. That'll give us time to drive down, no rushing."

She took the coffee and walked into the bedroom. "Where are we gonna stay?"

"I found a one-bedroom apartment, one block from Eva's. Second floor with a small balcony."

"How much?"

"Six-fifty with utilities."

"Can we afford it?"

"I've already put down a damage deposit an' paid the first an' last months' rent."

"What?" she said and came out of the bedroom pulling on a T-shirt.

He smiled. "I wanted it to be surprise."

"It is. Before you came along, I had my budget all planned."

"Sorry."

She smiled. "Don't be."

"Whatcha gonna do with your car?"

"I was gonna drive it down, but now I'm thinking of selling."

"Think Richard an' Ken will be interested?"

"They might. I'll ask them on Sunday. Whatcha gonna do today?" she asked.

"Gonna talk to Clint about paying me."

"How much?"

"One-twenty a night, Thursday to Saturday, an' I keep the tips."

"Tips?"

"Yeah, I'm gonna put a jar onstage an' stick a few dollars in an' see what happens."

"Is that normal?"

"Not really, but what the hey."

She left for work, and later he changed the oil in his truck, then took it to the river and washed it.

Clint was sitting in his usual spot when John walked into the LC and ordered a Blue and joined him.

"Hey, John," Clint said. "Where's Tina?"

"Work."

"She comin' tonight?"

John was about to say something risqué, but decided not to. "Don't see why not," he said.

"Good. Good help is hard to find in 'is town, what with people makin' big bucks with the oil companies. Know what they pay housekeepers out in the camps?"

"No. What?"

"Too fuckin' much, that's for fuckin' sure. I'm thinkin' 'a sellin' 'is shithole an' becomin' a chambermaid in one 'a those camps. Fuck, I'd even wear a fuckin' dress."

"You've been hanging out with Ken an' Richard for too long. You're swearing like a sailor an' thinking of cross dressing."

"Fuckin' A."

They laughed.

"So, you bring your guitar this time?" Clint asked.

"One-twenty a night, Thursday, Friday an' Saturday, nine 'til closin'. I keep the tips an' you keep the broads."

"You think?"

"Fuckin' A an' pardon the French."

"Done."

They shook on it.

"When you an' Tina leavin'?" Clint asked.

"First week in August."

"Sure hate to lose her. Best worker I got."

John finished half his beer, then thought about getting a part-time job to fill his days. So he went to the local employment office and found a notice from a construction company looking for labourers. He took down the name and went to their offices.

The young lady in front looked like she was getting ready to throw up her hands and quit. She was answering phones and trying to put paper in the fax machine and make coffee at the same time. After a few minutes she looked at John and smiled. "Can I help you?"

"I'm here to see if you still need any labourers."

"Brian!" she yelled into the back.

Brian came out dressed in a pair of coveralls, looking out of place in the office. He was a tall man with a red beard and a head full of white hair. "What?" he asked.

"This guy's looking for a job."

Brian looked at him. "Where you from?"

"Alberta."

"Whatcha doin' up here? Lost?"

John smiled. "No, just visiting an' waiting for college."

"Yeah? Whatcha taking?"

"Business," he lied.

"You ever do construction?"

"Worked on the rigs since I got outta school an' did do some construction before that, but not much."

"When can you start?"

"Whenever."

"Tomorrow, bright an' early."

"I'll be here."

"Fill out the forms before you go."

Later, he went back to Tina's apartment and looked in the freezer for something to cook. He settled on fish and had supper ready when she came home from work looking beat. "You look tired," he said.

"I am," she said and lay on the sofa while he rubbed her back. "I love that," she said. His hands moved further down her back. "That too."

He smiled. "You goin' to work tonight?"

"Yep, gonna see if Clint wants to sell, an' then I'm gonna make him an offer he can't refuse."

"I've thought about it."

"About what?"

"About owning a little bar with some cute barmaids."

"Yeah?"

"With big tits, of course."

She looked down at hers. "I could get me some implants."

"Don't need 'em," he said. "I'm not really a tit man."

"What do you like?"

"You."

"I know. But what turns you on?"

"You."

"I mean, what do you like about me?"

"Everything. Your looks, your bod, your loud laugh, your shyness, your boldness, your drive to get outta here."

She thought about that for a few seconds. "Yeah, I can live with that."

They had something to eat, and then took a drive before Tina had to go to work. "I love summers up here," she said.

"You gonna miss it?"

"A little."

"We'll be up for Christmas."

"Yeah, but it's still a long way off an' I've never really spent much time away from home, except when I came here for school."

"Where'd you stay?"

"In the hostel."

"Like it?"

"Not bad, but it wasn't home. Never was."

"El an' I are comin' up in October if we can get time off."

"Hunting?"

"Yeah."

"You ever think of going to college?" she asked.

"Now an' then, but I've got plans an' I'm going to take them as far as I can."

"I'll help."

"Just attend my concerts an' scream an' throw your panties on stage."

"I can do that," she said. "Every night."

At seven-thirty, they drove to the LC and found Clint stuck to his familiar stool. "Hey, Tina!" he shouted.

"Hey, Clint. Where's everyone?"

"Hump day. Prob'ly at home taking it literally."

"Yeah, right."

John sat with Clint, but after half an hour he decided to go back to the apartment, where he did two loads of laundry, cleaned up and then had a shower. He looked out the window at the countryside and felt good about everything: his life so far, his upcoming marriage and his plans for the next few months. And if he was good enough, and lucky, his plans for the next few years or decades.

On Friday night, John felt dead to the world. He had put in two days with the construction company and one night at the LC and wondered if he'd made the right move in taking on two jobs.

"Tired?" Tina asked.

"Dead."

"Me too, but it's Friday an' another week's over an' we've got another four to go, then we're outta here." She almost said *for good,* but caught herself. *But who knows,* she thought. *Maybe we* are *out of here for good*. She had no intention of staying any longer than she had to in her job. She couldn't wait to get into college, get a profession and make something of her life. "Whatcha wanna eat?" she asked.

"You."

She laughed. "Besides that."

"Whatever's nice an' easy."

"Me."

"No comment."

"Wanna order in? I'm lazy."

"Why not. Pizza sounds good."

"What kind?"

"Pepperoni, extra cheese."

She made the call while he took a shower. When he came out, Ken and Richard were sitting on her sofa looking like a bad dream. He went over and poked Ken. "What the fuck you doin'?" Ken asked.

"Just thought I was hallucinating."

"I'm one 'a your bad dreams. I'm not here. Gimme your wallet an' I'll disappear."

"I've no doubt you will. What're you doin' in town? I thought you weren't due 'til Sunday."

"Aberdeen's deader 'an Clint's sex appeal."

"Got 'at right," Richard said.

"Besides," Ken said. "Heard you was playing at the LC, so decided to have a look-see an' see if you need any help."

"With what?"

"Backup," Richard said. "Me an' Ken are the Flatt an' Scruggs 'a the Blue Injuns."

"Yeah," Ken said. "I'm the Conway an' he's the Loretta of the Blue Mountains."

"Fuck 'at noise," Richard said, and then looked at Tina who was smiling at this.

"You guys ever back up anyone?" John asked.

"Only in barroom fights an' brawls," Ken said.

"No, I mean it. I really wanna know."

"Yeah, we backed up some 'a the more famous an' infamous critters in this part of the country once or twice," Ken said. "Don't remember most 'a them, but we didn't get booed outta the country."

"Leas' not yet," Richard added.

"Well, drop around," John said. "Might give you a shot."

"That's all we ask," Richard said.

"What's the catch?"

"Free beer from Clint an' first dibs on the babes."

"Yeah," Ken said. "We're groupie gropers."

"Fuckin' A!" Richard said.

"Hey," Ken said, "that's a good name for a band. Ladies an' gents, Caesar's Palace is proud to introduce John Daniel an' the Groupie Gropers!"

"Sounds like one 'a those bands that swam across the Atlantic an' slimed New York," John said.

"Punk country at its finest," Richard said. "Could get some punk haircuts an' stick some safety pins in our noses an' ears an' yell swear words to bad music."

"Shoot," Ken said, "we're halfway there an' don' even know it."

There was a knock on the door and John answered it and paid for the pizza. He was glad Tina had ordered the largest one on the menu because the boys were going to help them finish it whether they liked it or not. "What's 'at?" Ken asked rhetorically.

"Dinner."

"Good. I'm tired 'a fish."

They dug in, and despite being lukewarm it was not bad.

"Who made 'is?" Richard asked. "Colder 'an Bill's first ex-wife."

"Prob'ly 'at new Chinese place just opened," Ken said. "Run by Greeks an' got some Lebanese cooks an' some Italian cab drivers to make it look authentic."

They laughed.

"Hey," Tina said. "You guys wanna buy my car?"

"What for?" Richard asked.

"So you don't have to take cabs home every time you come to town, or go to work."

"Does it come with ten midgets in the back?"

"Come on, it's not that small."

"Shee-it," Ken said. "It's so small we can hang it from the rear-view mirror on my firs' truck."

"How much can it hold?" Richard asked.

"How much what?"

"Cases."

She thought. "Ten in the trunk an' twenty in the back seat."

"Can't have nothin' in the back seat," he said. "Gonna be usin' 'at while my chauffeur drives."

"For what?" Ken asked.

"Me an' your wife are gonna play poker."

"Whatcha say?" Tina asked, getting the conversation back on the street and out of the gutter.

"How much?" Ken asked.

"Two."

"Two what?"

"Thousan'."

"Dollars or pesos?"

"Ha!"

"I take that as a no."

"Look at it this way," she said. "How much you pay for a cab down?"

"Two-fifty," Ken said.

"Cost you less than one for gas. Twenty trips an' you made your money back." They were thinking about it. "Could even run a taxi during your time off," she added.

"You set on two?" Ken asked.

"Negotiable."

"Give you a thousan'."

"Eighteen."

"Twelve."

"Sixteen an' that's my final."

"Fourteen an' that's my final."

"I can cover the other two," Richard said.

Ken looked at him as if he was out to lunch. "What you mean?" he asked. "You're payin' for half 'a this."

Richard looked at Tina. "Fifteen an' that's my final," he said.

"Done."

"When you leavin'?" Ken asked.

"Four weeks."

He reached into his jacket and pulled out a wad of cash.

"Holy shit!" she said. "Where'd you get that?"

"Never you min'," he said and counted seven hundred and fifty dollars and gave it to Tina, then looked at Richard.

"All right," Richard moaned, and pulled out his own private stash of cash. "Gonna have to get back to work after this."

"That's jus' poker money," Ken said.

"I know, but I enjoyed winnin'. First time I had a good streak in … first time I *had* a streak."

Tina put the money in her purse and looked at Ken. "Is that really poker money?"

"Yep," he said. "Not into sellin' drugs or booze." Then he looked at the time. "Gotta go," he said. "Gotta get a room. Gonna give her a month 'a pent-up lovin' to scream about."

"Who?" Tina asked.

"Whoever," Ken said. "Tired of my hand."

"Yeah," Richard said. "Me too."

They all looked at him.

"Gotta get 'is guy to a shrink an' soon," Ken said.

"I didn't mean *your* hand!" Richard said.

Ken said nothing, but looked around Tina's apartment. "Whatcha got left to sell?"

"Television an' stereo."

He looked at the furniture. "What about furniture?"

"It belongs to the government."

"Think they'll miss it?"

"Probably, but who would want it?"

"Yeah," he said. "Looks like something Clint would cream himself over. How much for your TV?"

"Two."

"It's highway robbery, but what the hell," he said, then pulled out his wad and counted out two hundred. "Gonna be back in three or four weeks. I'll pick it up then." He looked at his diminishing wad. "Let's get outta here before I buy more stuff I don't need," he said to Richard. "Wonder if Clint's got some rooms available?"

"Clint rents rooms by the hour," Richard said. "But you already knew that."

"Only once ..." Ken said, and then paused. "Only once a day an' sometimes in between."

At ten o'clock that evening, the LC was standing room only. John was on stage and Ken and Richard were backing him up and it was hotter than hell on a hot day, or so Ken had said. He was sweating as if he'd just gone a round with Clint's ex-wife. "Get use to that heat," he shouted. "That's what it's gonna be like in hell when we get there in a few hundred years!"

"Fuckin' A!" Richard shouted. "Me an' you is gonna be roommates right next to Hef an' Guccione!"

"You guys show any promise of sanity, I just might hire you to play in my band when I go commercial," John said.

"We're cheap an' easy," Ken shouted. "Like half the people in 'is joint."

"Fuckin' A!" Richard shouted, and then fantasized about standing on the stage of the Grand Ole Opry making eyes at the likes of Juice Newton and Dolly Parton.

"Gonna do Ricky Skaggs," John shouted. "Think you can keep up?"

"Which one?" Richard shouted.

"'Don't Cheat in Our Hometown'!"

"Wishful thinkin' in this den 'a sinners, but what the hell," Ken said. "Giv'er shit an' we'll follow."

"Kick it off an' I'll join!"

John began the song and Richard picked it up after a few bars. They were good, but they didn't realize how good they were. They'd never played professionally except at dances, and that was only for fun and spare change. They now thought seriously about forming the Groupie Gropers and shooting for the big time. Five minutes later, they took a break and went to the bar. "Hey, Clint!" Ken shouted. "Gimme beer!"

"Me too!" Richard demanded. "You're runnin' a fuckin' sweat-shop here! Should take you to the United Nations an' have 'em whip your ass!"

"Nah, he'd prob'ly ask for more!"

They laughed while Clint dished out two free beers. He watched them guzzle the drinks and hoped they didn't get too drunk tonight. Everyone was on the dance floor working up a thirst and business was booming. He hadn't realized Ken and Richard could play and wondered why they hadn't joined in on any jam sessions.

John came out of the bathroom and looked for Tina, who was working behind the bar. "Glass of water," he said. "Lotsa ice."

"Got them hopping tonight," she said. "Never seen it this busy for a long time."

"Should up my price, but a deal's a deal."

"Consider this an education for the big time."

"Wonder if Clint knows he's almost over the max?" John asked as he looked at the standing-room–only crowd.

"He keeps a close watch on the numbers," she said. "You tired?"

"Dead, but enjoying it."

"Gonna take a hot shower when I get home an' not gettin' up 'til noon."

"I'll join you."

"That's what I was hopin' for."

He smiled and watched as she went back to dishing out beer and doubles like they were going out of style.

"Hey, John," Clint shouted. "You should stay 'til September."

"No can do. Got things to do an' places to see."

By closing time, no one wanted to leave, but they damned well had to. John placed his guitar by the door and waited for Tina to cash out. Ken and Richard joined him with their fiddle and guitar. "Where you goin'?" he asked.

"Gonna sing for my supper," Ken said. "Don' know who she is, but she's out there somewhere."

"Me too," Richard said. "We'd invite you, but you're roped an' hog-tied tighter 'an Clint's wife used to be up in 'a rooms."

"Yeah," Ken said. "An' it wasn't Clint who did the tyin'."

"I heard he really did find her tied to a bed, naked as the day she was born."

Ken shuddered. "Only perverts would do that."

"Do what?" Richard asked. "Tie someone up?"

"Do Clint's wife."

"Wouldn't know. Never met her, let alone done her. Actually, I heard she was quite a looker: a looker with a hooker mentality."

"Clint croaks, she gets everything," Ken said.

"Yeah? Wonder where she's at."

"Hog-tied an' lovin' it somewhere."

"Hey, hon, I'm ready," Tina said as she joined them. She looked beat as they walked out of the LC in time to see Ken and

Richard leave with a group of people in the back of crew cab. They began walking to her apartment and Tina looked up at the sky. "Thunderstorm."

"How can you tell?"

She held her arms out and took a deep breath. "Can you smell it?"

"Smell what?"

"The moisture an' electricity. That's how you can tell there's going to be a thunderstorm." He said nothing, since she was so serious. "That," she said, "and I heard it on the radio earlier today."

He laughed. "And here I thought it was an old Injun trick."

"Think you can last four weeks?" she asked. "With your daytime job, I mean."

"Money's good. I never really did construction before, but I like it. Might even become a carpenter. I like nailin' things." She smiled. "You know what I'm thinkin'?" he asked.

"Of course. You know what I was gonna say?"

"Yeah."

"See, we're even startin' to think alike," she said. "I told you we were made for each other, an' don't you say it."

"Say what?"

"You were gonna say *fuckin' A*!"

"I guess we were made for each other."

"Fuckin' A!"

They laughed and continued into what they hoped would be a lucrative summer before they left for what they hoped would be a better way of life together, and a long one at that.

✴

He looked through the wire mesh at the trees and wondered if it was still summer in the Blue Mountains. Back home, it snowed in October and the rivers froze and the birds disappeared. That was when the caribou arrived and brought winter with them. In April, they moved north and took winter away. That was when the snows melted, the ice moved on the river and the birds came back to life. When he was in the army, he'd lost track of the seasons since it hardly snowed until Christmas, and then it was gone by Easter.

"Edward?"

He turned and looked at the woman in white and smiled.

"I'm amazed at how much better you're looking," she said. "It must be the sun."

He had been outside for the last two days taking walks in the yard with the others. Even when he first came here, he would see them walk by his window and wish he could join them. But at the time, they wouldn't allow him. His memories were nothing more than brief moments of time now, like flashes of a movie. Where was he? Was he in the hills again? Or did he go to the cabin? And what was it about the cabin and the two people? Is that why he was here? Was this jail? Was this the jail for slow and stupid people? Did they know what he had done? Did they know what William had done and said?

"Edward?" He turned to the woman. "You really should start cleaning," she said.

He looked at the rag in his hand, then looked at the windowsill. He lifted the rag and began cleaning.

"That's good," she said, and then he heard the door close.

This was just like the army. He'd cleaned up in the army: the barracks, the mess, anything they told him to. He'd cleaned up in the mission school, too. He'd liked cleaning the chapel. It was quiet there and no one had bothered him. He'd cleaned up the cabin, too, after he … After he what?

"What?"

He froze. He looked up at the wire mesh and tried to look at the trees, but the reflection in the window told him the dark man was back. He could feel his breath on the back of his head.

"I'll call you anything I want," he said. "You're too fuckin' stupid to do anything about it anyways!"

He was hyperventilating, his breathing coming in gasps. He knew what was coming and he didn't want to do it; not again; not ever again. He closed his eyes and hoped the dark man would leave him alone.

After what seemed like years, he lifted his head and looked out the window at the setting sun. He looked at the rag in his hand, and then dipped it into the pail of water and lifted it to the window, but the mesh was in his way. He pressed the rag to the mesh and water splashed against the windowpane and streaked toward the sill. The door opened and he instinctively looked at the reflection of the dark man in the window, his image distorted by the streaks of water.

"Edward?"

He turned and looked at the dark man questioningly. "Jim."

The dark man smiled. "You got that right."

That night, after supper, he could tell that God was going to be angry. The dark clouds in the north were growing larger and becoming darker. He hoped they'd poke him and send him to that place where his dreams couldn't get to him, but they didn't. He waited for a long time, almost holding his breath. Then the lightning began; flashes of light once every few minutes, and then every few seconds. He could hear the raindrops hitting the window as if they were trying to get in. It was becoming unbearable. Was God angry with him for being slow and stupid? Or was he angry at what he'd done to the dark man? Thou shalt not kill; that was what they had taught him in mission school. Thou shalt kill; that was what they had taught him in the army. It was confusing and he didn't want to do it. "Kill the son of a bitch!" the drill sergeant screamed. "Kill him, you stupid son of a bitch!"

He wanted to say that he was not stupid, but he couldn't. Floyd told him never to talk back or they would throw him in jail.

"Kill him!"

It was a direct order. He looked at the drill sergeant, and then at his gun: the one with the knife at the end. He looked at the man in front of him. He was drenched with rain; he was faceless.

"Kill him, you stupid son of a bitch!"

He lifted his gun, pointed it at the faceless man and stabbed. "I'm not stupid!" he screamed.

"Again!"

Again he stabbed. "I'm not stupid!"

"Again!"

Chapter Twelve

It was Friday, August 2, and Tina walked in the door and took a deep breath. "God, I'm tired," she said, then looked around the apartment "You cleaned up?"

"Yep. Washed all the walls, cleaned the bathroom an' the kitchen too."

"Wow, you're good."

He grinned. "I know."

She laughed. "You are good at that. And you can clean, too."

"I'm just full of surprises, as you'll find out in the next few hundred years."

"I sure hope so. Are you all packed?"

"Yep." The only things remaining in the apartment were a few pots, pans and dishes in the cupboard, and her television and stereo in the living room. She'd sold or given away most of what they didn't need or what they could purchase for less in Calgary. "As much as I'll ever be," he said.

"Can't believe we're leavin' tomorrow."

"Same here." He put his arms around her and held her from behind. "I can't believe how lucky I am to have met you."

She smiled. "You're gonna make me cry again."

"I mean it. I'd always said I'd never return, but I'm glad I did. Otherwise, I'd never have met you. You're everything I've never wanted because I didn't know what I wanted. Does that make sense?"

"Yes, it does, an' thanks."

"Do you know how beautiful you are?"

"You keep tellin' me, but I never get tired of hearing it."

"You are so very beautiful, fun, full of laughter an' giggles, so perfect."

She wiped her eyes. "See? You're making me cry."

"I love you."

"I love you too, very much." She turned and pushed her groin to his, felt his erection and smiled. Half an hour later, she had her head on his chest and he was stroking her hair.

"It is going to be an honour to be married to you," he said. "To call you my wife."

"Thanks."

"But more importantly, to be called your husband."

"My first husband," she said.

"I can live with that."

"Good, 'cause I gotta kill you before I can look for my second."

"Kinky, but you can certainly try."

"I don't think I can. Sometimes I don't think I can keep up with you." He raised his arms. "I know," she said, "you are the greatest."

"Thank you."

She kissed his stomach, and then moved down his stomach. He closed his eyes and took a deep breath as she took him in her mouth. They made love again, this time as if it was going to be their last. The smell of her womanhood permeated the air. He looked down at her. He was inside her and her legs were wrapped around him. She looked at him, and then closed her eyes. "You smell that?" he asked.

"Yeah."

"That's you. That's how you smell an' I just love that."

She wiped her eyes, and then he kissed and tasted her tears.

"I don't think I can move any more."

He smiled. A few minutes later, she was moving and her breath was coming faster and harder. "I'm coming," she whispered in his ear.

He slid in and out of her, grinding his pelvic bone to hers. She arched her back and moaned just as he released his load. She moved to get him deeper inside and moaned again. "Ooh, that feels sooo good."

A few minutes later, she held his face in her hands. "Tina Daniel," she said. "I like the sound of that."

He laughed. "So do I, but you don't have to take my name if you don't want to."

"What do you mean?"

"I mean this is the twentieth century."

"But I want to. Besides, I'm still old-fashioned in that respect."

"Thanks. I just thought I'd let you know I'm sorta modern when it comes to things of the heart."

"I know you are," she said, then looked at the time. "Geez, it's seven o'clock!"

He rolled off her and she went to the bathroom, and then he heard the shower and thought about the last month. The work had almost killed him at first, but it had got easier as he got used to it. It was not so much the work as it was working during the day and then singing at night. This was also the first time in his life that he'd lived with a woman and it was different. Not that he was a messy neanderthal with no manners and a closet full of dirty socks and shorts. Actually, he was something of a neat freak … but living with a woman was just different. He'd realized, after only a few weeks, that he couldn't have found a better woman to spend the rest of his life with. He was glad he didn't have to spend the rest of his life searching and wondering if she was the right one; he was certain of it.

"Geez," she said as she came out of the shower, "I don't know if I'm gonna be able to stand up for the next few hours."

He laughed. "You goin' in tomorrow?"

"Only to pick up my last cheque. You gonna shower?"

"No," he said. "I'm gonna go in smelling like you."

"Whatever."

He looked at the time and realized it was already going to eight. He looked at her and thought about going for broke.

"Don't you dare," she said as she pulled on her panties and pants.

He laughed again, then got up and dressed. She pulled on her T-shirt, grabbed her jacket and was out the door. He picked up his guitar and followed her. "You can run, but you can't hide," he shouted down the hall.

"Whatever!"

Ken and Richard were tuning up and making Clint's life miserable, but he'd had his best month in years, so he put up with it. "Hey, Clint," Ken shouted, "you miss us?"

"Like the clap," Clint said, and then laughed at his own joke. He was getting better at his comebacks, having learned from the best, namely Ken and Richard. They had left for work the Monday after John began singing and returned this week. They were both very sunburned, windburned and well done from working on the coast for almost a month.

John and Tina walked in a little after eight. She went behind the bar while he took his guitar up on stage and set up. Five minutes later, he was sitting at the bar with Clint, Ken and Richard. He still couldn't believe how dark they had gotten in the last month. "You guys look like Al Jolson," he said.

"Hung like him, too," Richard said.

"Al Jolson was a white man," Ken said. "You prob'ly *are* hung like him."

"Fuck 'at noise," Richard said. "Really? He was a white man?"

"Whiter 'an my arse an' that's the only place the sun didn't shine las' month."

"Fuck, I thought he was a black man."

Ken looked at his reflection in the mirror behind the bar. "Shit, I do look like Al Jolson," he said, and then broke into song. "Mammy! Mammy!"

They burst out laughing at his impression.

"Why'd they get a white man to play a black man?" Richard asked.

"It's a fuckin' movie," Ken said. "Sorta like Italians playin' Injuns."

"Yeah," John said, "sorta like Burt Lancaster playing an Apache."

"Yeah?" Richard said. "That use to be one 'a my favourite movies 'til I found out he was no Apache."

"You know the Apaches an' Navajos are related to the Blue People?" Ken asked him.

Richard was surprised. "Yeah?"

"Same type 'a language. Even got words similar."

"No fuckin' shit."

"I hear that's a couple 'a them."

"What 'a fuck they doin' way down there?"

"Probably grew brains an' decided to move to warmer climes," John said.

"Leas' some of us got brains," Ken said. "The rest of us stayed an' do nothin' but complain 'bout the cold an' the bugs."

"Wonder if they'll take me in if I tell 'em I'm their long-lost cuz."

"Prob'ly left 'cause they heard 'a you."

"What'll it be?" Tina asked.

John laughed. "Lime an' water."

"Another beer," Ken said.

"Me too," Richard added.

"You leavin' tomorrow?" Clint asked John for the tenth time.

"Right after closin' time," John said. Over the last two weeks, Clint had tried to convince him to stay, but his mind was made up. Besides, he had to show up for work next week. "Hey, Clint?" he asked. "Why don't you hire these two for a week?"

"Who?"

He nodded to Ken and Richard. "Flatt an' Scruggs."

"Call us Amos an' Andy now," Ken said.

They laughed as Clint thought about it.

"Can only give you 'nother week, then me an' Andy are back to work," Ken said.

"What's it gonna cost?" Clint asked.

"Two rooms, twelve free beer an' seventy-five a night each."

Clint thought about that one for a while. He hardly rented out any rooms these days since the bar was his bread and butter. And twelve beers was not much and one-fifty total was fair.

"Twelve each," Ken said as if he'd read Clint's mind.

"What?"

"Twelve beer each or no deal."

Clint recalculated this and wondered if it was worth it. He looked around the bar; it was already packed and it was only Thursday.

"Non-negotiable," Ken added.

Clint was about to say *six beers, one hundred and the rooms,* but Ken once again beat him to the punch. "Me an' Amos can keep 'em dancin' an' sweatin' up a thirst all night an' still have room for Jell-O."

"Hey," Richard said. "I thought I was Andy."

"Andy, Amos, same diff."

"Were they white too?"

"Fuck if I know. That's before my time." Ken looked at Clint, who was still thinking. "Gonna take my fiddler an' peddle his ass across the street if you don't put a smile on your face an' say yes in two secs."

"Yes," Clint said, and forced a smile.

Ken winked at John. "I can be your lead guitar an' agent too," he said. "If I can handle 'is miser, I can handle 'em sharks in L.A. or Hollywood."

An hour later, the trio took a break and Clint gladly opened three beers as they walked up to the bar. The place was packed and he'd had to get the bouncers to put a rope across the door since they were over the max and he'd seen the liquor inspector floating around counting heads.

"Gotta take a course in bein' an agent," Ken said as he looked around. "I think I ripped us off."

"How's the car?" Tina asked.

"Parked out back," he said. "Hopin' someone steals it so we can get a real one."

They laughed.

"Gotta pay somebody to steal it," Richard said. "No self-respectin' Injun would be caught dead in 'at tin can."

"Can't be that bad," Tina said. "It's good on gas."

"I want a gas guzzler that belches an' scares Injuns," Ken shouted. "Injuns an' pickups are the norm. Or haven't you noticed?"

"In a year you'll be drivin' one, I'm sure of it."

"Gonna drive 'at imitation car to Edmonton or Calgary an' trade it in," he said, and then looked at John. "When you think you'll need us for the big time?"

John shrugged. "Maybe next year. Who knows?"

"Why so long?" Richard asked. He was hoping they'd hit the big time before Dolly began sagging and her hairline started drooping.

"Gotta get a good van, some instruments and a kick-ass sound system, then I might send for you," John said. "Gonna cost more than a few thousand."

"We can get our own instruments an' we don' eat much," Ken said.

"Yeah," Richard added, "we're cheap."

They all looked at him and searched their minds for a good comeback. They couldn't think of one they hadn't used already, but he knew they were trying. "Fuck you both!" he shouted and then turned to Clint, who was watching this exchange hoping to pick up some pointers. "What you lookin' at?" Richard said. "Gimme 'nother beer an' kiss my white arse."

"Give him another," Clint told Tina, and then took out a little black book. "That's four already."

"What 'a fuck is that? You keepin' tabs on our drinkin'?"

"Somebody's got to."

"Fuck sakes," Richard said to Ken. "This guy's writin' down how much we drink!"

"Knew 'at little black book wasn't for all your woman friends," Ken said. "Only woman you had died 'a old age last year."

"Get the fuck back on stage or I'll shoot you."

"Ol' Rosa says you shoot nothin' but blanks."

"Yeah, Richard added. "And that's only when you can load up proper like."

"Fuck you."

"Up yours."

"Bite me."

Richard picked up his fiddle and he and Ken played "The Red River Jig." Thirty people jumped on the dance floor. Later, John got up to join Ken and Richard. He was going to miss these people and this place. He'd left more than a decade ago promising never to return, but he had. He'd arrived ten months ago, fallen in love and was now engaged to be married to a girl he couldn't get enough of. Things were certainly moving faster than the speed of light.

The next day, John watched as Tina came out of the apartment building for the last time and put a small box in the back of the truck. "That's it," she said.

They drove to the LC, where Clint had their last cheques ready. "You comin' in tonight?" he asked Tina.

"Be in, but I ain't working, at least not unless you really need me, then it's double time an' under the table."

"I can live with that," Clint said. "You?" he asked John.

"Be here at seven, then we're outta here at nine," he said. "Gotta be in Aberdeen by midnight or we turn into pumpkins."

"Hey, John!" Richard shouted as he walked in the back door looking like he'd seen better days. "Whatcha doin'?"

"Gonna go have somethin' to eat."

"Mind if I join you?"

"Sure."

"My treat."

"Gonna have a big one," John said. "Steak an' lobster an' the works."

"Sure," Richard said. "Why not?"

"Where's Ken?"

"Got a live one."

"Oh?"

"Not that. He's got a sucker for that tin can."

"That's my former tin can you're talkin' 'bout," Tina said.

"No offence, but we look like two clowns when we get outta that sardine can. Where we eatin'?" he asked.

"The hotel," John said.

"Wanna tell Ken we're over at the hotel restaurant?" Richard asked Clint. "You wanna come with us?"

"No, thanks. Gotta tend business."

"Oh yeah, that's right. You gotta water down the booze."

"Only the beer you drink, then I piss in it."

"No wonder it ain't got no kick," Richard said. "Sorta like your sex drive, or at least that's what Ol' Rosa says."

"She's a liar. Made her scream yesterday."

"That sounded like you havin' a hernia attack."

"Who's havin' a hernia attack?" Ken asked as he walked in. It wasn't even six and the bar was starting to fill up.

"Clint," Richard said.

"Hey, Clint," Ken said. "Gonna go for sup'. Wanna come? My treat."

"Can't. Got a business to run."

"Good. Was just askin' anyways. Wasn't gonna take you. What 'bout you?" he asked John and Tina.

"We're going to the hotel. Richard's treat," Tina said.

"I'll pay."

"How much?" Richard asked.

"How much what?"

"How much you gonna gimme?"

"For what?"

"My half 'a the sale."

Ken reached into his pocket and handed Richard a cheque.

"Nine hundred. Is 'at all?"

"Nine hundred for you an' nine for me."

"You sold it for eighteen?" Tina asked.

"Yep. That's why I'm takin' you for supper."

"Good, 'cause we're gonna order the biggest steak an' lobster they got."

"Good. Surf an' turf."

When they got to the restaurant, the Chinese owner and waiter showed them to a table, then took their order. They all looked out the window and watched the people walking and the trucks driving by. A few leaves on the trees were starting to turn yellow.

"What's that big building over there?" John asked and pointed to a large two-storey building with a cross on one end.

"That's the hostel," Tina said.

Richard looked at the building as if it were a dream. "That's a hellhole," he said.

"Got that right," Ken said.

"Want anything else to drink?" the Chinese waiter asked. Richard looked at him as if he were from another planet. "Anything else to drink?" he asked again.

"You guys should 'a discovered us first," Richard said.

"What?"

"Leas' we would've had gunpowder. Could 'a blowed 'em all back to Spain where they belong."

"Sorry, what?"

"Be worshipping Buddha an' communing with nature instead 'a some man they nailed to a cross for being a stand-up guy."

"Sorry, don' understand."

"Yeah," Richard said. "Lots 'a that goin' 'roun'. Gimme a Bud."

John looked at Richard and wondered what had brought that on. He began to think what would have happened had the Chinese or Japanese set foot on the New World before Columbus.

"What would 'a happen if the Chinese discovered us first?" Ken asked, still looking at the hostel.

"Who knows?" Richard said. "Be speakin' Chinese an' eatin' three-way combos. Be heaven, you ask me."

"Wouldn't be Canada," John said.

"One thing for certain. We wouldn't be Christians an' there'd be no hellholes or shitholes."

"Got 'at right," Ken said.

"Fuckin' A."

"Columbus was lost," Ken said for no apparent reason.

They all laughed as the waiter brought their supper, and then they ate in silence. Tina wondered what was behind the conversation, but she didn't think about it for too long; John had to get to the LC, and soon.

At nine o'clock, the bouncers had to block off the doors and control the flow of people in and out. John had just gotten off stage with Ken and Richard, and they were standing at the bar with David and Verna. Tina was behind the bar serving drinks.

"Do one more set," Verna pleaded with John.

"Yeah," David said. "Nex' time we hear you, it's gonna cost us or we're gonna have to buy your record."

John looked at Tina. "Go for it," she said. "We can leave later."

John took a sip of water, then looked at Richard to see if he was ready. He was, and the trio kept the LC going until eleven. Then John walked to the bar, leaned over and whispered to Tina: "I'm tired. Wanna leave?"

She looked around the bar, and then turned to Verna. "We're gonna leave. Take care."

"You too, an' don't forget to write or phone."

The next morning, they were at Tina's grandparents' house having coffee. "How long to Edmonton?" Tina asked.

"Thirty hours if we drive straight," John said. "Any need to stop in Yellowknife?"

"None."

"If we leave today, we could be there by tomorrow night ... if we don't stop along the way for this an' that."

She smiled. "You mean sex."

"Yeah, I mean sex."

"Then say what you mean."

"Sex," he said. "Warm, wet ..."

"Geez, I shouldn' 'a said that."

They went up to see Tina's grandparents, who were still camped in the same spot and still catching fish. "When are you leaving?" Sarah asked in the language.

"Today," Tina answered in the language. "It's a long way."

"You'll be okay?"

"Yes, we have everything and a place to stay."

"Is he nice?"

"Yes," Tina said and smiled.

Her grandmother knew she was telling the truth. She also knew she was in love, and that is all that mattered.

"When are you coming home?" Abraham asked.

"We'll be back at Christmas."

"Do you need any money?"

"No, we're okay."

John was cutting wood and listening to all of this. He wondered if he'd be speaking the language had he stayed in Aberdeen. Not likely, he thought. More and more of the young people couldn't speak the language and that meant the next generation would be totally unilingual. He wondered if Tina would bring up their children, if they had any, to be bilingual. But who would they talk to? The language was dying, and very few people knew it.

It being August meant the worst of the bug season was over and the sun had begun to set. But it was still summer in this part of the country. He looked at the river and marvelled at how pure and clean it was.

"Cold," Abraham said in the language.

"What?" John asked.

"The water is cold," he said in English. "Comes from ice up in 'a mountains."

"Looks pure an' clean."

"It is. How's the water down south?"

"Some rivers are okay, but others I wouldn't drink from."

"That's why we gotta keep this place clean. People down south gonna need clean water one 'a these days." After a few seconds he said, "Tina is the only thing we have left of her mom."

John looked at him. "I'll look after her."

"That's all I ask."

They stood by the river a while longer, and then Sarah called them for lunch. John and Tina later walked along the shore to think things over and to be alone. "Wanna leave?" he asked.

"Not really," she said. "But I have to if I'm going to get the education I want."

"Despite the last month, I don't think I could ever come back," he said. "For good, I mean."

She took his hand. "I don't think I could either, but I'm not gonna worry about it right now."

He stopped. "Wanna leave now? We could be in Calgary by tomorrow night."

"Okay."

They returned to the camp and told her grandparents, who'd already packed some drymeat, dryfish and bannock for them. They said their goodbyes and then drove to Aberdeen to pick up whatever they had left at her grandparents' house. Then they went to see Chief James and Lucy, and then to visit Chief Alfred and Eunice.

As they were leaving, Eunice gave them the name of the hospital where Edward had been living for the last ten years. "Olive says they asked her to visit," she said. "Guess Edward is gettin' better all the time, but they keep tellin' her not to expect too much. He still goes quiet now an' then."

As they drove out of Aberdeen, Tina asked, "Do you think we should stop an' see him?"

"Who?"

"Your uncle."

He shrugged. "I'd rather Olive sees him first, then maybe we can go. He won't remember me."

"Yeah, you're right," she said, looking down the long stretch of highway, and then at the Blue Mountains in the distance. "And he won't know me. I was born after he left an' he didn't stay too long when he got back."

✧

Today, for the first time since they'd buried William and Elizabeth, he went to church. It was a large church, ten times larger than the one back home. And there were ten times as many people. And a big organ, bigger than the one in the church in Aberdeen. The church was made from stone and it was tall. It almost touched the sky.

He remembered some of the prayers, but none of the songs. His mom and dad had prayed each morning and each night in the language. By the time he was five, he could pray and sing with them. By the time he was six, he was in mission school.

He remembered he was in the dorm and he tried to pray, but they were praying in a different language that only white people spoke. "Why are they saying it like white people?" he asked Floyd in the language.

Floyd was about to say something, but it was too late. "What did you say?" the missionary in a black robe asked in English.

"I don't understand," he said in the language.

"You are not permitted to speak that language in here!"

He looked at Floyd, and then at the missionary. "I don't understand," he said again in the language.

The next thing he knew, the missionary was pulling him down the aisle by the ear. He made him stand at the head of the dorm. "Stand there!" he almost screamed.

The missionary smelled; he smelled like the two men who came in at night: the ones who smoked in his bathroom. He smelled like nothing he had ever smelled before. He felt something warm on his leg. He was peeing and he couldn't stop.

The missionary stepped back. "Stupid Indian!" he screamed, and then slapped him. He slapped him so hard that he fainted.

"Edward?"

He opened his eyes and looked at Jim, who was smiling. Jim was always smiling. "It's time to leave."

Most of the people had already left the church. He wondered if they were going to sit outside the Chief's house and roast fish, drink tea and eat bannock. He smiled. They didn't have Chiefs out here. They had a mayor who wore a big gold chain around his neck. Maybe that was to keep him from running away. They did that to dogs back home: tied them up with chains ... but not gold ones.

"Margaret!" someone shouted.

He turned and looked for Margaret. She was a little white girl in a white dress and white shoes. He thought about his own Margaret and felt an immediate sadness. He thought about the young girl at Abraham's house. She didn't look like Margaret, but how would he know. He couldn't remember Margaret as a young girl, only as a young woman: a young woman with a stomach ache. He sat back in the van and took a deep breath. The city smelled different on Sunday. Maybe the white people all bathed on Sunday. Maybe that's why they all wore their best clothes. He never did see the missionaries bathe, and they were white. He never saw them change their clothes, but they must have. And they always wore black.

"I hear your sister might be coming for a visit?" Jim said.

He looked at Jim. "My sister is dead."

"Not that one. Olive, Olive Rowe. She *is* your sister, isn't she?"

He didn't answer. He was tired.

"Aren't you glad she's coming for a visit?"

He shrugged. "I don' know."

He tried to remember Olive, but it was a long time ago. Had she been there when he'd come back from the army? He couldn't remember. He remembered her as a young girl. She and Elizabeth used to look after him; they used to cook donuts for him. He tried to remember the People. He remembered his mom and dad, but they were dead. He remembered Margaret, but he could never forget her. He remembered Floyd, but only the Floyd before the truck hit him. He remembered Abraham and Sarah, but that was a long time ago. He remembered William and Elizabeth, but all he could remember is them being drunk. He tried to remember Elizabeth and William's son, but he was just a baby, and all babies looked the same. He tried to remember Margaret's baby, but she was not a baby; she was a little girl. Then he wondered why no one came to visit him. Maybe they did. Maybe they came when he was gone. When he was not here. Didn't they say Olive and Eunice came to visit him once? And who was Eunice? She was William's sister. In his mind, he pictured Eunice as a dark-skinned woman with messy hair and spittle hanging from her mouth. He pictured her wearing a dirty pair of coveralls. She was swearing and smelled like homebrew.

He was getting tired of the questions they kept asking over and over again. "I'm tired," he said.

"We know, but this is for your own good. You can't get better if you don't talk about it," they said. "The more you talk about it, the less it hurts; the less it hurts, the closer you get to going home."

He wondered if they were lying. They'd told him that in mission school once. *The faster you work,* they'd said, *the faster you go home.* He worked faster, but he never got home until months later. Then he only stayed for a few weeks before the boat took him back.

"You're making good progress," the man in white told him. "You're getting up on your own, dressing yourself, making up your own room, cleaning it. You're even starting to take walks in the yard by yourself, helping others."

The man was right. He was beginning to do things on his own, but hadn't he always? Or had someone always looked after him?

His mom and dad, his sisters and then Floyd. But they were all gone. Where? His mom and dad were in the ground, buried. "My mom an' dad are buried," he said.

"Yes, we know."

How did they know? Had they been there?

"Stay with us, Edward."

"Floyd tried to stop the truck."

"We know that, too."

Or had it been Floyd? The man he'd found on the highway had no face. The man he'd killed in the army had no face. The man in the cabin had no face. He shook his head, looked up at the ceiling and took a deep breath.

"Stay with us."

He knew the faceless man he'd killed in the army was not real. It was just a straw man held up by a piece of rope through its head. He didn't want to think about the dark man in the cabin. "Margaret's dead," he said.

"Who's Margaret?"

"A girl."

"Yes?"

"What?"

"Yes, we know Margaret was a girl. But who was she?"

"I wanted to marry her."

They smiled at him. "Was she your girlfriend?"

"Yes." She was a girl and she had been his friend.

"She had his kid."

"Who?"

Who had his kid? His sister? Of course she had his kid; she was his wife. Only wives could have their husbands' kids. That is what the Bible said. That is what they taught him in mission school.

"Edward?"

He looked at them.

"I think we've done enough today."

He smiled. He was glad it was over for now.

Later, as he lay in bed, he looked over at David, his new roommate. How long had he been here? He was young, and quiet most of the time; other times he shouted at people no one could see. Whoever David was shouting at disappeared when they stuck a needle in his arm and then strapped him to the bed.

He had taken a walk in the yard and was tired, but it was a good tired. A tired like after a long hunt when there was lots of meat. A tired like when he had a full stomach, a warm cup of tea and was lying on his sleeping bag listening to the People enjoying a brief respite from a very harsh way of life: laughing, telling stories and teasing one another.

He had never seen so many Indians in his life, except for that time in the movies just before they were all killed by the soldiers. But that was make-believe; pretend. And that Indian was no Indian, Floyd had told him. That was Burt Lancaster. See his blue eyes?

"It's a powwow!" Jim told him. "Don't they have powwows where you come from?"

"What's a powwow?"

"You'll see."

There were teepees, horses, drums and donuts. He watched some Indians singing and beating a drum like they were in the movies or something. An old woman with black hair and a long dress with flowers on it gave him a donut and said something he didn't understand. After a few seconds, she said, "Frybread."

He took it and felt the lard on his hand, and then he smelled it. It was a donut, not a frybread. It was sweet. Lard dripped down his chin as he looked up at the old woman. "Donut," he said.

She laughed and walked away.

"Hey, Jim!" he called, and then showed him the donut. "Donut!"

Jim laughed. "That's hardening of the arteries, but whatever turns you on."

He liked Jim. Maybe Jim would go home with him and look after him. But he knew he couldn't. "I've got another year of college," Jim had told him, "and then I'm going to be looking for work."

They danced, but it was not like the dances they'd had in the old community hall. This one had real Indians with drums and feathers and Indian screams. There were ten men beating on a drum and hundreds of Indians dancing, jumping around, twirling, hopping and shuffling. He wanted to dance, but he was not this kind of Indian; he was a Blue Indian and they only danced to fiddle and guitar. And they jigged and waltzed and square danced. But not him; he was shy. But he knew he'd have to jig when he married.... She had his kid?

He closed his eyes and drove the memory from his head. He was tired, but it was a good tired. A tired that comes from listening to Indians having a good time, dancing, drumming, laughing, teasing and eating donuts. Even if they do call it frybread, it was donuts to him.

Chapter Thirteen

Despite it being mid-December, there was hardly any snow on the ground: only a few patches here and there. John had told Tina he'd be back in Calgary on Thursday, but he'd decided to show up on Wednesday. He hoped she'd still be in class; he wanted to surprise her when she came home by wearing nothing but a pair of red jockey shorts. But he didn't get the chance. She was sitting in their apartment at the table with a book when he opened the door. "John!" she screamed and ran to him.

They hugged and kissed, and then he ran a hand over her groin. Her head went back and she moaned. He undid the button and removed her pants, then slipped a finger inside her; she was wet. They moved into the bedroom where he put his lips to hers, then moved to her tits, and then further down. She moaned when he kissed her pussy. When he entered her, she held his neck and threw her head back.

"You feel great," he said, and then made love to her.

Later, she lay her head on his stomach. "Geez, you're still hard. Did you come?"

He laughed. "Time enough later. I'm just gonna take my time with you, all day long."

"I can live with that."

And he did go all day; they made love three more times. "Don't you ever get tired?" she asked after the third time.

"I've been without for almost six weeks," he said. "But not really; I did have sex."

She turned to him. "Who with?"

He grinned and opened his hands. "Just me an' my hands."

She laughed. "Oh, okay. Long as I can have sex with them too."

He ran a hand over her stomach. "You have a wonderful bod."

"Thank you."

An hour later, after they'd made love again, the phone rang. Tina rolled over and picked it up. "Hello?"

He could hear it was Eva. "Is he home?"

"Yes."

"Good, I'll be there in half an hour."

"Eva's on her way," Tina said as she hung up, then laid her head on the pillow.

John had promised Eva a home-cooked dinner since it had been her birthday a few days ago and he couldn't be there.

Tina spread her legs and ran her hands over her pussy. "Geez, look at me. I'm just shiny."

He laughed and held her. "It is really going to be a pleasure to make love to my wife."

"Can I watch?"

"Sure, why not? You can even take pictures if you want?"

"Kinky," she said and spread her legs. "Take a picture of this." She laughed and turned her head away. "Geez, see what you make me do?"

"I can live with that."

"I miss you when you're gone, but thank God, or I'd never get any work done."

"You got that right." He ran his hands over her stomach.

She laughed. "Get off. I gotta take a shower before Eva comes over." She got off the bed. "Geez, lookit. My ass imprint."

He buried his head in the sheets and took a deep breath. "I just love the smell of your pussy."

"I can tell. You're down there most of the time."

"Can you blame me?"

"Whatever," she said, having no response for that. She walked into the bathroom, leaving the door open. He joined her in the shower. "See?" she said. "I don't even have to ask."

"Great minds think alike."

"So do perverts."

"Thank you."

A few minutes later, as John was preparing his specialty, or what he hoped would be his specialty—pan-fried chicken with pan-fried potatoes—Eva arrived.

"So," John said. "How does it feel to be out of your teens?"

"Feels no different."

She and Tina were in the living room and he was in the kitchen. When Eva wasn't looking, Tina opened her legs, smiled mischievously, put her hand to her crotch and then got very shy and laughed.

"What?" Eva asked.

"Nothing," Tina said. "Your brother's nuts!"

"Only since I met you," John said.

He couldn't have guessed Eva would take to Tina like she had. Usually she was the possessive type, never approving of the girls he went out with.

When they'd arrived in Calgary in August, Eva had hugged Tina like a long-lost sister and then begun showing her the sights: the best hair salons, the best clothing stores and so on. They'd become inseparable and he was glad. At least Tina'd have someone to keep her company when he went off to work.

His first shift after they'd arrived had lasted almost six weeks. By then, Eva had already shown Tina how to get around the university and how to use the bus system.

John's hunt in October hadn't gone ahead. During their time off, he and Elmer had picked up a bass player and headed to Lethbridge, where they'd played for two weeks in a bar owned by a guy who knew them from a previous gig. After that, John had made another demo. He'd recorded one of his own songs and one of Merle's called "Swinging Doors," which he'd given a little kick by almost going rock. He'd sent copies to as many radio stations as he could, and to Native newspapers. He'd also sent a few copies to Ken and Richard and told them to make sure they got onto the jukeboxes at the Saloon and the LC, and onto the little radio station in Aberdeen.

He and Elmer had then returned to work and put in another six weeks. By now, they were due for some serious time off. He and Tina were going to leave on Friday as soon as she got out of class, and then drive non-stop to Aberdeen. They'd be there late Saturday at the earliest, or early Sunday at the latest. And that would be just a few days from Christmas.

"You really do make a wonderful couple," Eva said. "Of course you're gone most of the time," she said to John.

"Thank God for that," Tina said.

Eva looked at her. "Geez, I don't wanna hear this!"

Tina laughed, then said to John, "Hey, I heard your song is getting airplay in Aberdeen."

"Really?"

"Yeah, they like your version of 'Swinging Doors.'"

"What about the other one?"

"I haven't heard, but Ken an' Richard called an' said it's on the jukebox at the Saloon an' at the LC. They even sent it to CBC in Inuvik an' to another radio station in Yellowknife. They said they've been sending requests to everyone they know for 'Swinging Doors' by John Daniel. They've even been sending requests to people they don't know, or people they've made up."

John laughed. "I hope they don't send me their phone bill."

"What's next?" Eva asked.

"Wait an' see an' hope."

"What about an album?"

"Costs too much. Besides, people are more into cassettes than records these days. I also got to try to get on a TV show."

"Which one?"

"Anyone that'll let me. It's more complicated than I thought. Now I'm wondering if I should go to Nashville, or at least to Toronto. More people an' more record producers."

"The only one standing in the way of your dreams ..." Eva said.

"... Is you," he finished. That was something their mom and dad had told them countless times as they were growing up. "Oh, well," he said. "It'll have to wait 'til I get back."

"Is El going up with you?" Eva asked.

"He's heading to Medicine Hat for a few days. Visit his folks."

"I didn't know he had folks."

"Me neither. I thought he crawled out from under some rock."
They laughed. "I don't know if he's going up. He said he might,
just to hunt an' visit the boys."

"Who?"

"Ken an' Richard."

"They sound like his kind of people. So," she said to Tina, "you
still set on spring?"

"Yeah."

"When?"

"I don't know. Maybe June. I'll be done for the year by then."

"You planning?"

"Not really. Just have to get a marriage licence, call the minister—Verna an' the girls said they'll look after the feast—an' get my
wedding dress an' bridesmaid."

"What about you?" Eva asked John.

"Gonna get a tux an' show up, say 'I do' an' get me a wife.
Nothing to it." They laughed. "Oh," he said, "gotta get me a best
man."

"Who?" Tina asked.

He shrugged. "El. If not, then David. If he's available. You?"

"Verna."

"You're just gonna have one each?" Eva asked.

John and Tina looked at each other. "That's all we need,"
Tina said.

"Have you been practising dancing?"

"I was trying to remember them jigs the last time I was up,"
John said, "but they all have different styles."

"You?" Eva asked Tina.

"I've jigged," she said and smiled at John. "Just never at my own wedding. This one's just practice for my second wedding anyway."

They laughed.

"Well," John said, "I'm hoping it's genetic."

"I was just thinking," Tina said. "They might make us jig if we show up for the dance on Boxing Day."

He shrugged. "Oh, well. Whatever happens happens. I'll just close my eyes an' make like John Travolta." He put three plates of food on the table and they all sat down.

"Wow!" Tina said. "You amaze me with your cooking an' your cleaning. I think I just might keep you."

"Thank you."

"Hey," she said, "I got a care package from home: caribou meat, drymeat an' bannock. It's in the fridge. I keep telling them I don't need bannock, I can make my own, but they keep sending it … and money."

"But it don't taste the same," John said. "I mean, everyone makes it their own way."

"Yeah. I like Eunice's bannock. I don't know what she does, but it's so light. Not like mine. Mine you can use for pucks."

They laughed.

"Did she hear from Olive?" John asked.

"Yeah, she said she's going to be back for the holidays."

"How was her trip to Edmonton?"

"I didn't ask, but we'll find out in a few days."

"I hope she took pictures. I'd like to know how he looks."

"I don't remember him," Eva said. "He was in the army when I was born, and we were gone by the time he returned. I wonder if he knew about us?"

"What gets me," John said, "is he never returned all the years he was in the army."

"I never knew him," Tina said. "But my grandparents told me he wasn't stupid or retarded, just slow. He did well for a few months after he got out of the army, but then ..." She didn't have to finish. They all knew what had happened: He had found John and Eva's parents at their cabin, frozen, and brought them into town. And then he had gone into his own world, a world from which he'd slowly been emerging over the last year.

John picked up Tina at the university and she looked beat. "I've got a real bad headache again," she said. She'd been getting headaches now and then, sometimes lasting for a week, and then they'd disappear. She wondered if they had to do with her change in lifestyle and her constant studies, which sometimes took more than a few hours a night. "An' I'm bruised," she said, grinning. "Down below. You really outdid yourself las' night."

"Thanks. What can I say? Must be the woman I was with."

"Well, I should hope so."

He laughed. "So you wanna stop an' pick up something?" he asked.

"For what?"

"Your headaches."

"Sure. I've got to do some last-minute shopping anyways."

They left that night and passed the sign that told them they were 100 kilometres from Aberdeen at seven o'clock on Sunday morning, three days before Christmas. Tina was still tired, but her spirits picked up when she saw the sign. "Finally," she said.

They arrived an hour later and it was still dark since the sun wouldn't rise until noon, and then only for a few minutes. When they pulled onto the main street and drove up to her grandparents' house, Tina could tell they were already up. They were always up early, at six or seven each and every morning. Abraham would make coffee for himself and tea for Sarah, and then he'd cook breakfast. Breakfast meant oatmeal and, on rare occasions, bacon and eggs.

Even before the car came to a complete stop, Tina was already getting out. She looked at John with tears in her eyes and smiled, then ran inside. He took his time gathering their bags and boxes. When he did finally go inside, Tina was already sitting at the table with a cup of coffee, eating boiled caribou meat as if she'd never had it before. She had strips of fat lined up next to her plate. He smiled at her. "You might get sick."

"It'll be worth it," she said.

Abraham shook John's hand and Sarah gave him a hug. "Thank you," she said. "Thank you for looking after Tina an' for bringing her home."

John didn't know what to say. He was about to say it was his pleasure, but somehow that didn't seem appropriate. He took his bag into their room, and then had a wash and a cup of coffee. He took a nap and woke up a few hours later to find a note telling him they'd gone to church.

Half an hour later, he was parked in front of the church waiting for Tina. It was cold, probably about thirty below, and every chimney he saw was spewing smoke straight up into the sky, which was only now getting bright. He looked at the cemetery and noticed they had buried two people in the last few weeks. He remembered Tina telling him that a couple of elders had passed away. He looked at the two crosses where his parents were buried and felt nothing. He wondered where Tina's mom was buried. Tina had photos of Margaret, but didn't look anything like her. She looked more like Eunice and Eunice's daughter, Sarah. *No wonder the white people say we all look alike,* he thought. He was jolted back to the present by a knock on the window. "Hi, sailor," Tina said.

"Hi, you sweet-tasting …" He stopped when he saw Abraham and Sarah walking up behind her.

She laughed. "We're going over to Alfred an' Eunice's. Wanna come?"

Alfred and Eunice's house was busy with the after-church crowd. They had a large coffee urn going and there was drymeat and bannock on the table and boiled and roasted caribou meat on the counter, and everyone was helping themselves.

"Who cooked?" Olive asked.

"Sarah," Eunice said. "She didn't want to go to church so I told her to stay home an' cook."

"She really outdid herself."

Sarah opened her bedroom door. "Did I hear my name?" she asked shyly.

"You did," Olive said. "I was just complimenting the chef."

"Thank you. Liz helped me." Then she saw Tina. "Tina!" she screamed, hugging her. "When did you get back?"

"This morning."

"When you're leaving?"

"Geez, I just got here an' you already want me to leave?"

Sarah laughed. "Come in for a while," she said. "Sit with me an' Liz."

"I knew she'd be here, or you'd be at her house. You two are stuck together like Mutt an' Jeff."

"As if!" Sarah and Tina both screamed.

Tina came out of the bedroom a few minutes later, laughing, and poured some tea. "Liz wants to know if you got any brothers," she said to John.

"Tina!" Liz screamed from the bedroom.

"I told them all you had is one sister."

John grinned.

An hour later, they were lying on their bed. "You glad to be home?" he asked.

"Yeah, but I'm glad anywhere I'm with you."

"Thanks."

"Wanna go out later?"

"Where?"

"Just thought you might wanna visit Ken an' Richard."

"Lots of time."

"Good, 'cause I'm still tired." She ran her fingers over his chest and felt the photo that Olive had given him earlier that day in his pocket. She took it out and looked at Edward Brian. "He looks old," she said. "And pale."

✧

He was staring at the snow in the yard. The snow was always dirty in the city: dirty, grey and wet. But not in the mountains: There it was white, like the snow on the Blue Mountains and the Teal River. He liked travelling on the river with dogs. You could stand up, or sit down, and just let the dogs run and run and run. When they got tired, they stopped and looked at you, like they were asking permission to rest.

Olive had told him they used to ride together in the sled with

Elizabeth, before Elizabeth went to school. Then it was just him and Olive. Then it was just him. Then it was no one.

He still remembered Olive's visit in October. She brought drymeat, dryfish, bannock and donuts. He smiled when he saw the donuts. She also brought him a pair of moose skin slippers with beads and beaver fur on the back.

After she left that first day, he held the slippers to his nose, closed his eyes and smelled. He remembered his mother sitting by the gas lamp in their cabin sewing shoes and slippers and making mitts. He wished he were back there again, sitting next to her. Then, for whatever reason, he cried for the first time since Floyd had left him alone on the highway. He cried, but it was a lonely cry, a cry that told no one how alone he was. He wiped away his tears, and then ate a donut.

Olive stayed two weeks, visiting almost every day, and she talked to him in the language and he liked that. He didn't understand a lot of it, but he knew a few of the words and some of what she said. She told him of the People: who had died, who'd got married, who'd had kids, who'd left and who'd came back. Most of them he didn't know. She told him the caribou had returned to the Blue Mountains and he wondered if the elders still sang in the hills for their return.

Olive looked like Elizabeth, but she was smaller. And she never drank or slurred her words. And there was no spit hanging from her mouth. "You remember William an' Elizabeth's kids?" she asked.

He looked at her and tried to forget William, but he couldn't. He kept picturing a dark man in dirty coveralls with messy hair and spit hanging from his mouth sneering at him.

"You remember them?" she asked again.

"Who?"

"William an' Elizabeth's kids: John an' Eva."

"He's a baby."

She laughed. "He's a big man now, twenty-five an' tall. He came home last Christmas."

He remembered a little baby crawling on the floor. "What's his name?"

"John. His name is John. He kept his last name. John Daniel."

"Who's Eva?"

"You don't know who Eva is?"

He shook his head shyly, as if being reprimanded.

"Didn't Elizabeth ever write to you?"

He pictured Elizabeth, but she was drunk with messy hair and she had a black eye. She was lying on the floor, motionless.

"She never wrote to you?"

He shook his head. "No."

"Eva is their daughter. She was six when she left. She's really pretty an' is going to college to become a nurse."

He said nothing for a few seconds, and then: "I've been here a long time."

"Yes, you have. I wish you could come home."

"They say I might, in a few months, when I get better."

"Mrs. Rowe?" It was Jim, smiling. "Visiting hours are over."

Olive grinned at him. "My name is Olive," she said. "I'd prefer Olive. Mrs. Rowe seems ancient, an' I'm not ancient. At least not yet."

Jim laughed. "Okay, Olive."

She looked at Jim's feet. "What size is your feet?"

Jim looked at his feet, and then at Olive. "Why?"

"Just asking."

"I wear size tens."

Then she left.

"Edward?"

He knew it was Jim. "Hi, Jim."

"It's getting late."

"There's a lot of lights."

"It's almost Christmas."

"I don't like it here."

"Well, it's up to you," Jim said. "You're the only one who can help you get better."

"You think they'll let me go home?"

"They will, when you're better."

"When?"

"A couple of months, maybe longer."

"Be spring. River will still be frozen." He suddenly felt very sad, almost ashamed. He wished he hadn't said that.

"What's wrong?" Jim asked.

"I think I did something bad."

"What?"

"I don't know. I think that's why I'm here."

"This is not a jail, Edward. This is a hospital."

He looked at the wire mesh. "Why they have these on the windows?"

"That's so no one can get in, to keep you safe."

"I don't feel safe. I feel locked up."

"What do you think you did?"

"What?"

"What do you think you did to be here?"

He tried to remember, but it was too confusing. Everything was mixed up. He remembered the faceless straw man, the faceless Floyd and the faceless man in the cabin. He remembered driving a snowmobile on the river. He remembered doing something to someone. He remembered standing on the bank of the river outside the cabin, looking up and down the river.

"Whatever it is," Jim said, "I'm sure you'll remember."

He said nothing. How could he tell Jim he felt shame and fear? It was as if he was hiding something. But what?

Olive had returned and she brought more drymeat, bannock and donuts. And this time she brought pictures; lots of pictures. She told him who all the people were, but he didn't know most of them. He remembered Chief James and some others. She showed him a picture of her husband and children, and of Chief Alfred and Eunice and their children. Eunice didn't look like William; she was a nice-looking woman with a big smile and long black hair. "Who's this?" he asked.

The young man was tall, dark and wore a grin: a happy grin. He was holding a young woman from behind. She was smiling, looking up at him. He was tall. She only came up to his chin. "That's John," Olive said. "That's Elizabeth's son."

"He's tall."

"She laughed. "Tall an' good lookin'."

"Who's this one?"

"That's Tina. Abraham an' Sarah's granddaughter. They're gonna be married."

"How's Abraham an' Sarah?"

"Oh, they're doin' fine. Getting on, but doin' fine. They've got lots of grandchildren."

He wanted to ask about Margaret, but she was dead. She was buried in the cemetery where they'd buried Elizabeth and William. He remembered driving back to Aberdeen with them in the back of his sled. He had put them on a sleeping bag and covered them with another. They were cold, almost frozen. They were frozen when he arrived in town and drove up to Chief James's house. He was cold, too.

Chief James was cutting wood when he stopped his snowmobile. The Chief looked at him and smiled. "You're cold," he told him in the language, and then looked at his sled.

"It's cold," he answered, and then clasped his arms around his chest as if to warm himself.

Chief James saw the sleeping bags. "What's that?" he asked in the language.

"Elizabeth an' William."

The Chief pulled back the upper sleeping bag and froze. They were dressed in clean clothes, their arms folded as if they were already in coffins. The Chief looked at him. "What happened?" he asked in English.

"It's cold."

"They froze?" he asked.

"I'm cold."

"Come inside."

They went inside and Lucy gave him some tea, but he couldn't move his arms. His hands were stuck to his chest. Lucy had to put the cup to his mouth.

A few minutes later, Chief James walked in with a policeman. "Is he okay?" Chief James asked his wife.

"He's cold," she answered in the language.

"Edward," the policeman said.

He looked up at the man dressed in white. "Yes?"

"It's almost time for supper. Are you cold?"

He had his arms around his chest.

Chapter Fourteen

"God, that feels sooo good," she whispered and wrapped her legs around his. Beads of sweat were dropping from him onto her face. He shook his head and more sweat showered her. She adjusted her legs, getting more of him inside her. "Do you know how good you feel?"

"Thank you."

"My pleasure."

"That's my line."

"And I just love your smell."

"That's my line, too," he said.

They laughed. "My grandparents are gonna be home soon," she said, then went into the bathroom and returned a few minutes later. "Wanna go up to the Saloon?"

"Sure," he said, pulling on his pants.

"Geez, at least put on some shorts."

"I didn't bring any."

"You're gonna give me a rep. Woo-hoo! I'm getting a rep … finally!"

The Saloon was packed, noisy and smoky. Ricky Skaggs was singing his heart out on the jukebox and, like before, when they walked in everyone looked at them for a few seconds and then got back to whatever they were doing.

"Hey, John! Hey, Tina!" Richard yelled from across the bar.

They both waved at him.

"Hey, Tina!" Verna shouted from the bar.

"Hey, Verna!" Tina shouted. "Wanna beer?" she asked John.

"Sure."

She ordered two beers, then gave him one. "I'll be over in a bit," she said. "Gonna sit with Verna."

John walked through the sea of people to Richard and Ken. "Ian an' Bella are gonna pay us to play," Ken said. "Wanna join us for a few?"

He shrugged. "Sure. When?"

"Seven 'til closing."

"I can do a few."

A few minutes later, Tina joined them. "Hey, Ken, Richard."

"Hey," they responded.

By nine, the Saloon was even more packed, noisier and smokier. Richard and Ken began at seven and had the place jigging and waltzing. They decided to have a jigging contest: five bucks to enter, winner takes all. Twenty couples signed up and it took an hour to get through everyone.

John was watching the different styles and taking notes when Verna called out, "Las' couple is Tina Joseph an' John Daniel."

He looked at Tina, who was grinning from ear to ear. "Come on," she said. "Not gonna marry you if you don't know how to jig!"

They got up, and despite it being his first time it must've been genetic, because he danced like a seasoned pro. The entire bar whooped their approval, and John and Tina won a hundred dollars. Tina was exhausted and out of breath.

"Geez," Richard said as he sat down, "you didn't tell us you know how to jig."

John laughed. "I didn't know I could."

"You must 'a been practising," Ken said.

"Only in the shower," John said. "An' even then I don' watch."

Twenty minutes later, he was onstage doing some classics by George, Hank and Lefty. Actually, the stage was just a small space in the corner and the dance floor was about twelve by twelve. As he was singing, he noticed that Tina was holding her head with her eyes closed. After he finished, he went over to her. "How you feeling?" he asked.

"Gettin' a headache."

"Well, we should go."

"Don't wanna be a party-pooper."

"Whither thou goest ..." he said.

"Thanks," she said and got up. As they stepped into the cold night air, she felt immediate relief. "It must've been the smell of smoke."

They arrived at her grandparents' house to find them getting ready for church. "Are you coming to church with us?" Sarah asked in the language.

"Not tonight," Tina answered. "I've got a headache."

"Are you okay?"

"Yes. I'll be okay."

Later, just before midnight, Tina was lying on the bed with a wet cloth across her forehead. She looked at the time. "It's almost midnight," she told John. "Turn the radio on."

John did, and he heard about ten people counting down to midnight on the little radio station. "Ten, nine, eight, seven, six, five, four, three, two, one. Happy New Year!"

✧

The radio in the hall was loud. They were counting down to midnight and the new year. He remembered they used to shoot guns at midnight in Aberdeen and shake everyone's hand. The last time he was there, someone shot a flare into the night sky right after church. It was bright red and lit up the whole town. Everyone stopped what they were doing and watched as if it were an alien spaceship. He watched until it fell between some houses, and then it was dark and quiet, like it was the end of the world. People looked around as if someone had taken the fun out of the moment, and then another shot rang out. "Hap' New Year!" And just as quickly as it had gone, the joy was back. Guns were fired into the air. "Hap' New Year!"

He walked home with his bible and hymnbook, hoping he wouldn't see William and Elizabeth; he didn't. He went into his house and there they were: lying on the floor, their arms folded across their chests, pale faces, frozen faces. He looked up and saw he was still in the Chief's house; his arms were still stuck to his chest, frozen.

"Edward?" the policeman asked. "What happened?"

He looked at the officer and wondered who he was. Where had he come from? What was he doing here?

"Did they freeze?"

He shivered and tried to pull his arms free, but he couldn't feel them. They had no feeling. They were dead. "They're dead."

"Yes, I know," the officer said. "Did they freeze?"

He was still looking at his arms. "They're frozen."

"They must've been drinking," Chief James said.

He wondered how his arms could drink. Were they drunk? Frozen drunk? Maybe they drank homebrew. "Homebrew."

"Well," the officer said. "I figured as much."

"What happens now?" Chief James asked.

"Not much we can do. I'll get the nurse in charge to issue death certificates so we can bury them."

He pictured them burying his arms and wondered how he was going to drive his Ski-Doo. How was he going to eat? Who was going to dress him? Who was going to wash and shave him?

Chief James took him by the hands and pried them from his chest. He pulled them free. "They're alive. They're not dead."

"Are you okay?" the Chief asked in the language.

"Yes," he answered.

"Pardon me?"

He looked up at the attendant, the one who came in at night and smoked in the bathroom. "What?" he asked.

"I asked if you're okay."

He looked around his familiar room. He was sitting in his chair by the window. The night attendant was holding his hands. "Yes, I'm okay."

"You should get into bed now."

He walked to his bed and climbed in.

"Edward?"

"Yes?"

"Happy New Year."

"Hap' New Year."

Chapter Fifteen

They were approaching Edmonton late on the afternoon of Saturday, January 4, and Tina was getting up after having slept most of the way. "You feeling better?" John asked.

"Yeah. What's the time?" She looked at her watch, and then at the sun. "Geez, what day is this?"

"You slept a long time."

"Feels like it. I feel better now, more rested."

They stopped at a gas station, and while John filled up, Tina went to the washroom and returned wearing a blue dress and a blazer.

"Wow," John said, and Tina blushed.

The building didn't look like an asylum. It looked like an old hospital. They were shown to a waiting room and a short while later, Edward Brian walked in and looked at them.

Tina recognized him from the photograph. "Edward?"

"Yes, ma'am."

She smiled. "I'm Tina Joseph. Abraham an' Sarah are my grandparents. This is John."

John looked like William, but he was not as dark and he was taller. And no spit hung from his mouth. "Hi."

"How are you?" Tina asked.

"Fine."

She was about to ask if he liked it here, but it didn't seem appropriate. "We got some drymeat an' bannock for you."

He smiled, then took the bag from her. "Thank you."

She gave him another bag. "This is from Olive an' Eunice."

He took the bag, but didn't look in it.

"It's some shirts an' pictures from Aberdeen."

"Thank you."

"Where's Jim?"

He turned to Jim, who was standing near the coffee area. How did they know Jim?

"I'm Jim."

"Hi, I'm Tina Joseph. This is John, my fiancé."

"Hi. How's Mrs. Rowe? I mean Olive."

Tina smiled. "She's fine. She sends her best an' asked me to give you these."

Jim took the plastic bag and looked in it and his eyes went wide. "Wow!" He pulled out a pair of moose skin slippers. "Wow!"

"She said it's their way of saying thanks for ..." She was about to say *for looking after Edward*. "... For everything," she said.

"Wow!"

Edward was glad they'd sent Jim some slippers. Jim liked his so much he had almost given them to him, but they were used. And you do not give used slippers to friends; you give new ones. He looked at John and remembered a baby crawling on the floor. "You were just a baby."

John grinned. "Yes, I was."

"You're tall."

"How are you?"

Edward shrugged and looked at the white walls, the white furniture, the white wire mesh and the white floors with grey specks—grey specks so small that you had to get down on your knees and put your face almost to the floor just to see them. "Tired."

"Well," Tina said, "we should be going. We've got a long ways to go."

Edward was tired, but not *tired* tired. He was tired of this place. He wanted to ask if John and Tina were going back to Aberdeen. And if they were, could they take him? They could be back by tonight.

"It was nice to meet you," Tina said.

Edward looked at her, but she was a stranger; he was a stranger.

"We'll tell my grandparents we saw you."

Edward thought about Abraham, Sarah and the little girl with no name. She was Margaret's daughter. Then where was Margaret's husband? She didn't have a husband. How did he know that? He never asked Abraham and Sarah, but he didn't have to because he knew. Someone took his hand. He looked up at the tall Indian. "John."

John smiled. For a few seconds, he had thought his uncle was in a world by himself, but he knew his name and said it as if he were prepared to say goodbye. "It was nice to meet you."

"Thank you."

"You're welcome. We'll be sure to drop by an' visit again. Soon, I hope."

Edward watched them leave, and then walked to his room. He opened the bag and smelled the drymeat, then took out the photographs and went through them. Their names and what relation they were to him were written on the back. He had a lot of nephews and nieces. He was an uncle. He'd never had an uncle or an aunt, or if he had, they'd never told him.

"Well, Edward?" Jim said, looking down and grinning.

"Well, Jim."

"Well, how do they look?" Jim asked.

Edward looked at Jim's feet. He was wearing his new slippers. "They look good."

Jim moved his feet, like he was trying to get comfortable, or like he was getting ready to jig. "They're a little tight."

Edward grinned. "That's the way it is. They'll stretch."

"They're comfortable an' I love the smell of leather."

Edward laughed. "That's moose skin, not leather."

"Okay, Edward. But they *are* nice. I hope she didn't spend too much on them."

"She didn't buy them, she made them. You want some drymeat?"

Jim laughed. "No, thanks. That stuff is too wild for me. They were a nice couple."

"Who?"

"John and Tina."

"They're getting married."

"Yeah, I sort of figured."

"He's Elizabeth's son. He's ... I'm his uncle."

"Yes, you are."

"I'm an uncle," he said proudly.

Jim laughed. "Whose daughter is she?"

"She's Abraham an' Sarah's ... I don't know."

"They must have some nice-looking women up there. Even your sister Olive is a nice-looking woman."

"She's married," he said.

"So am I, but it doesn't hurt to look. That reminds me, I've applied for a full-time job in Vancouver when I finish."

"Finish what?"

"When I finish college."

"When's that?"

"I graduate in June," Jim said proudly.

"You're leaving?"

"I've got a family to think about an' my wife wants to be closer to hers."

"Her what?"

"Her family."

"You're leaving?"

"Yes, Edward. I'm leaving, or I hope to leave."

"My mom an' dad left." Jim said nothing. "Floyd left. William an' Elizabeth left. Margaret ..."

"Did Margaret leave?"

"She died."

"How did she die?"

He thought. "They say she drowned."

"When?"

"Long ago."

"I'm sorry."

"You're leaving."

"Yes," Jim said. "I'm leaving, but I'll be back to visit. I promise. Hey," he said, like he had an idea, "I might even visit when you go home. We can do some fishing an' crack a few."

"Crack a few?"

"Brewskis."

"Brewskis?"

"Yeah, you know … beer."

"I don't like beer."

Jim laughed. "Okay, you can have tea an' I'll have a few." He looked at his watch. "Hey, it's almost suppertime. It's burger night."

Chapter Sixteen

John and Tina were driving south from Edmonton toward Calgary. A few days ago, they had been freezing their asses off in forty-below weather; today it was ten above and the chinook was like a breath of warm, fresh air. The sky was a bright, crimson red. "Red sky at night …" he said.

"… Sailor's delight," she finished. "Hi, sailor."

He grinned. "It *can* be a sailor's delight."

She moved closer and ran her hands up his leg to his crotch. "It *can* be."

He laughed. "I can, you know."

"I know you can. Wanna?" she teased.

"Ha! You're just saying that 'cause I'm driving."

"Of course I am," she said, and then looked at the sky. "It really *is* beautiful."

"It is. I've never seen it like this, or maybe I've never looked."

A few kilometres later, they were standing outside his truck, which was parked in a vacant viewing area, and watching the sunset. He held her from behind, his face in her hair, his hands caressing her groin. She reached behind and felt his erection through his pants, then laid her head against his shoulder while he lifted her dress and ran his hands over her thighs. She moaned. He ran a hand up to her pussy to find her without panties. His fingers ran over her pubic hair, and then found her moistness. She moaned as he slipped a finger in, and then turned to face him. She put her arms around his neck and kissed him passionately as he moved her to the open passenger door, then lifted her dress. She undid his pants and then reached inside and held his cock, moving her hands back and forth. She looked up and down the highway, opened her legs and waited. He bent his legs, felt her thighs on his and then entered her. She moaned, and then wrapped her legs around him. "Oooh God, I'm gonna come." He pushed his cock deeper into her and felt her breathing turn to gasps. She clung to him, moaning, wanting him to get deeper and deeper. "Oooh." She shuddered. "God, that feels good."

He felt her wetness on his cock and thighs and slowly lowered her feet to the ground. She stood shakily while he turned her away from him. She leaned over onto the truck seat and felt him lift her dress from behind. She opened her legs, then felt his cock sliding between her cheeks, and then sliding into her dripping woman-hood. He thrust and held it there: deep inside her. His thrusts began slowly, then became faster and deeper. She closed her legs and moaned. "Geez, that feels sooo fuckin' good."

His breathing was coming faster. He held her hips from behind and thrust again and again. He gave one final thrust and moaned, and then stood motionless. After a few seconds, he slowly removed his cock from her wetness and she turned to him shyly. He ran his hands down to her pussy. She was wet, sticky and smelled like heaven on earth. He put his hands on her face, brushed her hair aside and kissed her. "I love the hell out of you."

She put her arms around his neck and began sobbing softly. "I love you so very much."

They held each other in the waning light, and then he looked at her and smiled. "Wanna elope?"

She laughed. "Ha! Are you serious?"

"I've never been more serious in my life about anyone or anything."

"You really wanna marry me?"

"I did propose didn't I?"

"Yeah, but I guess I never really thought we'd go ahead with it. I thought maybe you'd back out."

"I love you, Tina, an' I want you to be my wife. But more importantly, I want to be your husband."

"You want to elope?"

"Okay. It's sudden, but okay."

She laughed just as a large tractor-trailer went flying by. "We should get going," she said. "Before we get arrested an' you give me a rep."

A few miles further down the highway, she rested her head on his shoulder, a hand on his thigh. "Yes."

"When?" he asked.

"Whenever you want."

"I go back to work on Wednesday. We can get the marriage licence on Monday an' do it then."

"Who'll stand with us?"

"I'll call El an' there's Eva."

"I want a dress."

"You've already got one."

"I know, but it's soiled."

He laughed. "So will your wedding dress."

"Woo-hoo!"

"Pick up one on Monday an' we'll get the rings, too."

"Just the four of us?"

"Just the four of us."

"What about your parents?"

"We're eloping," he said. "You an' I. Then we're gonna call everyone an' yell surprise. Well?" he asked.

"Well, after careful consideration, I've decided why the fuck not!"

He laughed. "Then it's set an' there's no backing down."

"None whatso-fuckin'-ever!"

"Good, I like a woman with conviction an' determination, an' a mouth like a sailor."

"You'd better, 'cause you ain't gettin' away, ever."

"That's exactly why I want to do it now, so I can say you're mine. But more importantly ..."

"... To say you're mine."

"Exactly."

"Great minds ..."

"Perverts an' deviates, too."

They laughed. "See that sunset?" she asked.

"Yeah?"

"Drive into it."

"Whatever you say!"

Tina woke up on Sunday morning to find John making coffee and cooking breakfast. "Well, what do we do?" she asked as she walked into the kitchen.

"Gotta call El," he said and picked up the phone and dialled El's number. "Hey, El," he said. "Me an' Tina are gonna elope."

"Yeah?"

"Yeah."

Elmer sounded like he'd had a rough weekend. "Where?" he asked.

"In town. Gonna need a best man."

"Don' know if I'm the bes' man in town right at the moment, but I'm here. When?"

"We'll let you know."

"Okay. If I don't answer, call 911 an' break down my door an' gimme CPR. Better yet, get some big-busted blonde to gimme CPR. Don't care if she's a nurse. It can even be 'at tall hooker I seen the other day. I think her name's Big Rhonda."

John laughed, hung up and then handed the phone to Tina. "Can you break the news to my sister?"

Tina called Eva. "Guess what?" she said.

"What?"

"Me an' your bro are gonna elope."

"You're kiddin'?"

"Nope."

"When?"

"Tomorrow or the nex'. Gonna need a bridesmaid."

"You're askin' me?"

"Yes."

Eva screamed. "I'd be glad to!" And then she got serious. "You aren't pregnant, are you?"

"No," Tina said. "Why?"

"It's jus' you've been sick these last few weeks."

"Well, I don't have morning sickness an' I have no cravings for pickles an' ice cream, or anything weird, except for your brother."

"Geez, I don't wanna hear that."

"Well, I'd better go. Gonna have some weird breakfast."

"Tina!"

They laughed and hung up, and then Tina yawned. "Geez," she said, "I must've slept two days. I'm taking a shower." She took off her nightgown and stood in the kitchen naked and unashamed.

He smiled at her brazenness. "Can I join you?"

"Sure, I need someone to do my back."

It was then that he noticed her hips were bruised. "Your hips."

She looked at them. "Geez, I didn't think you were that rough."

"I'm sorry."

"I ain't complaining."

"I know."

"I never bruise this easily. Not even when I played soccer an' basketball in high school."

After they had showered, Tina called her grandparents. "We're going to elope," she said to her grandmother.

"Elope? What's that?"

"It means we're going to get married right away."

"Are you pregnant?" Sarah asked in the language.

"No, we just want to get married right away."

"You can't wait?"

"We could, but we don't want to."

Her grandfather came on the line. "You're gonna elope?" he asked.

"Yes, Grandfather," she answered in the language.

"Then we won't have a wedding up here?"

"John?" she whispered.

He was on the other extension. "We can elope an' still get married again," he said. "Later."

"Grandfather," she said in the language, "we'll have a wedding up there too."

"This is confusing," Abraham said.

"We're gonna get married by a JP here. Up there, we'll have a minister an' it'll be in a church."

"You're not gonna get married in church?"

"We're gonna get married an' it'll be legal, but it won't be in a church. We can do that later."

"You're gonna have two weddings? One down there an' one up here?"

"Yes," she said. "It'll be all right."

"If it's not against the law, then I guess it's all right."

She laughed. "It's not, an' it will be."

"What are we going to tell the People?" he asked in the language.

"Tell them we eloped, but we are going to have a church wedding up there in June."

"It's still confusing, but we'll tell them."

"Thanks," Tina said. "I knew you'd understand an' it will be all right."

"What can I say?"

"You can give me your blessing, Grandfather."

"You're my granddaughter. You'll always have it."

"Thank you. *Mussi cho.*"

"You're welcome."

"Goodbye. I'll call you in a few days."

John then called his parents, who gave their approval. His dad even suggested that John and Tina drive over on Monday evening and he'd have the local JP ready for them. They agreed that would be better than having to look for one in the Yellow Pages.

The next morning, John went to city hall and got a marriage licence while Tina was in class. He bought two wedding bands, and then he and El went looking for tuxes. They settled on two dark blue business suits. "Hey," El said. "We can use 'em if we ever get invited to sing on the Grand Ole Opry."

"Yeah," John said. "Or if we ever have to go to court."

Tina and Eva went looking for dresses during their lunch break and found something modern, low cut and without frills, lace and ribbons. "We can use them at other events," Tina said.

"Like what?"

"Like *your* wedding."

"As if!"

After class, John picked up Tina and El picked up Eva. Two hours later, they were all standing in Don and Katherine Olson's living room. And despite it being a private affair, more than a few of John's high school friends were showing up.

"We only told a few of your friends," Katherine said.

"Yeah," Eva said, "and I only called five of mine."

"The more the merrier," John said.

Half an hour later, John and El stood while Tina and Eva walked into the living room. Tina looked at John with tears in her eyes, and when she stood near him, he leaned over, took her left hand in his right, put his left hand behind her, squeezed her ass and whispered, "Thank you."

"John!" Katherine Olson whispered.

Fifteen minutes later, he did as Justice of the Peace Sheila Robinson told him: He kissed his wife, and then whispered, "Thank you for allowing me to be your husband, Mrs. Tina Daniel."

"The honour is all mine, my first husband."

"Whatever."

☼

His mind was going again. Or at least that's what it felt like. He focused on staying in the present, hoping the fog wouldn't return. He was going to be alone again. Jim was leaving; he'd be gone by summer. He wanted to go home. He wanted to live in his house, cut his own wood, haul his own water, and clean up and do his laundry like they taught him in mission school and in the army. But they wouldn't let him. They told him he had to get much better so that he could look after himself. "How do I get better?" he had asked.

The man in white, Doctor Stilman, smiled. "You have to tell us what's bothering you. Why do you leave? Go into your head? You've told us it's a fog, but you've not told us what's in there. What's in there that makes you go quiet and silent?"

It was the river, the hills, the mountains and the cabin. It was a drunken, dark Indian screaming at him, while his wife lay on the floor, passed out. It was William and Elizabeth, his brother-in-law and his sister. They were drunk; they were always drunk.

"Once you deal with that, then maybe you might be able to go home."

Maybe? Might? Home? He looked at Jim, who was smiling, nodding at him, confirming they were telling the truth. He was scared; scared of the ... What was it he was scared of? There was the river; the cabin; the dark man, William; and the woman, Elizabeth. What was there to be scared of? They were dreams, nothing more than dreams. He had to get better, or he'd be alone again. And he didn't want to be alone in here. In here, if you were alone, you were … What were you? You were alone forever, and he didn't want to be alone forever. He wanted to go home; home to the Blue Mountains and the People. He focused on the wire mesh. It was just wire mesh, and this was just a room with one window and two beds.

"Edward?"

He turned to the attendant, Steve. "Yes, sir?"

"Bedtime."

Chapter Seventeen

It was Wednesday, March 26, and John was on the phone with Ken. "Hey," Ken said, "when you're coming up again?"

"No idea."

"Well, Easter's comin'. You should come up then. Pay us a visit an' sing a few. You know you're popular up here? People think you're big time."

"Ha!"

"Really. We get Clint to play it at 'a LC ever' chance we get, an' it's pop'lar in 'a Saloon too. Me an' Richard been tryin' to get 'em to play it on CBC an' other radio stations too."

"So I've heard."

"You got it on cassette?"

"It *is* on cassette."

"I mean mass produced, like."

"Not yet. Costs too much."

"Yeah? Well, if you ever get it mass produced, people want it."

"Really?"

"Really. I copied it five times already an' gave it out to chicks who liked it. Making you some fans."

"An' gettin' laid?"

"That too, but that's just fringe benefits. So, you comin' up?"

"I'll see what Tina wants to do. She's been busy studying."

"Well, let us know if you're comin'."

John hung up. He had just gotten off work and was looking at spending time with Tina. Since they'd eloped, he'd come home only once and this, his second time, he wanted to spend looking after her and doing her every which way he could.

When she came home from the university, he told her of the phone call from Ken. She had a headache again and was tired. "If we leave on Friday," she said, "we'll be up there on Saturday, late. If we leave on Sunday, we'll be back here on Monday, very late. An' I have an important class on Tuesday."

"It's up to you."

"Would you do that for me?"

"I'd do anything for you."

"It's a long way."

"I can break the speed limit."

She smiled, and then looked at her class schedule. "I can miss class tomorrow. If we leave tonight, we can be there late tomorrow. That way we'll have Friday an' Saturday to do whatever we want. If we leave Sunday, we'll be here late Monday. I'm gonna have to make up for one day, but it'll be worth it."

"It might do you good to be home for a while."

"I can stop at the health centre, too. I need to pick up an application for a summer job. I'd like to see if I can get on at the Helena Hospital." She looked at him. "Would you mind if I took a job up there?"

"Not a prob."

She was lying on her stomach on the floor, where it was cooler, and holding her head in her hands. "Geez," she said, "I don't know what it is. Keeps coming an' going. Maybe it's just too much thinking."

He sat beside her and began massaging her back. He lifted her T-shirt and pressed his hands into her soft brown skin. "That feels good," she said.

A little later, they were both naked on the floor and she had her head on his chest and he was stroking her hair. "Thank you," she said.

"As always, my pleasure"

"You do me good."

"I know, but it really is my pleasure."

She laughed. "I meant being with you does me good."

"I know, but it really is my pleasure."

"Whatever."

"So, do you wanna?" he asked about the trip to Aberdeen.

"Are you up to it?"

He looked down at his cock. "Gimme a few minutes, okay. I've just gone a round with my wife."

She laughed. "Geez, maybe I should leave before she comes home? Hey, I am your wife!"

"And I'm your husband."

Twenty-four hours later, they were just over a hundred miles from Aberdeen. It was seven in the evening and the sun was setting over the Blue Mountains; winter was still officially in the land of the Blue People. The snows were still knee-deep to a big Indian and the only grass visible dotted the windswept hills and mountains.

Tina had fallen asleep and was just getting up and noticing familiar landmarks. "We're almost home. Two more hours. I wonder if we'll see any caribou?"

"Haven't seen any. Not even tracks."

"Maybe up further. You brought your gun?"

"Yep."

"Good."

"You know what?"

"What?"

"I notice everyone up north measures long distances in hours, not miles."

"We do?"

"Yep. Like it's two hours to Aberdeen, not two hundred klicks. And I also noticed that people from Aberdeen have their own accent."

"Really?"

"And they have a bad habit of saying 'really.'"

She laughed. "Really?"

"Really."

Two hours later, they drove down main-street Aberdeen and despite the sun having set, it was still light out. "Feel better?" he asked.

"Much."

"Headache?"

"Gone."

"Saloon's open."

"Maybe later."

"Good. I'm tired," he said.

"Same here. I could sleep forever."

They pulled up to Abraham and Sarah's house and she ran inside while he got their bags. When he went in, she was eating caribou meat and Sarah was putting out drymeat and bannock. "Are you eating well?" she asked Tina in the language.

"Yes, but I miss the food."

"Are you sure? You're getting thin."

"I am?" she asked in English. "It must be all the studying an' worrying I do about classes."

"Is it difficult?"

"It's a lot of work, but I'm doing well."

"John," Abraham said, and then shook his hand. "You're married."

John grinned. "Yes, legally."

Sarah hugged him while Abraham shrugged. "Heard of someone gettin' married by JP once."

"John an' Mary," Sarah said.

"Yeah," Abraham said. "Them. They don't live together now."

"We're married," Tina said. "But if you want, we can get married again in the summer when I get back."

"I'd like to give you away. Did anyone give you away?" asked Abraham.

"No."

"No feast?" Sarah asked. "No dance?"

"None."

"They didn't even throw rice?"

"No."

"How can they call that a wedding?"

Tina laughed. "Grandmother, Grandfather," she said in the language, "we'll get married in June in the church."

Later, John and Tina lay in bed and listened to familiar noises, and smelled familiar smells. "Missed it?" he asked.

"Yes. You?"

"A guy can get used to it."

"I'm not asking you to move here."

"I know."

"I'd be happy anywhere with you as long as we can come back for Christmas an' every so often."

"We'll work something out."

"To tell the truth," she said, "before you came along I always thought I'd return an' live my whole life here."

"And now?"

"Like I said, I'd be happy anywhere with you. Besides, I think I'd rather work somewhere I don't already know the people. There's a few nurses who told us we'd have a hard time working in our own community, what with things being so confidential an' all. Maybe that's why the nurses who come here don't stay that long, an' rarely associate with the locals."

A few minutes later, John heard her breathing slow and become steady.

Friday was Good Friday and everything was closed and Tina and her grandparents had gone to church. John walked up the main street hell-bent on visiting Ken and Richard, who lived right next door to one another in one of five six-unit apartment buildings in the community. He knocked on Ken's apartment, but someone opened Richard's door: It was Ken. "Hey, you big son 'a bitch!" he shouted at John. "When the hell you get into town?"

"Yesterday."

"What? How come you never come 'roun'?"

"Tired."

"Tired? Fuck sakes, nothin' few beers can't cure."

"Close 'at fuckin' door, you dork!" Richard shouted. "You think heat grows on trees?"

Ken laughed. "Come in."

John stepped into Richard's apartment. It smelled like beer, vodka and cigarettes. "Smells like Clint's socks," he said.

"Yeah," Richard said. "Who hell are you? Don Fuckin' Rickles?" John laughed and Richard got up and shook his hand. "How the fuck are you? When you get in? Wanna beer?"

"Good, yesterday, no thanks."

"When you leavin'?"

"Sunday."

"So soon?"

"Tina's got class an' I got work."

"Knew it was her had the class."

"Up yours."

"You an' Ken wish."

They laughed.

"This is Kathy an' Mary. An' 'at guy passed out is Lawrence."

"Hi," John said.

"Gettin' there," Kathy said, nodding and grinning. "Who're you?"

"Who is this?" Ken asked. "This is John Fuckin' Daniel."

"Hey, you're the guy that sings."

"So they tell me."

"Your record is at the Saloon an' it's been playin' on 'a radio for months now."

"Yeah," Mary said. "These guys forever sendin' us requests, people think we're foolin' 'roun' with them."

"You are," Ken said.

"Yeah, but only on weekends an' only 'til we meet some real men."

Everyone laughed at that.

"Your chances are little to none in 'is town," Richard said.

"Yeah," Mary said, "you got 'at right. So, whatcha doin' in town?"

"Came up with my wife."

"Who's your wife?" Kathy asked.

"Tina."

"You're the one married Tina."

"Yep."

"Nice girl."

"So I've heard."

"How long you know her?"

"Over a year now."

"Long enough."

"So what's to do in town?" John asked Richard.

"Absolutely nothin', 'less you're into goin' to church. What's to do in Calgary?"

"Nothin', 'less you're into goin' to church."

"Cow town, caribou town, different place, same shit."

"Well, just thought I'd drop in an' say hi."

"Whatcha doin' tomorrow?" Richard asked.

"No idea."

"Wanna go huntin'? I'll buy gas."

"When?"

"Soon as gas station opens."

"When's 'at?"

"Eight bells."

"I'll be here. You'll be ready?"

"With bells on," he said, and then looked at Ken. "An' don' say nothin' or I'm leavin' you."

"Fuck sakes," Ken said. "We're not married, you know."

"I meant I'm not takin' you into the hills with us."

"Hey, say hi to Tina for us," Mary said.

John returned to Abraham and Sarah's and made some tea, then began cooking some chicken he and Tina had brought from Calgary. He placed the chicken in a frying pan, added a ton of butter, potatoes, carrots and some spices. After he got it nice and hot, he shut the stove off, lay down and fell asleep. He woke up when he heard Tina and her grandparents coming in. He heard Sarah and Tina talking in the language, and then Tina laughed. She came in, took her jacket off and lay beside him. "What did she say?" he asked.

"She asked if you knew how to cook."

"And?"

"I said you do everything: clean, cook, do laundry."

"And?"

"She told me to keep you." He smiled. "Hey," she said, "Eunice said she got a call from Olive. She said Edward is doing real good. They're even thinkin' of lettin' him come home in a few months, if he keeps gettin' better."

"Yeah? For good?"

"No, just for a visit. They say it's still too early to tell if he's ready to come back permanently."

"Well, he seems to be able to look after himself. He's not a psycho or a nutcase like I thought he'd be. Guess I watch too many movies."

"Probably, but he's going to need help when he gets back. Eunice said she an' Alfred could see his needs are looked after so long as he doesn't need twenty-four-hour care."

"I still don't know him. I just met him that once an' he seems to be …"

"Normal?"

"Yeah, he's normal as you an' me."

"Are we normal?"

"Not likely."

✧

Olive came to visit again. She and her husband and kids drove down from Whitehorse and they all visited him. She brought some shirts and some bannock, but no donuts. And they didn't stay long. Their kids wanted to get going and see the city.

Doctor Stilman and Jim kept asking him questions about his life growing up, in mission school, in the army and out of the army. He kept telling them the same things over and over again. They knew about his parents and how they died. They knew about Floyd and how he died. They knew about Margaret and that she was dead. They also knew William and Elizabeth had died. They knew that already. They also knew he dreamed of the river and the cabin and the … What else did he dream about? He dreamed of Floyd and he dreamed of his parents, but those were good dreams, most of them.

Doctor Stilman was a good man. He was always smiling, like Jim. But he was white and he had a beard: a white beard.

His hair was grey: dark grey. "Can you tell us again about the cabin, Edward?"

Why did they want to know about that? More and more they asked about the cabin. Did they know? What did they know? What did he know? Jim was sitting in again, like he had done for the last few ... How long had he been telling them the same thing? Only a few months, but it felt like forever. "The cabin?"

"Yes. What's in the cabin?"

"Dark, fog, noise."

"What else?"

"Screaming, shouting, yelling."

"Is there anyone in there?"

"A dark Indian, screaming, yelling."

"What is he yelling?"

He was now breathing hard and fast.

"Edward, stay with us. What is he yelling?"

He looked at Jim. "I think I did something bad."

"What did you do, Edward?" Jim asked. "What do you see?"

"I think he killed her."

"Who?"

"William."

"Who did he kill?"

"The woman."

"What woman?"

"The woman on the floor."

"Who is she?"

"His wife, my sister."

"Olive?"

He looked at Jim. "No."

"Who?"

The doctor looked in a brown folder. "Was it Elizabeth?" he asked.

"Elizabeth an' William."

"Yes, those were their names. They're your ..." Doctor Stilman looked in the brown folder again. "They were your brother-in-law and sister.... Edward?"

"Yes."

"Why ..." The doctor seemed to search his mind for the right words. "Why, after all these years, are you making such progress?"

"Progress?"

"Yes. Why are you able to talk and talk about the cabin and what you found?"

"Why?"

"Yes. Why are you telling us this now?"

He looked at Jim. "He's leaving."

"Who? Jim?"

"Yes."

"Yes, I know. He's been here for a long time. He'll be finished school and moving on."

"I'll be alone."

"You'll never be alone."

He was slipping away.

"Can you stay with us, Edward? Don't leave."

"I don't want to stay."

"I meant stay with us right now; stay focused on the moment, here and now."

"Focus?"

"Yes, focus. Jim has to leave and move on with his life, and so do you. You have to get better so we can send you home where you can look after yourself and do what you want."

"I want to hunt an' trap."

Doctor Stilman smiled. "Of course you do. And the faster we deal with your issues, the faster you'll go home."

"I want to go home."

"You will."

He was getting frustrated. They kept asking him about the cabin, and he kept telling them. But they kept asking him over and over again. "Were they alive?" Doctor Stilman asked.

"Who?" he asked. He could tell the doctor was getting frustrated, too. Not angry, just frustrated.

"William and Elizabeth."

He tried to focus. "They were drunk, passed out."

"Yes, we know that. Were they alive?"

He thought. "She was dead."

"Was he dead?" Doctor Stilman asked.

"Who?"

"William."

"He was screaming."

"At what?"

"At me."

"What was he saying?"

He forced out the words. "She had his kid."

"Who had his kid? Elizabeth?"

"She was dead."

"Who?"

"Elizabeth."

"How did she die?" Doctor Stilman asked.

"She was drunk. She was dead."

"Edward?"

"Yes."

"Are you cold?"

He looked at Doctor Stilman. "Cold?"

"Yes. Are you cold?"

"No."

"Why do you keep your hands tucked in your armpits?"

He looked at his hands. "They're cold."

"Are they cold now?"

"No."

"Were they cold then?"

"When?"

"When you found them?"

"Who?"

"William and Elizabeth. Were your hands cold when you found them?"

"No."

"When did they get cold?"

"They said they were going to bury them."

"Bury who?"

He looked at his hands, and then pulled them from his sides. "They're not dead. They said they were going to bury them."

"Who's not dead?" Doctor Stilman asked.

"My hands."

"Of course they're not dead. Why would they bury them?"

"They said …"

"What did they say, Edward?" It was Jim.

"They said they were going to bury them."

"Why?" Jim asked.

"They were frozen."

"What? Your hands?"

"Yes."

"Why were they frozen?"

He almost shivered. "They were cold."

"Why were they cold?" Jim asked.

"I was on the river."

"What were you doing on the river?"

"I was ... I was bringing them back."

"Who? William and Elizabeth?"

"Yes. They were frozen."

Jim looked at Doctor Stilman, who nodded. "Edward?"

"Yes?"

"Were they alive? Were William and Elizabeth alive when you found them?"

"She was passed out."

"Was she alive?" Doctor Stilman asked.

He was suffocating, breathing hard. "She died."

Doctor Stilman sat back. "I think we've done enough for today. Edward?"

"Yes?"

The doctor smiled. "You did very well."

"Thank you, sir."

Jim poured him a glass of water and he drank it. "You can take it easy now," Jim said. "Can you make it back to your room?"

"Yes, Jim."

Jim showed him to the door. He took a few steps out, and then stopped and listened, forcing his ears to reach for the door and beyond, move into the room.

"Well, Jim. Your assessment?"

Jim took a deep breath. "It would appear, contrary to the reports, that they were alive when he found them. At least William was."

"I agree. But Elizabeth is a question."

"I agree."

"He *is* making remarkable progress."

"I couldn't agree with you more. He is taking more responsibility for his needs—washing, dressing, cleaning up his room—and he's more mobile."

"Who knows, he just might be able to make significant progress so that we can send him home."

"He's been gone a long time."

"Ten years. Did he have any visitors recently?"

"Just two young people from his hometown: Tina Joseph and John Daniel," Jim said, a smile in his voice. "They're engaged."

Doctor Stilman laughed. "Oh, to be young again."

"Edward?"

He turned to the man in green, the one they called Steve. "Yes, sir?"

"It's getting late. You should be in bed."

He looked at his reflection in the window; he was in his white nightgown. He looked down at his feet; he was wearing his slippers. He smiled. He was getting better and he might be going home soon.

Chapter Eighteen

It was April and Tina was lying face down on the sofa in their apartment in Calgary. "I talked to Verna," she said.

"And?" John asked.

"They're moving to Norman Wells an' she may not have time to plan the wedding."

"It's only two months away."

"I know."

He brought her some tea and a couple of Aspirins. "What would you like to do?"

"I don't know. We're both down here an' it's going to be up there, but it's so hard planning."

"We don't have to, you know."

"I know, but my grandparents want me to."

"I mean, we don't have to do it in June. We can do it in the fall, or at Christmas. Or even later."

"You don't mind?" she asked.

"Not at all. We're married already, you know."

"Can I tell my grandparents we can do it at Christmas?"

He shrugged. "If I have to, I'll take time off an' drive up an' plan it myself. I'll even do all the sewing, cooking an' whatever else has to be done."

She smiled. "I know you will. You know, my grandfather has a cabin upriver. I'd really like to take you there sometime."

"Yeah?"

"We went up about five years ago, but it's so far an' it's so much work to get up there."

"Maybe we'll use it one of these years. Take some time an' jus' take it easy."

"I use to love being up there. The hills an' mountains, an' the quiet, an' fresh bannock cooked on a wood stove."

On Friday, May 23, Tina turned twenty-four and was almost done her first year at school. John drove in as soon as he got off work and picked her up at the university. He didn't like what he saw: She looked pale and tired. She held on to him and she felt light: frail. "Happy birthday," he said.

"Thanks."

"You've lost weight," he said as they drove off.

"I know. I've been told. I haven't had a good night's sleep since you left. Must be the exams. I've been cramming an' staying up late an' drinking too much coffee for my own good."

"Are you sure you're okay?"

She smiled. "Yeah. Now that you're back, I'm better. An' I'll probably get a good night's sleep tonight," she said, and then grinned. "Very late tonight."

He smiled. "I'm hoping."

"Hope no more. You an' I are gonna raise the roof." Then she got shy. "Geez, I still can't believe some of the things you have me saying."

"What?"

"I never talked like this in my life, never."

"So, you just needed someone like me to bring out the pervert in you."

"Perversion, brazenness, whatever. I just love it. There's so much more freedom than I thought it would be."

"What did you think it would be like?"

"I thought it would be like any other relationship I'd seen: Me at home, pregnant, cooking, cleaning and waiting for you to come home from work with your supper ready. When you're here, I don't have to do anything. An' you take care of the rent, the utilities, the bills ... an' you take care of me."

"That's what I enjoy: looking after you."

"And you don't mind?"

"Not at all. I'm so ..." He slowed down and she noticed tears flowing down his face. "I'm so very much in love with you," he said.

"I love you too."

"All my life, I've been trying to forget about where I came from, who I was, who my parents were, who my people were. But today, I'm glad of who I am, an' I'm so glad things turned out the way they did: with you in my life."

"And I'm never leaving."

"Promise?"

"Promise."

❖

"Can you tell us again what went on in that cabin?" Doctor Stilman asked.

How many times had he told the doctor and Jim? A hundred? "The cabin?"

"Yes. From the time you drove up to the cabin."

"They were drinkin' again."

"William and Elizabeth?"

"Yes. They were arguing again, fightin'."

"William was fighting Elizabeth?"

"Yes."

"What did he do?"

"He gave her black eyes again."

"What was the first thing you saw when you looked in the cabin?"

"He hit her."

"How did he hit her?"

"He hit her an' she fell."

"Tell us again how she fell."

"She fell an' hit her head."

"Where did she hit her head?"

"On the table."

"Did she get up?"

"No, she just lay there."

"Did she move?"

"No."

"Then what happened?"

"He kept calling me stupid an' calling me names."

"Why?"

"I told him not to hit her."

"Did he hit her again?"

"He kicked her."

"Did she get up or move?"

"No."

"What happened next?" Jim asked.

"He said she had his kid."

"Who had his kid?"

"He said Margaret had his kid."

"And who's Margaret?"

"Margaret is … was my girlfriend. She was Abraham an' Sarah's daughter."

"How old was Margaret?"

"Same as me."

"She died?"

"Yes. July 1963."

"How do you remember that?" Doctor Stilman asked.

"I saw her cross. That's what it said: *Margaret, Beloved Daughter of Abraham an' Sarah. Born 1944. Died 1963.*"

"She was nineteen," Jim said.

"Yes."

"She had William's child?" Doctor Stilman asked.

"Yes."

"Where's the child now?"

He shrugged. "I don' know. Maybe he's in Aberdeen."

"He. So it was a boy?"

He shrugged. "I don' know." He remembered the young girl at the feast with Abraham and Sarah. She was in their house a few days later. This is Margaret's daughter, Sarah had said in the language. "She was a girl."

"What was her name?"

He shrugged. "I don' know. They never tol' me."

"What happened next?" Doctor Stilman asked.

He looked puzzled.

"What happened after William hit Elizabeth? What did you do?"

"I picked her up."

"Did she get up?"

"No, she was gone."

"Gone?"

"She was dead."

"Did William know she was dead?"

"I tol' him."

"What did he say?"

He saw William sneering. "He said she's passed out an' he called me stupid."

"And then what happened?"

"He pushed me."

"How?"

"He pushed me on the head an' I fell."

"Where did you fall?"

"On the floor."

"And then what happened?"

"He kept pushing me an' calling me stupid."

"And then?"

He saw William raise his fist. "He was going to hit me."

"Did he hit you?" Jim asked.

"He tried."

"And?"

He saw himself deflect William's fist, and then hit him. "I hit him."

"Where did you hit him?" Doctor Stilman asked.

He watched his own fist as it disappeared into William's throat. "Right here," he said and pointed to his throat.

"What happened next?" Jim asked.

"He fell."

"Did he get up?"

He watched William kneel, and then fall next to Elizabeth. "No, he fell."

"Did he get up?"

"No."

"What about Elizabeth?" Doctor Stilman asked. "Did she get up?"

"No, she was dead."

"Was William dead?"

He looked at the doctor, and then at Jim. They were waiting for an answer. "He fell."

"What happened after he fell, Edward?"

He thought about what he had done. "I took them back."

"Back to where?"

"I took them back to town."

"What did they ask you?"

"Who?"

"The RCMP. What did they ask you?"

He remembered the officer. "He asked what happened."

"What did you tell him?"

"He asked if they froze."

"What did you tell him?" Jim asked.

"I told him they're frozen."

Doctor Stilman sat back. That meant it was over for today. He had told them the same thing for years, and for years and it had ended the same way: Doctor Stilman sat back and Jim smiled. But today, Jim didn't smile. "Did I do something wrong?" he asked. "Something bad?"

"No, Edward," Jim said, "you didn't do anything wrong or bad."

"Are you mad?"

Jim smiled. "No, I'm not mad."

It was okay. Jim had smiled.

"That's it for today, Edward."

"Yes, sir."

Chapter Nineteen

On Wednesday, June 11, Tina left the hospital and went back to the apartment. She breathed a sigh of relief that it was over. For the first time in a long time she hadn't had any classes in the afternoon, so she'd decided to get some tests done to see why she was losing weight and getting tired. She walked into the apartment just as John called. "Hey," he said, sounding different.

"Is anything wrong?"

"No, I'm okay. Jus' had a close call."

"What happened?"

"Almost los' my fingers."

"What?"

"Just got 'em banged up pretty good. Nothing serious: a few bruises an' some sore bones."

"Where are you?"

"At the hospital."

"Are you okay?"

"Yeah, nothing to worry about. I'll be home in half an hour. I jus' have to figure out if I'm gonna go back again. Anything happens to my fingers, I can kiss my other career goodbye."

"I'll be waiting," she said and hung up. A few minutes later, the phone rang again.

It was her grandmother, and she noticed the concern in Tina's voice. "What's wrong?" she asked in the language.

"John got hurt at work. He's okay. Nothing serious."

"Are you sure?"

"Yes, he'll be home in a few minutes."

"He should find different job."

"Money's too good, he says."

"Well, tell him to look after himself. You jus' got married, you know."

"I know."

"His auntie Eunice and his auntie Olive are going down to visit Edward."

"When?"

"Next week. I'm sending a parcel with them."

When John walked in, Tina looked at his left hand, which was in a cast, and then hugged him carefully. "Are you okay?" she asked again.

"Yeah, just bruised an' one cracked bone."

"What happened?"

"Greenhorns."

"Can you still ..."

"Yes," he said and smiled, "I can still ..."

She laughed. "That's not what I meant. I meant can you still play the guitar."

"Not right now." He waved his left hand. "But they said there'd be no permanent damage."

"Good. I married you as is, so you lose a hand, I'm gonna get our marriage annulled an' then you're gonna have to chase me all over again."

"Sounds like fun."

She smiled. "Hey, didn't I chase you?"

"No. How'd your tests go?"

"Long an' boring."

"What they find?"

"They tol' me I'm married to a nutcase."

"I could've told you that."

"I'm kidding. They said they'll know in two weeks. That reminds me, your aunts are coming to Edmonton."

"When?"

"Nex' week."

"Do you think we should drive up?" he asked.

"My grandmother's sending a parcel."

"Good. We'll go."

"When do you go back?"

"Cast comes off in two, three weeks, an' they tol' me to take it easy for another month. An' don't worry; I'm on compensation 'til I go back in July. An' I've got a few weeks comin' to me too."

"Good. I got a job in Helena."

"I'm glad."

"You are?"

"Of course. When's your last day of school?"

"Friday," she said. "All I've got are a few exams an' I'm done for this year."

"So, when do you start?"

"I'd like to stay until I get the results from my medical. I told them I'd start first Monday in July."

"When do you want to go?"

"Whenever you can drive me."

"We'll see after you get your results in."

"Sounds great. Hey, do you think Eva would want to come to Edmonton?"

"I'll call her later."

"Are you up to it?" she asked.

"I'm up to anything right now."

"Good, 'cause I'm horny."

❖

He opened the door, took a few steps and stopped. He listened: stretching his ears so that they moved across the hall and through the door. He had done this many times in the last few months and was getting good at it. The people who walked by didn't even notice. "When are you leaving?" Doctor Stilman asked Jim.

"I was going to start in July, but I asked if I could start in August. I told them I had a case I'd like to see to its conclusion and they didn't seem to mind. I'll probably pack in July and then move."

"That's good. His story's still the same," Doctor Stilman said. "It hasn't changed."

"No, it hasn't."

"According to the report, they were drinking and froze to death. That's when he found them and brought them to town."

"And they didn't do any autopsies?"

"None. They just took him at his word."

"Would you have?" Jim asked.

"Probably."

"So, what do we do?"

"What would you do?"

"It's obvious William killed his wife. Accidentally, but he killed her nonetheless."

"Yes," Doctor Stilman said. "And it's obvious Edward killed William in self-defence."

"Yes."

"So what would change if the authorities knew?"

Jim was silent for a few seconds, and then said, "Nothing, in the long run."

"You're right. So what would you do?"

"In terms of what you and I know of the events as they actually happened?"

"Yes."

Jim sighed. "You're asking me a difficult question."

"Yes, I am."

"You're asking if I should, or would, withhold information that's important, but which, in the end, wouldn't change anything."

"That's what I'm asking," Doctor Stilman said.

"Personally, if I knew he was going to be in here for the rest of his life, I wouldn't make a concerted effort to …" Jim didn't finish.

"I'd do the same, but …"

"But," Jim said. "If we're thinking about releasing him, what's to say he won't disclose this to someone who isn't as …"

"Compassionate?"

"Exactly."

"So, there's the dilemma. Do we let the authorities know? They may reopen the case and Edward will have to relive memories he doesn't want to relive. It's a cut and dried case of self-defence if ever I saw one."

"Or do we let it be?" Jim said. "If we do, and Edward discloses to someone who reports it to the authorities, then we may have to come forward."

"A potentially embarrassing situation."

"And career threatening," Jim added.

"So?" Doctor Stilman asked. "What would you do?"

"Are you asking me as my mentor? Or as one professional to another?"

"I'm asking you as a friend."

"Off the record?"

"Definitely."

"I've known Edward as a gentle soul who wouldn't intentionally hurt anyone."

"Agreed."

"And," Jim added, "if I were to send him home, I'd say the events in the reports were ..."

"Accurate?"

"Perhaps *accurate* is not the word. *Unchanged* seems more benign."

"Good."

"But we have to remember that he's not here because of what he did, or didn't do. He's here because of what he saw and how it affected him and his ability to look after himself."

"True."

"So what do we do?" Jim asked.

"Exactly what we discussed."

"And if he decides to tell someone of the events as he knows them?"

"I'd be prepared to ..." Doctor Stilman didn't finish.

"I would too."

"Thanks."

"I'm only doing what I think is best for Edward."

"I am too, but I'd sleep better if I knew he wasn't going to tell anyone."

"So would I," Jim said. "Anyhow, it's getting late and I've got to pick up my wife." The door opened and Jim came out, looked at him and frowned. "Edward?"

"Yes."

"What are you doing out here?"

"Nothing, just thinking."

"About what?"

He looked at Jim. "I wouldn't tell."

"Wouldn't tell what?"

"I wouldn't tell." It took Jim a few seconds, but he got it. "I wouldn't tell," he said again.

Jim smiled. "I know you wouldn't."

"I'm …"

"You're what?"

"I want to go home."

Jim looked at him for a long time. "You will."

"Thank you."

"You're welcome." He looked at his watch. "I've got to pick up my wife, Edward."

"Yes, sir."

"Good night, Edward."

"Good night, Jim."

Chapter Twenty

John knocked on the hotel room door. "Come in," Eunice answered.

Olive laughed. "You gotta open it."

Eunice opened the door and laughed. "Geez," she said, "I only came south three times in my life an' twice was with my husband." She looked at Tina and frowned. "You're losing weight."

"Yes, so they tell me."

"Are you eating okay?"

"Yes. It's just I have these headaches from time to time an' I get tired, but I figure it's stress from being back in school an' all the homework."

Eunice gave her a bag. "It's drymeat an' other goodies. Maybe it'll help you gain some weight."

"I got some tests done to see why. They should be ready nex' week."

"Good." Then she looked at John's hand. "What happen to you?"

"Accident on the job."

"You okay?"

"Yeah," he said and wiggled his fingers. "Just a few bruises an' one cracked bone." He turned and there was Eva standing behind him. "This is my sister, Eva."

Eunice took one look at her and hugged her, then began crying. Olive came over and she too hugged Eva and started crying. "You are so pretty," she said.

"Thank you," Eva replied.

"You look jus' like Tina."

"No," Eva said, "Tina's so much more beautiful."

Tina got shy. "How's my grandparents?" she asked.

"They're okay. Don' worry about them, they'll live for 'nother thirty years."

Tina smiled. "I'll be fifty-four. Probably with grandkids."

"Geez, I never thought about that," John said.

"What?" Olive asked. "Grandkids?"

"Yeah."

She laughed. "Me neither, but my oldest is gonna be a daddy in a few months."

"An' you're gonna be a …"

"Don't say it."

They laughed.

"How's Edward?" John asked Olive.

"He's doin' good. They want to send him up nex' week to see how he does, jus' for two weeks. They're gonna send Jim too. I like that man. He cares for Edward."

"You should come with us to see him," Eunice said.

"When?"

"This afternoon."

❖

He was more alive than he had ever been. It was like the time he joined the army. He was going to learn to fight, to hunt Germans and Japanese like John Wayne. But it hadn't been like that. Sure, they'd taught him how to fight, but then they'd put him and Floyd in the kitchen, and then they'd moved him to cleaning up, just like in the mission school and hostel. But this time it was different; this time he was going home. It was only for two weeks, but if he did okay they might even send him home for good. And best of all, Jim was coming with him. Maybe he could show Jim how to hunt, fish and trap.

His sister, Olive, had even come down to visit him. And she brought more drymeat, bannock and donuts. He smiled when he saw the donuts. And she brought Eunice. Eunice was William's sister, but they didn't look like each other. Eunice was nicer and didn't drink and always smiled at everyone.

They'd taken him out yesterday and done some shopping, and then had supper. They'd brought him back late at night and he'd fallen asleep right away. He'd been tired. Tired, but happy. They'd even talked to him in the language and he'd tried talking, but he'd had to think about what he said and make the changes in his head. And sometimes he said the words wrong, but they didn't laugh at him. They corrected him, but they didn't laugh at him.

They came back late that afternoon and brought his nephew John and John's wife, Tina. They'd got married and were happy, even though she was skinnier than when he'd last seen her. Still, she looked happy and enjoyed being teased by Eunice and Olive, while John sat back and grinned.

He wanted to ask John what had happened to his hand, but he didn't. He was still too shy or unsure of himself. But John noticed him looking. "I got hurt working," he said. "Almost broke it, but it's okay."

They also brought another girl: Her name was Eva and she was John's sister. That meant she was William and Elizabeth's daughter. He thought she was Tina's sister for a while, since they both looked the same. And they both looked like Eunice, but younger. "I don't know you," he said to Eva.

"I was born after you left."

He thought about it. "I was in the army."

"Yes, I've heard."

She was very nice and polite.

"So, how does it feel to be going home?" Tina asked him.

He grinned. "It feels good. I'm tired of this place."

"Me too," she said. "I'm tired of the south, an' I've only been here for a little over ten months. What're you gonna do first?"

He smiled and shrugged. "I don't know. Fish, maybe."

"I'd like to fish," Jim said. "Should I bring my rod an' reel?"

"Sure," Eunice told him. "We got lots of fish in the Teal."

"Good huntin', too," he said. "But only in the fall when caribou are fat."

Jim laughed. "I'm not a hunter. I've only fished."

They talked for a few minutes, and then Jim left. They all went to a large store, and then they had dinner. It was steak and he liked that, but it didn't taste like caribou.

"What do you miss the most?" Eva asked him.

He wanted to say his parents, but they were dead. "I miss the food an' the people an' the water an' the caribou an' fishing an' hunting an' everything. You?"

She shrugged. "I don't know. I left when I was six an' I don't remember too much of ... home."

"You don't remember?"

"No, I can't."

"I didn't remember for a long time either. But Doctor Stilman an' Jim, they helped me remember."

"That's good," she said to him. "I'm so happy for you." Then she began crying.

"What's wrong?" he asked.

"I can't remember anything."

"Some things are not good to remember."

She smiled. "I guess you're right. I was young an' I shouldn't expect to remember anything."

"So, Eva," Eunice said, "are you ever going up for a visit?"

"Maybe I'll go up next Christmas when John and Tina get married."

He looked at John and Tina. "You're getting married again?"

Tina laughed. She had a nice laugh. "Yes. We were married by a justice of the peace, but my grandparents want us to get married in a church."

"Abraham an' Sarah."

"Yes."

"I remember them." He wanted to say that he remembered Margaret too, but he didn't. She was dead. He wanted to ask about Margaret's daughter; he didn't. "There's gonna be a dance?"

"Yes," she said, rolling her eyes. "We're gonna have to jig, but we've jigged before."

"When?" Eva asked, astonished.

"Yeah, when?" Olive asked.

"Las' Christmas. We was in the jigging contest at the Saloon."

"You were what?" Eunice asked.

"We won," Tina said.

"You did?" Eva asked, and looked at John in amazement.

"I think they might've given it to us 'cause we were gonna get married," Tina said.

"Probably," John said.

He thought about the dances they used to have. He remembered Crazy Charlie dancing and hollering and having a good time. Crazy Charlie wasn't crazy; he was just funny and liked to have a good time and dance. He used to wear these cowboy boots with his jeans and his red shiny shirt with tassels on them. He wondered what Crazy Charlie was doing now.

Chapter Twenty-one

One week after they'd gone to see John's aunts and uncle in Edmonton, Tina walked out of the doctor's office and smiled at John. "They want to do more tests. It's gonna take a while, so you can leave if you'd like."

"Anything wrong?"

"No, nothing to worry about. They said the tests were inconclusive and they need to do more to determine what's ailing me. It'll be okay. Maybe another two hours."

"You sure?"

"Yes, I'm sure. Now get outta here before my husband comes an' kicks your ass."

"I'm sure I can handle the dork with one hand," he said, showing his bandaged hand.

She laughed. "I'm sure you can. Jus' don't jump in the sack with him. He'll kill you."

"What do you take me for? A pervert?"

"I'll take you any which way I can."

"Ain't got a comeback for that."

"Good, now get lost."

"You got it. Need anything?"

She grinned. "Later. Hey, they might pump me full of drugs. Maybe it'll be a new experience for both of us."

"Are you sure you want to leave tomorrow?"

"Yeah," she said. "If we leave bright an' early, we can be home by Friday night."

❖

Jim was excited about going up north and had asked a lot of questions about the land, the community and the Blue People. He'd told Jim as much as he could, but it had been a long time since he'd been back. And from what Olive told him, a lot of changes had happened and a lot of elders had died and children were having children.

"When did your parents pass away?" Jim asked.

"A long time ago, in the fifties."

"And you just have … had two sisters?"

"Yes, Elizabeth an' Olive."

"No brothers?"

"No."

"Any aunts or uncles?"

"I had an aunt, but she died. I had two uncles, but they died too."

"An' Eunice has three children an' Olive has four and is going to be grandmother soon."

"Yes."

"Can I ask you a question about Margaret?" Jim asked.

"Yes."

"Did she have any more children?"

"I don't know. I don't think so."

"And they never told you her daughter's name? Abraham and Sarah."

"No, they jus' told me Margaret died. I was going to ask Olive an' Eunice, but ..."

"But what?"

"We was havin' a good time."

"Yeah," Jim said, "I understand. You have six nieces an' nephews."

"I guess."

"Olive has four an' then there's John an' Eva."

"Yes."

"Who's Tina's parents?"

He had to think for a few seconds. "I don't know."

"You never asked?"

"No."

"But she is Abraham an' Sarah's granddaughter?"

"Yes."

"I can't wait to get up there," Jim said. "To see the land of the midnight sun."

He smiled. "It stays up all night. Kids play all night."

"I've heard about it, but I've gotta see it to believe it."

"Lots of mosquitoes, too."

"Really?"

"Yes."

"What else is there?"

"People. People an' land an' animals."

Chapter Twenty-Two

On Thursday afternoon, the day after Tina had had more tests done and after they'd packed and shopped, they drove north to Aberdeen. It was a long drive and Tina was exhausted, but like before, her spirits picked up when she saw the Blue Mountains in the distance living up to their name. They had been driving almost non-stop, taking time only to eat and fill up. Tina ate sparingly, saying she was tired from the medical and a hectic year. "Can we stop in the mountains?" she asked.

"Anywhere you want."

"There's a place, a hill, about an hour an' a half out of Aberdeen. It was where they sent Chief Francis back to the Old People in the sixties."

"What's that?"

"What's what?"

"What do you mean they sent him back to the Old People?"

She took a deep breath. "You want a history lesson?"

"Sure."

"Our people, the Blue People, believe the world an' all the animals were created by the Creator in the Blue Mountains, in one of the valleys they call the Redstone River Valley. Anyways, the

Creator took some red soil an' created the People. It's these Old People that all Blue People come from. An' when we die, our People, a long time ago, used to burn the bodies so that they could be returned to the land, an' the soul could carry on to the Old People who still live in the mountains."

"Nice."

"It is, isn't it?"

"Yeah."

"Anyways, back in 1965, my grandfather said they took Chief Francis up to the hills an' sent him back to the Old People."

"Who's Chief Francis?"

"He was the old Chief who signed our Treaty back in 1921: Chief James's father; Chief Alfred's grandfather."

"Do they still do that?" he asked.

"Do what?"

"Send people back."

"No. My grandfather said even back then, in sixty-five, the minister tried to stop them."

"Why?"

"I don't know. I guess they thought it was barbaric."

"Personally, I'd prefer that than being put in the ground."

"Same here," she said. "Hey, if I die before you, an' that's unlikely, I want you to do that to me."

He laughed. "Yeah, right. You'll outlive me by twenty, thirty years. You promise me, if I die, you'll do that to me."

"Really?"

"Sure, why not? It's not gonna bother me none. I'll be croaked. But just make sure I'm really croaked an' not just sleepin'."

She laughed. "I will."

"When was the last one?"

"Chief Francis. An' before him I don't think they done that since before the 1920s."

An hour later, they stopped about fifty miles from Aberdeen. They got out of the truck and Tina walked to a small creek and dipped her cup in. "It's cold," she said. "My grandfather said this was where they sent Chief Francis back."

Up at this altitude, there were no large trees, only small clumps of willows. John looked across the valley at the distant mountains that were twenty miles away. He turned north to a ridge five miles away. "That's where the caribou normally come by," Tina said.

"This is an awesome land."

"It is. Awesome, but harsh an' barren. Lots of our people think we should go back to the old ways, but my grandfather always tells me that it was a hard life."

"I guess."

An hour later, around ten at night, they cruised into Aberdeen and drove slowly down the main street and past the Saloon. This being Friday, the bar was open and they passed a few people who waved at Tina; she waved back. They drove to her grandparents', who were waiting for them. Sarah was happy to see Tina, but looked her up and down. "You're well?" she asked in the language.

"Yes, Grandmother. I'm just tired. And yes, I know I've lost weight, but I've had a long year at school."

"You've seen a doctor?" Abraham asked.

"Yes, I went to see one a few days ago an' they should have my tests in two or three weeks."

"And you," Abraham said to John and looked at his hand. "You should be more careful."

"I was, but they had some young people who didn't have any experience."

"Where's your cast?"

"They took it off."

Tina was already eating smoked fish roasted in the oven. She gave John a plate and he dug in. "This is good."

"When do you start work?" Abraham asked Tina.

"Two weeks."

"You got a place to stay?"

"Yes, they're gonna give me a place. It's small, but we don't have much stuff."

"That's good."

"I hear Edward is coming home," Sarah said to John.

"Yes, he is. They should be up tonight. We passed them this side of Yellowknife."

❖

They'd left Edmonton on Thursday morning and it had taken them all day to drive to Yellowknife. The next day, Friday, Jim called Eunice, and then they drove further north. Jim said it would take them the whole day, but he didn't mind as long as he got there. His nephew John and John's wife, Tina, Abraham and Sarah's grand-daughter, passed them on the highway. They stopped and talked to them, and then they left them in a cloud of dust. After a long time, they passed a sign that said Aberdeen was still two hundred kilometres away. It seemed like forever, and then he saw them: the Blue Mountains. They were far, far away, but they were blue. "The mountains," he said, hardly able to contain his excitement.

"Where?" Jim asked.

He pointed. "There."

"We've been driving through nothin' but mountains."

"These are hills. Those," he pointed again, "are mountains."

Jim looked at the time, then up at the sun. "It's ten an' the sun is still up."

"It's not gonna go down."

"So I've been told, but I still can't believe it."

An hour later, they stopped at almost the same spot where John and Tina had paused and looked at the scenery. "This is great," Jim said. "I've never seen land like this. It's so big."

"There's lots of it," he said, and then looked around. He wondered if he had ever been here in the winter. If he had, it had been a long time ago: long before he went in the army. That was over twenty years ago.

"Let's go," Jim said. "We'll be there after midnight."

An hour later, they were coming up to Aberdeen and he could see the river through the trees. "Teal River," he said.

Jim looked through the trees at the river. "It is?"

"Yes."

"Do you know that *teal* means blue?"

"No."

"Well, it does."

A few minutes later, they pulled off the highway and drove into Aberdeen. It was different than he remembered it. There were more houses, more trucks, more people and more garbage on the side of the road. They passed a large brown building that had a sign on it: *The Saloon*. "That must be the bar," Jim said.

"I guess." He wondered why he felt like a stranger. He wanted to visit Jim, but Jim, the Aberdeen Jim, was dead. He wanted to visit Julius, but Julius was dead. He wanted to visit Ol' William, but Ol' William was dead. He wanted to visit Margaret, but Margaret was dead.

"Where does Eunice live?" Jim asked. "She said she'd have the keys to the house where you an' I will be staying."

"I don't know." He pointed to a house. "That's where Abraham an' Sarah stay."

"Maybe Tina will give us directions."

"Maybe."

Jim slowed down, and then stopped. Someone looked out the window. A few seconds later, the door opened and out walked Abraham, smiling. "Hello, Edward. How are you?" he said in the language, and then shook his hand.

"I'm well. How are you?" he answered in the language and smiled.

"It's good to have you home," Abraham said in English, then reached over and shook Jim's hand. "My name is Abraham Joseph."

"You're Tina's grandfather."

"Yes."

"We're lost. We need to find Eunice's house."

"Down the road, can't miss it. Chief Alfred has this big green Ford with a blue canopy." He looked at Edward. "You look good."

"Thank you."

"Eunice is expecting you."

"Thank you."

"They knew you were coming late, so they cooked for you."

"Thank you."

"I hope you have a good time while you're here," Abraham said. "An' I hope you come back soon."

"I will."

Abraham smiled. "Sarah went to sleep. We'll see you tomorrow."

"Yes."

An hour later, they were in the house where they would be staying for two weeks. Eunice had made the beds, bought them some groceries and even made them supper. It was fish, bannock and tea, and he and Jim liked it. Afterwards, he washed, brushed and got into his nightgown, and then looked out the living room window. He saw two young people and one old man walking down the road. They were drunk and laughing. One of them looked at him and waved and he stepped back from the window.

"Edward?" Jim said.

"Yes?"

"It's getting late." He looked at the time, then out the living room window at the sun. "We *are* in the land of the midnight sun."

"Yes."

"It's amazing. Do you know that it's pitch black in Edmonton right now?"

"Yes."

"Well, we have two weeks to enjoy it. Let's get to bed. I'll take the bedroom on the left; you take the one on the right."

"Yes."

The bed was comfortable. Much more comfortable than his bed in Edmonton. And it smelled different, like flowers. And the ceiling was different.

"Good night, Edward."

"Good night, Floyd."

"Pardon me?"

"Good night, Jim." He wondered why he'd said Floyd's name. He hadn't thought about Floyd for a long time. Maybe it was because he was home.

Chapter Twenty-three

It was July 1 and, despite the doors being wide open, the community hall was hot: almost unbearable. Everyone was sweating, especially Ken and Richard, who were playing for the dance. They'd begun with a waltz, and then played a jig, and now a square dance. Chief Alfred was calling the dance and twenty-four couples were dancing and kicking up dust.

Jim had heard Edward talk about the dances, but now he knew what he had meant. It was lively, full of laughter and fun. And the feast they had had only a few hours ago was full of caribou meat, moose meat, fish, bannock, turkey, ham, salads and kettles of tea.

Olive, who had arrived a few days ago, greeted Jim like a long-lost brother, hugging him and Edward and crying. She had also picked Jim up for a square dance, but this one had more couples.

A few minutes later, the dance stopped as quickly as it had begun, and the people all went out for a smoke or to get some fresh air and try to cool off. Jim and Edward joined them.

Jim watched Edward, who seemed to be getting more comfortable with the community and its people. Tonight, he was smiling and happy. People, mostly elders, were coming up to him and welcoming him back to the community.

Chief Alfred approached them. "How are you guys doin'?"

"Great," Jim said. "This is great."

"They're gonna jig nex'," he said.

Half an hour later, Ken and Richard began playing the "Red River Jig" and everyone waited for the first couple to get up. Finally, Olive took Jim by the hand and led him onto the dance floor. "I don't know how to jig!" he shouted in protest.

"So fake it!"

He tried to imitate the Chief's steps, but he was not as coordinated or as light on his feet. Despite his crude steps, the entire community hall erupted in hoots and cheers. He thought it would be over in less than a minute, since that is what had happened the last time they'd jigged a few hours ago. Instead, he noticed more and more women getting up and joining Olive. They were surrounding him. "Honour dance!" she shouted at him.

"What?"

"They're honouring you."

"Why?"

She had tears in her eyes. "For looking after my brother."

At least twenty women kept him dancing for about ten minutes, and when he finally sat down he was sweating, but feeling great. Edward clapped him on the back. "You did good!" he shouted.

"Thank you. But you should be up there."

"I never dance."

"What? I thought you said you like dances."

"I like dances. I don't dance."

"Why?"

He looked around. "Too shy."

Jim laughed aloud. "This is great!"

"Yes," Edward said, and then he noticed Abraham talking to Tina. He wondered where Margaret's daughter was. Then he saw Tina take John's hand and lead him onto the floor, and they began jigging. Again, the community hall erupted in whoops, hollers and cheers.

Sarah then got up and took Tina's place, and then Olive, and then Eunice, and then Tina's aunts, and then some other women he didn't know. Finally, Tina got up and jigged again with John. Then it was Abraham's turn to jig with Tina, and then her uncles, and then Chief Alfred, and then more men.

Jim was sitting next to Eunice and Olive. "They make a nice couple!" Olive shouted to Jim.

"They do!" he shouted back. He knew Olive, Edward and Eunice were John's only living relatives other than his sister and his cousins. He also knew Tina, but he didn't know her parents. "Who's Tina's parents?" he asked Olive amid the noise.

"Her mom was Margaret. She died long ago. Tina was raised by her grandparents, Abraham an' Sarah."

Jim thought nothing of it at that precise moment, but then he remembered Edward mentioning Margaret and that she'd had William's child. Tina was Margaret's child. And John was William's son. *It couldn't be,* he thought. *Maybe Margaret had another child.* "Did Margaret have any other children?" he asked.

"No," Olive answered. "Jus' Tina."

"Who's her dad?"

She shrugged. "Margaret never tol' nobody."

Jim was now very confused, and the fiddle music and the shouting, hollering, whooping and cheering didn't help any. He wondered if there was some mistake. Surely, they couldn't be ... Didn't they know? "She doesn't know who her dad is?"

Olive shrugged again. "I don't think so. Don't think nobody knows."

Jim remembered meeting Eva in Edmonton and thinking how much she and Tina looked alike. And how much they both looked like a younger version of Eunice. And wasn't Eunice William's sister? If he was thinking was he was thinking, then ...

"Anything wrong?" Olive asked.

"No," he said. "It's so hot." While they danced, he looked at Eunice, and then at Tina, and then at John, and then at Edward. He was now utterly confused.

John and Tina were laughing. "I'm exhausted," she said, and then got scared. "John?"

"Yeah?"

"I think I'm gonna faint."

"Are you okay?"

"I've got a headache an' I'm having trouble breathing."

John was suddenly concerned. He took her arm and led her out of the building. Abraham and Sarah followed. "What's wrong?" Sarah asked in the language.

"I think I'm gonna throw up," Tina said, then bent over and did just that. She took a few gasps of air, and then stood. "I'm still a little woozy, but ..." She bent over and puked again. A few minutes later, she shook her head. "There. I'm feeling better."

"Are you sure you're okay?" John asked. "Do you want to go to the health centre?"

"No, I'm feeling better."

"Are you pregnant?" Sarah asked in the language.

Tina frowned, and then smiled. "No," she answered in the language. "I had my period last week."

"Are you sure?"

"Yes."

"You live in the city an' eat white man's food," Sarah said in English. "What you expec'?"

"I'm tired."

John took Tina's arm and led her to the main road and they walked to Abraham and Sarah's house. Abraham and Sarah followed. "You don't have to come with us," Tina said. "I'll be okay. You can go back to the dance."

"We're tired too," Abraham said. "Your grandmother is not young any more, you know."

Sarah looked at Abraham. "What you mean I'm not young any more? You, you're not young any more."

They all laughed.

✧

Despite his confusion over the changes in the community, he was glad to see that the feast and dance on the first of July hadn't changed. It was still fun. He also liked the foot races, canoe races, bicycle races, kids' races, pudding-eating contest, egg-throwing contest and tug of war. He and Jim joined the men's side in the tug of war, but the men lost three times in a row. He liked the dance and he liked it even better when Olive and the women danced with Jim. He knew they were thanking Jim for looking after him. Even at the feast, when they welcomed him back home, they asked Jim to stand up and Chief Alfred and Chief James both thanked

Jim for looking after him. Then they gave them gifts: shirts, hats, pins and another pair of moose skin slippers each. He was tired, but it was a good tired. The kind of tired that you didn't want to end. He washed his face, brushed, and then looked at himself in the mirror. He was getting darker. He was becoming an Indian again.

"Edward?"

"Yes, Jim?"

"Can I ask you some questions?"

He walked into the living room and looked at the time. It was almost three o'clock and the dance was still going on. They had left early, right after Abraham and Sarah. "Yes."

"Do you remember you said Margaret had William's child?"

"Yes."

"That was Margaret Joseph?"

"Yes."

"Abraham and Sarah's daughter."

"Yes."

"When?"

He shrugged. "I don' know."

"What was her name? Margaret's daughter."

"I don' know. They never tol' me."

"Did you ever meet Margaret's daughter?"

"I met her once when I came home from the army. I met her twice then. She was a kid."

"And they never told you her name?"

"No. Is something wrong?"

Jim looked at him. "No. I'm just thinking, that's all. Hey, it's bedtime."

"Good night, Jim."
"Good night, Edward."

Jim thought about it for a long time after Edward had fallen asleep. William married Elizabeth and they had John and Eva. William had one sister, Eunice. She married Alfred and they had three children. Elizabeth had one brother, Edward, and one sister, Olive. Edward had no children; Olive had four. William, in a drunken rage in a cabin up the Teal River, had confided in Edward that Margaret, Abraham and Sarah's daughter, now dead, had had his child. When did Margaret die? When was Tina born? She was younger than John, but older than Eva. And she looked like Eva and Eunice. Eunice was William's sister and John and Eva's aunt. Tina was William and Margaret's daughter, therefore Eunice was Tina's ... And John and Eva were Tina's ... "I hope I'm wrong."

Chapter Twenty-four

Tina seemed to be sleeping more and more in the last month. Usually, John didn't have to wake her up; she'd just get up after he had made coffee and breakfast. He placed the cup of coffee on the night table and looked at her. She had lost weight. More so in the last few months. Her once-firm legs were no longer firm, she tired and bruised easily, and her eyes, once laughing and smiling, were now weary.

"What are you looking at?" She was up. "You're not some kind 'a peeping Tom, are you?"

"No, jus' lookin'."

"Damn! I was hopin' you'd say yes."

"I can do that. An' I do enjoy looking at you. You're so beautiful in the morning, an' in the afternoon, an' at night."

"Thanks."

"I mean it."

"I know. That's why I love you: You're sooo romantic."

"Only with you."

"I should hope so."

He laughed. "And I love you too."

"And I love it when you tell me."

"Are you feeling better?"

"Yes," she said and took a deep breath. "I was just tired, full of smoke, dust, cheap perfume and God knows what else was floating aroun' the community hall."

"I really think you should go to the health centre."

"I'll be okay. I'd rather wait until they get back my tests. Maybe I've got some kind 'a sleeping disorder. You know that disease where people like to sleep all the time? Where they're tired for no reason?"

"So you're saying I'm no reason."

She laughed. "If they tell me I got that disease, I'll just tell them it's you that's keeping me up at all hours of the night an' day an' sometimes in between."

"What do you want to do today?"

"Take it easy an' rest. You?"

"Whatever."

"You can go up to the Saloon if you'd like."

"Don't feel like it. I'd like to take a run into the hills later."

"I'll go with you. We can take my grandparents up to their tent, an' then get some water for them."

"Sounds like a plan to me."

Jim was glad when Edward said he'd like to go to the cemetery. They found Margaret Joseph's grave. The headstone was simple: *Margaret, Beloved Daughter of Abraham and Sarah. Born 1944. Died 1963.* She had been nineteen when she'd drowned. He figured Tina must have been born in 1962. Hadn't Edward and Floyd joined the army in 1961? That's why Edward had been confused about whether Margaret had had a boy or a girl: He had been in the army and Tina hadn't even been born. Everything was becoming clear and Jim did not like it. Was he the only one who knew? He made a mental note to call Doctor Stilman.

"Jim!" Edward called from the other side of the cemetery.

Jim walked over to Edward, who was standing beside a grave.

"This," Edward said, motioning to a grave, "is my friend: Floyd Chinke. He looked after me in 'a hostel an' in 'a army."

Jim looked at the grave, and then at Edward.

"How do you feel?"

"Tired, but good."

"And do you think you can return?"

"When?"

"Whenever Doctor Stilman says you can."

"When is that?"

"Probably next month, or sooner."

"I lived here when I was young, an' after I got out of the army. Before I went ... Before I went to Edmonton."

"Can you live here on your own?"

"Yes."

"Then I don't see any reason why Doctor Stilman can't allow you to come home."

"For good?"

"For good."

Later that afternoon, Jim called Doctor Stilman. His name was Ron, but Jim never called him that: He preferred Doctor Stilman. "So, Edward is doing well, I presume?" the doctor asked.

"Yes, he is. Personally, I would like to think he's ready to come home. Eunice and her husband, the Chief, Chief Alfred, are willing to look after his needs, as long as it's not a twenty-four-hour job. And it isn't. He's taken charge of the household duties since we've been up here, including the cleaning and the laundry and some of the cooking."

"That's great. Is it everything you thought it would be?"

"That and more."

"I was up in Inuvik a couple of times, once in the winter and another time in the summer. It was great, but I prefer the winter. Cold, I can handle. Bugs, I can't."

Jim laughed. "Same here." Then he became more serious. "I've come across something that might interest you. It has nothing … It has nothing to do with Edward's condition, but it might have some other implications, for lack of a better term."

"Yes?"

"Do you remember Edward telling us that William told him that Margaret had his child?"

"Yes."

"Margaret, as in Margaret Joseph, and William, as in William Daniel?"

"Yes."

"And do you remember he said William and Elizabeth had a son, John?"

"Yes."

"And do you remember that he couldn't remember Margaret's daughter's name?"

"Yes."

"I found out her name."

"And?"

"Her name is Tina: Tina Joseph."

"Yes?"

"Do you recall his nephew John? I told you that he came to visit Edward last December."

"Yes."

"And do you recall that John brought his fiancée with him?"

"Yes."

"His fiancée's name was …"

"Tina Joseph," Doctor Stilman finished, and then let out a sigh. The silence was confirmation that he understood what Jim was talking about, or thinking about.

"Yes," Jim said. "I've asked Olive and apparently no one knows who Tina's dad is. Margaret didn't tell anyone before she passed away."

"No one?"

"No one. I'd bet money that if we pull Tina's birth certificate, the space under father will be blank."

"You think?"

"I think," Jim answered. "I'd like to know if you can call the health centre in Aberdeen and get that information."

"I can. I can do that today, right now."

"I'd appreciate it, and I'm hoping I'm wrong. I'm hoping there was another man."

"There had to be," Doctor Stilman answered, but it was more hope than anything else.

"And if we're not wrong?"

"I don't know. This is all so clear and yet so confusing."

"I've thought about it all night, ever since I found out."

"Who else knows?"

"I would say no one. I'm assuming William told no one but Edward, or else someone would have come forward by now. I'm also assuming Margaret didn't tell anyone prior to her death."

"But why would William tell only Edward?"

"You've got to remember that he was married, an' at that time no one talked about their affairs. If it was an affair."

"What else could it be?"

"I'm just thinking out loud," Jim said. "And I've not had a good night's sleep. And here's more thinking out loud: Margaret was young an' William was a married man. But from what I've learned about Margaret an' from what Edward has told us about William, why would she have an affair with someone like him?"

"Strange bedfellows."

"Yeah, and we also have to remember that Edward said Margaret was his girlfriend: He was sweet on her."

"Yes."

"I'm assuming that William told Edward to goad him into hitting him, or perhaps, as Edward has told us in his roundabout way, William was simply an alcoholic and a mean one at that."

"Let's hope he wasn't telling the truth," Doctor Stilman said.

"Or maybe Edward got it wrong."

"But if you're right …"

"Then it's only right we tell them. I've spent time with Edward's sister, Olive, and William's sister, Eunice. And I've had the pleasure of meeting John's younger sister, Eva."

"Yes?"

"I must tell you that Tina does bear a striking resemblance to Eva, and they both look like a younger version of Eunice."

"I'd imagine Eva would look like Eunice, what with Eunice being her aunt."

"Yes," Jim said.

"I guess it all hinges on what we find on the birth certificate, an' if that proves nothing, then it all hinges on what Edward has told us."

"It does. Moreover, Edward does not know that Tina is Margaret's daughter, but if he does stay in Aberdeen he will eventually come to the same conclusion. If he hasn't already."

"Are you suggesting ..."

"No, I'm not suggesting we keep him in the centre because of this. Quite simply, he is ready to come home. I would recommend that he does. What I'm saying is that if we are right with regards to John and Tina, then it's up to us to step in. Not to do so would prove, could prove, unprofessional, and embarrassing."

"Yes, embarrassing," Doctor Stilman said. "John and Tina could be incestuous."

Jim took a deep breath. "Innocent, but incestuous nonetheless."

"And they're already married."

"Yes, they were to be married in June, but they eloped in January."

"Oh, God."

"Yes," Jim said. "Which is why we should find out about Tina's father, if that's on the birth certificate."

"Yes, by all means. I'll do that right away."

"I'll wait for your call, and I'll try not to jump to any conclusions until we know all the facts."

"Yes. Is there anything we might've missed?"

"Not that I can think of, but I'm hoping I'm wrong. They are a very happy couple in love."

The hills were green, the distant mountains blue and the fireweed along the highway pink, dark pink. "Thank you," Tina said.

"My pleasure."

"You do me good."

"I know."

"I mean … whatever."

He laughed. He still had his cock in her. He looked up and down the highway for any dust plumes, which would tell them they'd have to get back into their pants, but there were none, yet.

"Geez," she said. "We've made love on two highways already. I wonder what the Guinness Record is for this?"

"I wonder if we're the first ones on this highway?" he asked.

"We're the first ones today."

He laughed, and she began coughing, and then stopped. "Are you okay?"

"Yes, my love, my husband. I feel fuckin' great. Emphasis on *fuckin'.*"

"I love it when you talk dirty."

"You keep doing me this good, I might let you tie me up."

"Kinky, but I'm open to new challenges."

"But I don't trust you. You might tie me up an' leave me, or forget about me."

"Truck coming."

She turned and saw the dust plume about two or three miles away. "That truck is not the only one comin' on this highway … Geez, what's wrong with me? What have you done to me?"

"What?"

"You just drive me nuts, make me talk crazy."

Edward had gone to his old house, where Olive was staying, and Jim was waiting for Doctor Stilman's phone call. He almost didn't pick it up when it rang. "Hello?"

"Jim, it's Ron."

"Yes?"

"Well, you were right. There's no father's name on the birth certificate."

"So what do we do now?"

"I'd suggest you find out if anyone knows who her father is. That is imperative. If we can find someone who knows it is not William, then we're out of our dilemma, I think. But then it's going to be Edward's story against his or hers."

"I'd bet a pile of money that Edward's will carry credibility. He is not capable of lying. He's capable of withdrawing into his head, but not lying."

"Or maybe he was wrong."

"Yes, you're right. We're here for another week; perhaps something or someone will turn up and prove us wrong."

"We can only hope."

After another hour, Jim was tired of thinking about possible explanations. It was plain and simple: William and Elizabeth had had two children, and one of them was John. William and Margaret had had a relationship that produced Tina, but no one but William and Margaret knew about it, except Edward. William was indeed John's father; there was no doubting that. William was also Tina's father; Jim was hoping he was wrong about that. And Margaret did not have any other children, only Tina.

Jim walked out into the night air and down to Chief Alfred and Eunice's. He did enjoy it up here, but the twenty-four-hour daylight was taking its toll on him. He had trouble getting to sleep at night. Eunice finally told him to put tinfoil over his window, and that helped.

As he approached the house, he noticed they were having a fish roast again. That meant fresh fish roasted on the fire, fresh bannock, and tea made from mountain water. The second night he and Edward had been here, they'd had one and it hadn't finished until one in the morning. Even then he'd thought his watch was wrong: The sun had been above the horizon to the north.

From a distance, he could see Olive and Edward. He could also see John, Tina and the two young men who'd played at the dance. There were also a couple of elders whose names he had forgotten. They were all laughing and joking, and they all smiled when he joined them. He enjoyed their easygoing manners, their joking and their teasing. All this in spite of the problems they, as a people and as a community, were facing. The idyllic life that Edward had talked about was all but gone. Drugs, alcohol and the problems it brought were the norm. No one lived off the land any more. There were no dog teams, community hunts and fish camps, except along the river close by the town, and then it was only the elders who went there.

Only on three occasions did someone—children—come up and look at him. They had all said the same thing: "You're a black man." And he had answered them the same way: "Yes, I am." And they had smiled broadly and left. Eunice had told him that he was the first black man the children had seen. "We had one up here once. He was a teacher, but that was a long time ago."

"Hey, Richard!" Olive shouted. "Play some Hank Williams."

Richard played a lonesome song on the fiddle that Jim had never heard before. He had never even heard of Hank Williams before he came up north. Apparently, he was some great country singer from the south who had died in the early fifties and was a legend among legends.

John and Tina were smiling at each other, like they had a secret. She sat on his lap and he said something in her ear; she rolled her eyes, and then blushed. Jim kept looking at them, hoping he was wrong.

"John," Ken said, "come sing something."

John picked up his guitar. "What do you wanna hear?" he asked Tina.

She shrugged. "Anything. Just don't make me shy."

He strummed a few chords and then sang, "'*I know you're married, but I love you still.*'"

Everyone laughed and Tina blushed. "My husband ever find out," she said, "you're in big trouble."

"He's probably a wimp, or a pervert."

"I'd like to think the latter."

"You wish," John said and everyone laughed, and then he sang a song he had heard by Ricky Skaggs called "I Wouldn't Change You If I Could." Overall, it was beautiful, peaceful, serene. Sort of the calm before the storm.

"When are you gonna have kids?" Olive asked Tina.

Tina smiled shyly. For one brief moment, Jim thought she was going to say that she was pregnant. "We've decided to wait," she said. "I've got a couple more years of school, an' John has work an' music to concentrate on."

✧

Jim was still awake an hour later when he walked in, tired but happy. "Are they still up?" Jim asked him.

"No, everyone is going home."

"Are you having a good time?"

"Yes, it's like long ago."

"Edward?"

"Yes."

"Can I ask you more questions?"

"About what?"

"About what William told you?"

"When?"

"When you were up at the cabin."

"That's a long time ago."

"Yes, but it's important."

"Why?"

"Let's just say it's important."

He shrugged. "Okay."

"Did William … Did William tell you how Margaret became pregnant?"

"He said …"

"Yes?"

"He said … It wasn't nice."

"Can you tell me what he said? What did he tell you?"

"He said …" He remembered William shouting at him, screaming. "He said she didn' want to, but he knew she wanted it."

"Wanted what?"

He didn't know how to say it. "He was with her."

"Yes, you've told us, and you've told us Margaret had a child: his child."

"She didn't want to."

"How do you know, Edward?"

"He said she didn't want to."

"She didn't want to what? Didn't want to have his baby?"

"She didn't want … She didn't want to be with him. He called her a bitch."

"Why?" Jim asked.

"She didn't look at him."

"She didn't look at him?"

"Yes."

"Why?"

"He said she was too good for him."

Jim paused, as if considering something, and then asked, "Edward, did William rape her?"

He took a deep breath. The truth had finally been revealed. "Yes. She didn't want to be with him."

"What were his words? If you can remember."

William was shouting at him. "He said, 'She didn't want to, but I knew she wanted it. They all want it.'"

"Want what, Edward?"

"He said they all wanna be …"

"They all wanna be what?"

"He said the f-word."

"Did he say they all wanna be fucked?"

He hung his head. "Yes."

"I'm sorry I used that word, Edward."

He shrugged. "That's okay."

"I've recommended to Doctor Stilman that you can come home."

He smiled.

"But," Jim said, "that decision is still up to Doctor Stilman an' he'll let you know when we get back to Edmonton."

"Thank you."

Chapter Twenty-five

It was Friday, July 4, and John and Tina were on their way to Helena, hoping to get her settled and ready for work on Monday. They had to check in to the apartment, buy groceries and take care of other things. "Think I should ask Clint for my old job?" John asked.

"If you'd like, but wouldn't that affect your compensation?"

"I've no idea. Could take it under the table."

Jim picked up the telephone and called Doctor Stilman. "Well, I've found out one more bit of information in this puzzle."

"Yes?"

"I've learned, according to Edward, that William may have raped Margaret."

"That would explain a lot of things," Doctor Stilman said. "Why she would go out with a man like that. Why she didn't tell anyone the name of her baby's father. Why she didn't put his name on the birth certificate. Why she didn't tell anyone."

"Yes."

"But why didn't she report it?"

Jim took a deep breath. "From what I've learned of the

community, I'd say things like that weren't reported twenty years ago. It's still a pretty traditional community in that respect."

"I can understand."

"And try as I might, I cannot find any other explanations. Tina *is* Margaret's daughter, and her father *is* William Daniel, John's father."

"I, too, can't find any other plausible explanations."

"So, what do we do?"

"We have to tell."

"Who?"

"I think it would be best if we tell Olive, then perhaps she can help us or, if need be, she can tell John and Tina."

"That's exactly what I was thinking. When?"

"Can you handle it?"

"I've come this far."

"Have you been keeping notes?"

"Yes, everything I've learned and heard from Edward, almost verbatim."

"Good. When will you tell her?"

"I've only got a few more days. I'd like to leave on Monday morning if I can. It'll take me two days to get back to Edmonton." He looked at the calendar on the wall. "I'll tell her tomorrow: Saturday."

"What can I say? I wish we didn't have to, but it is for the best. It *has* to be."

"Yes, you're right. I'm hoping if we tell her, she can come up with something. But she's the one who told me that no one knows who Tina's father is. Margaret took it to her grave."

"That's right. She drowned not too long after she gave birth."

"Yes, summer of sixty-three."

"Do you suppose?"

"Suicide?"

"Yes."

"My thoughts as well," Jim said. "But we'll never know. The river, the Teal, is swift and cold as ice. From what I've heard, anyone who's ever fallen in has drowned."

"The summer I spent in Inuvik, three people fell into a lake and drowned. One of them was supposed to be a good swimmer, but after a minute, hypothermia sets in and there's nothing you can do."

"I feel like I'm in a mystery novel."

"You'll feel like that often in this profession we've chosen."

"I'm beginning to understand."

"Well, if you need any help, you can call me here or at home."

"Thanks," Jim said, and then hung up and went for a walk along the river. He tried to picture the meeting he had to have with Olive. How does one tell someone something as bizarre as this? And what would be her reaction? What will she say and do? He looked at the river, and then at the hills and the mountains. It was indeed a beautiful land, almost untouched. He looked down the riverbank and saw garbage scattered here and there and the occasional empty bottle of whisky and a few cans of beer.

"Jim!"

He turned and saw Chief Alfred carrying a paddle and a gas tank for an outboard motor. "Hi, Chief."

"What you're doin'?"

"Just admiring the scenery."

Alfred looked at the hills and the mountains. "Seen it all my life. When we go south an' come back, the first thing you see is the mountains, then you know you're home. Hey, I'm gonna check my nets. Wanna come?"

"Sure."

They walked down the bank, took Alfred's boat and went upriver to his nets. "So," Alfred said after he had finished looking at them, "what's on your mind?"

"Pardon?"

"You've been quiet for a few days now." Alfred picked up the paddle and they floated downriver.

"I've got things on my mind."

"Anything I can help with?"

"Not likely, but thanks."

"I'm the Chief," Alfred said, "an' that means I'm everythin' to everyone. I've helped mos' people in one way or 'nother, even when they don' need it, or want it. I'm the unofficial counsellor, referee an' much more to my people."

Jim looked at Alfred and saw a man with compassion and understanding that can only come from a lifetime of listening to others. "I've got a problem, not mine, but a problem or a concern."

"Is it about Edward?"

"No, he's okay. It's about something else."

"You wanna talk about it?"

"I've got to meet with Olive. It's about one of her family members."

After a few seconds, Alfred asked, "Is it about John?" Jim looked at him. "He's the only other family she has here."

"Yes," Jim said, and then he asked, "Do you know who Tina's dad is?"

Alfred shrugged. "No. I don't think nobody knows. Margaret never said."

"So I've heard."

After a few moments, Alfred asked, "You found somethin'?"

"Yes."

"About Tina's dad?"

"Yes."

"How?"

"From Edward."

"Edward knows?"

"Yes."

"Is it Edward?"

"No, it's not Edward, but he says he knows who it is." Jim wondered if he had already said too much to Alfred.

"He was sweet on her."

"Yes, I know."

"He talked about her?"

"Yes, he's talked a lot about her." He could tell Alfred was thinking.

"This is what you want to talk to Olive about?"

"Yes."

"I was just a young man when Margaret drowned. Edward lef' before Tina was born an' he never came back 'til seventy-three."

"Yes."

"An' you say he knows who her father is?"

"Yes."

"An' it's not him."

"No, it's not him." Jim then realized that he might have to tell Alfred that it was his brother-in-law, since Eunice, his wife, was William's sister.

"Is she gonna like it?" Alfred asked.

"Who?"

"Tina."

"No."

Once again, he could tell Alfred was thinking. "You wanna tell me?" he asked.

"Well, ever since Edward started getting better, he's been talking about what happened when he found William and Elizabeth."

"Yes, I remember the year."

"He began to remember what went on up there."

"He said they froze."

Jim stopped. Perhaps he *had* said too much already, but he had come too far to turn back now. "They didn't. That's all I can tell you right now. But it really doesn't matter. What happened … what really happened wouldn't change anything." He watched Alfred. "Can you accept that?"

Alfred shrugged. "Yeah."

"But before …" Jim sighed. "William told Edward something."

"William was alive, then," Alfred said, and it wasn't really a question; it was more of a statement.

"Yes."

"What did William tell Edward?"

"He told him about Margaret."

It took Alfred a few seconds to understand what Jim was telling him and to formulate the words and construct the sentence he didn't want to formulate or construct. "William was Tina's father?" he asked. Jim's silence was affirmation enough. "Fuck sakes."

"I've only found out recently," Jim said. "An' even then I didn't have proof. And it's still only … It's still only Edward's word we have to work with right now. And he doesn't even know it. He doesn't know Tina is Margaret's daughter."

"How can he not know?"

"Oh, he knows Margaret had a daughter; he just doesn't know she's Tina."

"Who else knows?"

"So far, just me an' Doctor Stilman, Edward's doctor in Edmonton."

"But we don't know for sure."

"I'm not a hundred percent sure, but I've got no other explanation. Tina was born in May 1962, which means Margaret got pregnant in August 1961. It wasn't Edward, but he has the only answer because I've asked Olive who her … who Tina's father was, but she doesn't know. Nobody knew. Even you didn't know."

"But we don't know for sure."

"No, we don't. Have you ever seen John's sister, Eva?"

"Not recently, but I've seen pictures of her. Why?"

"Have you noticed she looks like Tina, especially around the eyes and the mouth?"

"I never noticed. 'Course I wasn't lookin'."

"And another thing: Eunice is your wife and William's sister."

"Yeah."

"As an outsider, I've noticed she looks like an older version of both Tina and Eva."

"Fuck sakes," Alfred said and continued paddling. "Excuse my French, but now I can see the resemblance. I always thought that, but I never worried about it. Eunice is related to Abraham an' Sarah, but it goes way back."

"Can I ask you something else?" Jim asked.

"Yeah."

"How did Margaret die?"

"She drowned."

"Was it an accident?"

Once again, Jim could tell Alfred's mind was churning. "I guess we'll never know."

"She never told anyone who the father was; she never put the father's name on the birth certificate."

"Are you sure? Not of that, but of what Edward tol' you an' what you found out."

"I'm almost sure of everything. And Edward may be slow, but one thing we know is he is not capable of lying. I wish I hadn't found out."

"If you hadn't, nobody would've."

"But now we have to tell them."

"Of course. But are you sure?"

Jim took a deep breath. "I wish I could say I wasn't."

"We have to find out if anybody could know, other than Edward."

"But who else would know? From what Edward has told us, William may have … William may have raped her."

"Margaret?"

"Yes."

"He wasn't a nice man."

"So we've learned."

"What else you learned? About William an' 'Lizabeth."

"From what Edward has told us, we believe William killed Elizabeth. He hit her and she fell and hit her head on the table in the cabin. It was an accident, but he killed her nonetheless."

"An' what happen to William?"

"He tried to fight with Edward, but ..."

"Edward was in the army," Alfred explained.

"Yes. That's what I meant when I said if you knew, if anyone knew, nothing would change."

"Yes, I see."

"I have to talk to Olive."

"Yes," Alfred said.

"And then we have to find out if there's anything we've missed."

"Let's hope."

"And if there's nothing, then we have to tell them."

"They're married."

"Yes, I know, but we still have to tell them."

Alfred hung his head as if in deep thought. "An' there's no other explanation?"

"None."

"Now it all makes sense."

"I was hoping it wouldn't."

"Me too."

They paddled to shore, and then carried Alfred's catch up the long riverbank, walking like two men who didn't want the climb to end ... but it did. As they got to the top of the bank, Alfred lowered the tub of fish and looked at his watch. "When?" he asked.

Jim lowered his tub. "The sooner, the better."

"Give me a time an' place. I'll arrange it."

"Six o'clock. Our place."

"We'll be there. I'll bring Olive an' Eunice."

It was quiet, almost eerie. For some reason, Jim thought the two women were angry with him for being the bearer of bad news. Maybe they were, but that was the least of his problems. Edward spoke only when one of them asked a question. Olive and Eunice sat and listened, and then asked the same question Alfred had asked: "Are you sure?"

"Yes," Jim answered. "I'm almost a hundred percent sure." He watched Eunice's reaction: William had been her brother. "I'm sorry. I'm sorry I had to find out."

"It's not your fault," Eunice said.

"Who else did she go with?" Olive asked, and then looked at Edward. But he was silent and he didn't understand the question.

Jim looked directly at Olive. "I'm positive he was never with her."

"Do you remember when she went back to school that fall?" Chief Alfred asked. "Remember she was quiet, different?" Jim could tell they were remembering a time from the distant past. "Remember she came home at Easter an' stayed?" Alfred continued. "She never tol' no one until she was showin', an' then she never tol' nobody who the father was."

Then, for whatever reason, it all clicked for Edward. "William was Tina's father," he said. It was more of a statement than a question.

"From what you've told us," Jim said, "that's what we've concluded."

"William was John's father."

"Yes, now do you see the problem?"

It took Edward a few seconds, and then he said, "Yes, sir."

Jim smiled. "You don't have to call me *sir.*"

"Yes, sir."

"So, we have to tell them," Eunice said.

"Yes," Jim answered. "We have to tell them."

"But what if we're wrong?" Olive asked.

"Are you sure we can be wrong?"

It took a few seconds for her to answer. "No."

"I was hoping you, or anyone, could come up with another explanation."

"Where are they?" Alfred asked.

"They went to Helena this morning," Olive said. "She has to work on Monday."

"How do we tell them?" Eunice asked.

Jim took a deep breath. "I'll tell them."

"You?" Olive and Eunice asked.

"Yes. I've already told Alfred and now I've told you two, and Edward. I think I know … I hope I know how to tell them."

"We should be there," Olive said. "For support."

"Yes," Eunice added.

"What about Abraham an' Sarah?" Alfred asked. "Do we tell them?"

Jim sighed. "Not until after we've told John and Tina," he answered. "If … When they split up … When they separate, I doubt if John will ever return. If that's the case, we may not have to tell Abraham and Sarah. We can just tell them they …"

"They what?" Olive asked. "Got a divorce?"

"We can tell them they didn't get along," Jim said. "Do they have to know the truth?"

Olive and Eunice each took a deep breath. Jim took that as confirmation Abraham and Sarah didn't have to know.

"How are they gonna take it?" Eunice asked, and then realized she had a new niece and her children had another cousin.

"They are so much in love," Olive said. "But they have to know. They have to."

"When can we do it?" Jim asked. "I've …" He looked at Edward. "We've got to leave on Monday."

"We have to do it right away," Alfred said. "There's no waitin'. Not in this situation."

"Who else knows?" Olive asked.

"Besides us, only Edward's doctor, Doctor Stilman. Do you know where they're living in Helena?"

"Tina said they got an apartment in the nurses' residence."

"Do they have a phone?"

"Not yet. They said they're gonna call when it was hooked up."

"It's not likely they're gonna have it hooked up 'til Monday or Tuesday, or later," Alfred said. "We have to look for them."

Someone banged on the door. "Daddy! Mom!" It was Sarah, Alfred and Eunice's daughter.

Alfred went to the door. "What's the matter?"

She was out of breath. "Abraham an' Sarah. They called. Tina's in a' hospital. She's sick."

Half an hour later, Jim was driving the van to Helena with Abraham, Sarah, Olive and Edward. From what they'd learned, Tina had taken sick and fainted, and John had taken her to the hospital. They were keeping her for observation. Behind them, Chief Alfred, Eunice and their daughter Sarah followed. Eunice kept looking at Sarah and wondering how she'd take the news. She'd probably be excited. She and Tina had always got along like sisters. Now she could see the resemblance. Eunice wondered if she should tell her. *Not now,* she thought. *Maybe later.*

When they arrived at the Helena Hospital, they found John sitting in the waiting room, his head bowed. "John?" Chief Alfred said.

John looked up and they could tell he had been crying. He looked at Abraham and Sarah, his face blank. "What's wrong with Tina?" Sarah asked.

"She's sick, real sick."

"What's wrong?"

"I think I'd better answer that." They all turned to see a white man wearing a jogging suit and carrying a stethoscope. "I'm Doctor Everett," he said. "Can I have some introductions?"

"I'm Alfred. I'm Chief of Aberdeen, an' this is my wife, Eunice, my daughter Sarah, an' this is Olive Rowe. She's John's aunt. An' this is Abraham an' Sarah, Tina's grandparents. This is Jim an' this is Edward Brian, John's uncle."

Doctor Everett looked at Abraham and Sarah. "I'm afraid I don't have good news. Tina is very ill."

"What wrong with her?" Sarah asked for the third time.

"Acute lymphoblastic leukemia."

No one said anything for a few seconds. "Leukemia," Abraham said. "That's cancer."

"Yes, it is."

Sarah hung her head and began crying.

"Is it bad?" Abraham asked.

"I've been in touch with her doctor in Calgary, where they ran some tests. We don't have the resources to do any further tests up here. We've recommended she be sent to Edmonton for tests and treatment as soon as possible."

"Can I see her?" Sarah asked.

"Yes. She's sleeping, but I'll let you see her. She's going to be out for a few hours, or perhaps all night. I've given her a rather heavy dose of a tranquilizer to help her rest."

They all went into Tina's room and Sarah cried even more. Jim noticed that Olive, Eunice and her Sarah were also crying, silently. Tina didn't look well. She looked pale and sickly. Perhaps it was all the white in the room.

Edward wanted to leave. He had had enough white rooms in his life. He sat in the waiting room, looking at nothing and wondering why he had to remember all this. Why did he remember what William told him? He now knew John and Tina couldn't be together. They were half-brother and half-sister. They were related.

Abraham led his wife out of Tina's room and the rest followed.

"We're going to have her on tomorrow's plane to Edmonton," Doctor Everett was saying. "John will accompany her."

"What's gonna happen?" Abraham asked.

"I can't say for certain, but they'll do more tests, and then hopefully begin treatment right away. I must warn you that the leukemia is advanced, but each individual is different. She's young, so her chances of making a full recovery are good."

"Can we go with her?" Sarah asked.

Doctor Everett thought about it, and then said, "I'm afraid we have room for only one escort, and that's usually reserved for the husband or the wife."

"I'll take care of it," John said to Abraham and Sarah. "I'll make your travel arrangements tomorrow."

Sarah took his hand. "*Mussi,* my boy." Then she started crying again.

Jim watched them, and then wondered when they'd tell John and Tina. This was one tragedy after another. What would happen next?

Alfred pulled Jim aside. "What do we do now?" he asked.

"What would *you* do?"

"I'd leave it for now."

"So would I."

"What are you talking about?" Eunice asked in the language.

"We're gonna leave it for now," Alfred said.

She didn't say anything.

"I'm sorry we dragged you here," Alfred said to Jim.

Jim shrugged. "It had to be done."

"Are you going to go right back? We can find a place for you to stay."

"No, I think Edward and I should leave. We'll be back in Aberdeen around midnight." He looked at Edward. "Given what's happened, I think we'll leave tomorrow. Do you mind, Edward?"

"No, sir."

"We'll be in Edmonton late Sunday night or early Monday morning. Abraham and Sarah should be there by then." He looked at John. "John and Tina too."

"She's going to be sleeping all night," Doctor Everett was saying, "but you are welcome to stay. I'll see to it that you have coffee and tea in the waiting room all night."

"We'll stay," Alfred said.

Abraham took Edward's hand. "My son," he said in the language, "it was good to see you."

Edward did not smile. "Yes, sir."

"My son," Sarah said, also in the language, "it's time to come home."

"Yes, ma'am."

"When?" she asked.

Edward looked at Jim. "When am I comin' home, sir?"

"We'll find out when we get to Edmonton, but I'm sure it'll be soon. I'd say in about a month or two."

"Be August or September," Chief Alfred said. "Moose time."

Edward smiled.

"When you come home," Abraham said, "me an' you will go huntin' moose."

"Yes, sir."

"I'm your friend," Abraham said in the language.

"My friend," Edward said in the language.

"My daughter left because the Creator decided it was her time. I'm not going to lose a granddaughter. The Creator will look after her. And I've never had a son."

"Yes, my friend."

"You have a lot to learn when you come home. We are here."

"*Mussi.*"

❖

As they drove onto the highway leading to Aberdeen, Jim asked, "What did he say?"

"Who, sir … Jim?"

"Abraham."

"He said he lost a daughter, he's not gonna lose Tina."

"I hope not."

"An' he called me his son."

"I wish you were his son."

"I am, sir … Jim."

"I think I'm beginning to understand."

"Thank you."

"You're welcome."

Chapter Twenty-six

The 737 rumbled down the runway, and then lifted off. John couldn't take his eyes off Tina. She had put on a brave face when they'd told her about the test results from Calgary. "Don't worry," she'd said. "They probably made a mistake." This morning, she'd woken up to find them all looking at her. "Geez," she said, "I'm okay. You didn't have to all come down."

"Cancer is not funny," her grandfather had said.

Now Tina was on a stretcher in the back of a 737 on her way to Edmonton for more tests and treatment. And treatment meant chemotherapy, and chemotherapy meant pain and the loss of her hair and more pain. John remembered a girl in high school: Alison had been a grade ahead of him, a great basketball player and intelligent. She'd had leukemia, but John didn't know what kind. They had been looking for a bone marrow transplant, but hadn't found one and she had died. He wondered if they'd have to search for a bone marrow donor for Tina. Other than her grandparents, she had her uncle Robert, her aunt Caroline, and seven cousins who would best qualify to be a donor. And if they didn't match, John would do anything it took.

"John?"

He looked at Tina. She was still sleepy and she looked frailer than ever. "Yes?"

"I need a drink of water."

He looked at Nicole, the nurse, who nodded, and then the stewardess brought a glass of water and John held it while Tina drank from the straw. "How do you feel?"

She smiled weakly. "I feel I can go a roun' with my husband."

He grinned. "I'll tell him."

"You know where he is? If I can't fool aroun' with the man I love, I'll fool aroun' with the man I'm with."

"I can live with that."

"Are you two married?" the nurse asked.

"We'd better be," Tina said, "or I'm on the wrong plane with the wrong man."

Nicole smiled. "Are those your parents?" she asked.

"No, they're my grandparents."

"You're kidding? They look so …"

"Young?"

"Yes."

"You're not the first to assume they were my parents. And they do look young, but they're sixty-three."

John was glad Abraham and Sarah were with them. They had been up all night and finally fell asleep soon after the aircraft levelled off.

"I think you should give my husband a tranquilizer, too," he heard Tina say to Nicole. "Then maybe I can take advantage of him."

He smiled. He knew she was putting up a front. "Be gentle," he said, and Tina and Nicole both laughed at him.

He woke up feeling rested when they landed in Yellowknife, helped Tina to her feet and took her to the washroom. "Wow," she said, "too bad we aren't at thirty-thousand; we could join the mile-high club."

"You wish."

"Up yours."

"Promise?"

"I promise," she said. "John?"

"Yeah?"

"I don't want you to worry."

"I have to. You're my wife."

"And you're my husband. I'm ordering you not to worry."

"I know. I just want to tell you that I love you."

"Good, now pull my pants up before I jump you."

"I can live with that."

"I don't think we have the time, unless you want them to break down the door."

He held her in the small washroom. She felt frail, weak and tiny. "I do love you."

"I know. I just love the hell out of you."

As she settled into the stretcher, she asked, "Did you call Eva?"

"Yes."

"What she say?"

"She said she'd meet us."

"She's driving up?"

"With Elmer."

"Geez, I don't know what's the big fuss. I'll be okay. Nothin' a little chemo an' some chemicals can't cure these days. Hey, I hope you like bald women."

"I'll learn."

"Bald all over," she whispered.

He laughed, and then looked at Nicole, who hadn't heard. "I like that," he said. "If you do go bald, I'll shave every inch of hair off so we can look like twins."

"I'm gonna hold you to that."

"Good, 'cause you ain't gonna have much to hold."

"Geez," Nicole said. "Are you sure you're married? Married people don't talk like that."

They laughed, and then Tina closed her eyes and went to sleep. "So," Nicole asked, "how long have you been married?"

"Six months an' a few days."

"How long have you known her? All your life?"

"No, a year an' nine months."

"Any kids?"

"None, yet."

"You're young. Have some fun first."

"She's going to university in Calgary."

"Yeah? What's she taking?"

"Nursing."

"Really?"

"Really."

"That's good. We need more nurses up here."

They arrived in Edmonton at seven-thirty to find Elmer and Eva waiting for them. They were both very concerned and Eva hugged Tina and started to cry. When she finally stopped, Tina said, "I keep tellin' people that I'm going to be okay, so I don't want no one worryin'. Worry about Nicole's first husband's second wife."

When they arrived at the hospital, they put Tina in a room by herself, and then a Doctor Markham told her what to expect. "We're going to do more tests tomorrow, and then we'll decide on the best course of action. And that, Mrs. Daniel, may mean chemo."

"I'm ready to go Kojak," she answered. "An' so is my husband. He promised to shave all his hair off if I go bald."

"Well, you can tell him not to get excited just yet. We still don't know if chemo is the best course. We may have to find you a bone marrow donor. Speaking of which, do you have any brothers or sisters?"

"None. Only child."

"How about your mom and dad?"

"Orphan, raised by my grandparents. I also have an aunt an' an uncle and six, no, seven cousins."

"Well," Doctor Markham said, "that's a start, but let's not jump to conclusions yet. Tests, then a solution and a cure."

"Sounds like a plan to me," Tina said. "John?"

"Yeah?"

"Get a room an' get some sleep."

"There's a good apartment hotel close by," Doctor Markham said.

An hour later, John checked into the hotel. The apartment had a bedroom, a living room and a kitchenette. He and Elmer and Eva sat and drank tea, and then they went to sleep. Elmer took the sofa and Eva slept in the bedroom. John could not sleep. He took a pillow and lay on the rug in front of the television, tuned in *Cheers* and went brain-dead, or at least he tried.

Chapter Twenty-seven

Three days later, Jim and Doctor Stilman were having coffee in the staff lounge. "So, how was the trip?" Doctor Stilman asked.

"Tiring, exciting, eventful and full of surprises," Jim answered.

"You think we should recommend Edward's release?"

"I'd recommend it, but only after a few weeks of debriefing. He's gone through a lot, what with this new turn of events. I think we should be sure of what went on in that cabin, and his comprehension of it."

"I agree. Now, what of Tina? Did they catch it early enough?"

"I'm not sure yet. I'll call in the next day or two and find out."

"When do you think they'll tell them?"

"Well, we did have a long discussion about it, and they all agreed it should be done as soon as she's capable of handling it. That will probably be after her first chemo."

"Which is?"

"I'd say in early August, but once again, I'll find out."

"This is really something," Doctor Stilman said. "I mean, it's like a soap opera: one bad thing after another."

"Yes, it is. And unfortunately, there is no happy ending."

"None."

"And what of her grandparents? Will they know?"

"They've decided against telling them. They'll just recommend John and Tina separate and get on with what's left of their lives."

"Well, I'd have to agree with them on that. What else can we do?"

"We can't let them continue their relationship any longer than we have to. Thank God, she can't … Well, at least their sex life is curtailed for the time being."

"Let's hope so."

Jim rubbed his eyes. "Geez, why'd I choose this profession? I could've been a contender."

Doctor Stilman laughed. "My dad wanted me to be a lawyer."

"Why didn't you?"

"Ocean's too full of them."

"What?"

"You hear the joke?"

"No."

"What do they call fifty lawyers at the bottom of the ocean?"

Jim shrugged. "What?"

"A pretty good start."

Jim laughed.

"I got another one. Two lawyers are talking. One says to the other, 'Did you hear about Bob Crane?' The other says, 'No, what happened?' 'He's in the hospital lying at death's door.' 'Really,' the other says. 'You gotta hand it to him: He's at death's door and still lying.'"

Jim laughed. "You should have been a comedian. You might've been another Rodney Dangerfield."

Chapter Twenty-eight

It was Monday, July 21, and it had been over two weeks since John, Tina and her grandparents had arrived in Edmonton. Elmer had gone back to work and Eva had returned to Calgary, where she was working at a hospital for the summer.

After ten days, Tina had finally convinced her grandparents to return to Aberdeen. They'd agreed to leave on the condition that she call them every day to let them know what was happening; she did. Abraham and Sarah had visited Edward before they left and found out he was going home in August if everything went well. And there was no reason to think it wouldn't. Soon after they'd left, Tina had begun chemotherapy and radiation treatment. It was not easy for John to watch as she dealt with the side effects: nausea, pain, more weight loss and the beginning of the loss of her hair.

"You're not going to do it, are you?" she asked as he brushed her hair and more fell out.

"Do what?"

"Cut your hair."

"I did promise my wife."

"You are not to cut your hair. The hell with your wife. She don't like it, you can move in with me."

"Well, if that's the case, then I'll have to move in with you."

"Good, we can call her an' let her listen to us havin' sex."

"Kinky."

"Can I ask you to do somethin' for me?" she asked.

"Anything."

"Get lost."

He laughed. "Are you serious?"

"Yes. I'm gonna be goin' through some tough times in the next few weeks an' I don't want you here."

"Why?"

"I don't want to see your pain. It's a real downer."

"What'll I do?"

"Go back to work."

"I don't go back 'til next Thursday."

"Then why don't you fly up an' bring our stuff an' your truck back down. I start classes in six weeks. I'll be done an' recuperated by then."

"You sure?"

"Are you doubtin' I'll get better?"

"I'm not doubting that. I just wanna know if you're sure you want me to leave."

"Yes, John, I want you to leave. I want you to fly up to Helena, get your truck, our stuff an' some dryfish, drymeat an' whatever else you can steal an' come back down, go to work, an' I'll go back to university."

"Sounds like a plan."

"It is: mine."

"Are you sure?"

"You wan' it in writing?"

He smiled. "I'll do it, but only for you."

"Good, now get outta here an' let me get some rest. Geez, I never thought I'd be kickin' you outta my bedroom."

"An' this is the only time I'll let you do that."

"Promise?"

"Promise."

He leaned over and kissed her while she copped a feel. "Oooh, is that for me?"

"Always."

"Promise?"

"Fuckin' A."

She laughed, and then started coughing. "I'll be okay," she said. "Just go an' get my dryfish an' drymeat an' other goodies."

"I'll be back in …"

"And I don't wanna see you for another week, at least. Take your time."

Two days later, John was approaching the place on the highway just south of Aberdeen where he and Tina had made love. He stopped and thought about that moment. He could remember the scent of their sexual escapade. He looked across the wide open valley to the mountains in the distance. It looked empty and desolate. Ken had told him they had seen thirty thousand caribou in this area, but that was a long time ago. This was also where Tina had told him of the Old People and the time they sent Chief Francis back. "Hey," she had said, "if I die before you, and that's unlikely, I want you to do that to me." And he had promised he would.

He took a container from the back of his truck and filled it with water. She swore this water made the best tea in the world, and it did. He washed his face in the icy mountain water; it was refreshing. He was never a religious man, but he said a prayer. And he said it aloud just in case the gods were listening. Or just in case the Old People were out and about. "If you're out there, I hope you can hear me. I just want her to get better. She doesn't deserve this. I'll do anything." He then realized it was such an overused expression, a cliché, but he meant it. He wondered if he could give his life for hers. If he had to die so she could live, would he do it? He didn't have to think about it: He'd do it. What would his life be without her?

Fifteen hours later, he was passing Yellowknife. Thirty hours later, he was in Edmonton and had broken a promise: He had returned early. She was glad for the drymeat, the dryfish and the water, but she was now on a liquid diet.

Chapter Twenty-nine

"Well, Edward," Doctor Stilman said, "it's been three weeks since you've been back, and Jim and I have recommended that you be sent home."

He smiled. "Thank you."

"We've been talking to Chief Alfred and Eunice, and they have agreed to help you readjust. And Olive is still there; she'll have your house ready for you. And everything else is set."

"How do you feel about it?" Jim asked.

"I want to go home."

Jim smiled. "And you will. You've come a long way in the last few months. I think you'll do just fine."

"Thank you."

"Is there anything else we might've missed?" Doctor Stilman asked. "About the events before you came here?"

"I told you everything."

"Well, that's all. I think you should get ready. We have you booked on tomorrow's plane. Jim will be taking you up again. Chief Alfred and Eunice will be meeting you in Helena with Olive, then you're on your own."

"Thank you."

"Well, Edward," Doctor Stilman said as he got up and extended a hand, "it's been a pleasure knowing you."

He took the doctor's hand. "Thank you."

Jim opened the door for him. "I'll drop in and see you before I leave for home. I'll be back bright and early to pick you up."

"Early?"

"Six in the morning. Our plane leaves at eight, so we have to check in at seven, which means we leave here at six."

"Yes, Jim." He walked into the hall and didn't stop, nor did he listen. He had stopped and listened enough since he'd arrived years ago. He was going home and there was no need for any stopping and listening.

"What do you think?" Doctor Stilman asked.

"We've done as much as we could."

"I think so. But what do you think about what I've done?"

"I think it was the only thing to do, personally and professionally."

"If I hadn't, it could've been embarrassing later on."

"So, they've agreed not to reopen the case?"

"According to the sergeant, there was never any case to begin with. And there's no one to corroborate Edward's story, therefore he doesn't think there's any need to investigate further. And he agrees that even if all the facts came out, nothing would change. He also took it to his superiors and they came to the same conclusion. So, unless there's a public outcry, which I think is highly unlikely, nothing's going to be done."

"That's good," Jim said. "I think when I agreed to our former plan I was under the gun, so to speak. Coming to conclusions, jumping to conclusions, the whole nine yards."

"Same here. I have to keep reminding myself that I need to get all the facts, review them, then come to some viable and plausible conclusion in a calm, rational manner. Anyhow, how are John and Tina?"

"She's been in chemo and he's just returned from up north. He had to pick up his truck."

"So, I take it they haven't been told yet."

"Not yet," Jim said.

"What are her chances of making a recovery?"

"I don't know. I think fair to middlin'."

"Unsure, eh?"

"She's young. She has that in her favour. She's also in love. That too can work in her favour, but ..."

"But if she makes a full recovery, her world will be torn apart."

"Yes. And if there's anyone who doesn't deserve it, it's them."

"Children should not have to bear the mistakes of their parents."

"Yes," Jim said. "And these two are bearing the mistakes of the same parent, and they don't know it. At least not yet."

Chapter Thirty

On Thursday, September 18, John drove to Calgary, paid some bills and then drove to Edmonton. It had been a little over three weeks since he had last seen Tina and he looked forward to being with her. She had lost her hair, but was optimistic. "I'm going to get better," she said. "I've got too much to live for an' a little cancer is not going to stop me. An' you have to believe that too."

"I have no doubt you will get better," he said. And he didn't. She was young, strong and had the right attitude.

"Now get the hell back to work," she told him. And he did, but he was quiet and put in as much overtime as he could just to keep busy.

He parked his truck, ran across the street to the flower shop, picked up a dozen roses and then went into the hospital. He noticed Sheila was working today. Sheila was a nurse and almost the same age as Tina. "Hi, Sheila," he said.

"John, when did you get in?"

"Just now. She still in the same room?"

"No, they moved her."

"Yeah? What room?"

"They moved her upstairs. Intensive care."

"What? When? Why?"

"Two days ago. I think you should talk to Doctor Markham."

"Can I see her?" he asked.

"Yes. I believe Doctor Markham is up there right now."

Even before the elevator opened completely, John could see Doctor Markham talking to a nurse. The doctor spotted John and began walking toward him. "John, I'm glad you're here."

"What's wrong? Why's she up here?"

Doctor Markham took a deep breath. "I'm not going to blow wind up your kilt," he said. "She's not getting any better. The chemo slowed it down, but it's still progressing."

"What? Why?"

"I've no idea, but it happens all too often."

"So, where is she? An' what else can we do?"

He turned and led John down the hall. "There is another procedure we'd like to try."

"What's that?"

"Bone marrow transplant. You heard about it?"

"I've heard about it."

"Good. It's successful in some of the cases we've treated."

"Some?"

"It's not got the greatest odds, but we are getting better at it."

"So, what are you telling me?" John asked.

Doctor Markham took off his glasses and rubbed the bridge of his nose as if he'd had a long day. "It doesn't look too promising. A bone marrow transplant is our only option right now."

"And how long will that take?"

"I've already contacted the Helena Hospital and they're going to do some tests on her family members to determine if anyone is compatible. Even then, John, it's difficult to know if we'll find a match. Her selection is limited. She has two grand-parents, an aunt, an uncle and seven cousins. I'd be much more comfortable if she had siblings; her chances would be that much better."

"She doesn't."

"I'm aware of that. That's why the community is getting together to test as many people in the hopes we'll find a match. They're going back through her family tree and getting in touch with potential donors. They've gone as far as second and third cousins. Some people, even though they're not related, are volunteering."

"How many?"

He shrugged. "The last time I called Eunice and Olive, they said they had over thirty."

"When will you know?"

"Next week. If we find a match, we'll bring them down and do the procedure the week after that."

"Is there anything else that can be done?" John asked.

"Chemo, drugs and bone marrow are pretty standard. Eunice suggested that you and your sister be tested as well. She said she and her husband and their three children will be tested."

John thought nothing of it. He knew that he and Tina were related, but it was distant: third or fourth cousins. "Nothing else?"

"I'm afraid not." Doctor Markham stopped. "Well, here it is," he said. "John, she's lost whatever weight she gained and her hair is still gone. I've tried not to give her too much medication, but …"

"Is she sleeping?"

"She may be up."

Only when he saw her did he realize she might lose this battle. She had lost weight and her hair was gone, and she was pale, very pale. He remembered seeing *Love Story*, but Ali McGraw, even if she was white, hadn't looked this pale, nor had she lost any weight. She had been fat and healthy right until she died in that movie. *This is not the fucking movies*, he thought. *This is reality*. "What are you lookin' at?" Tina whispered.

He smiled. "Hi, my wife."

"Hey, my husband." He leaned over, put his lips to hers and kissed her lightly. "I'm sorry," she said.

"For what?"

"For not being able to give you a good fuck."

"Me an' my hands are doin' fine for the time being, but it's not the same."

"Pervert. You might get me jealous."

"Well, you'd better hurry an' get better."

"I will. I promised you, didn't I?"

"You did."

"And I've never broken a promise, have I?"

"No, you haven't."

"So there," she said, and then closed her eyes. A few seconds later, she was sleeping again.

Chief Alfred and Eunice were having coffee at the restaurant in the Blue Mountain Hotel. They had driven Abraham and Sarah down to be tested. Despite their age, they had insisted on it. In addition, two vanloads of people had come down to be tested. Ken and Richard were among them, as were David and Verna.

Alfred and Eunice had suggested to their three children that they also be tested, and none of them had questioned their reasoning.

Doctor Everett, who had been in touch with Doctor Markham, had said that Tina's uncle, Robert, and her aunt, Caroline, were the best bet, followed by her cousins. He'd also told them Tina's chances would have been better had she had a brother or a sister. "She don' have none," Abraham had said.

Eunice had looked at Alfred and said nothing. An hour later, they had left the hospital and taken Abraham and Sarah to the store, and then gone for coffee. The few birch trees planted in the community were already turning yellow. "Thank you," Eunice said.

"For what?" Alfred asked.

"For sayin' we should get tested."

"It's only right," he said. "You're her aunt."

"Yeah, but ..."

"I know it's being sneaky, but it's best this way, for now."

"Why these things happen to us?"

"They happen to anyone. That Esau family, they have at leas' one cancer in their family every other year. Nobody knows why."

"I mean with Tina an' John an' Eva, all of us."

"I don't know," Alfred said. "If he had stayed away, none 'a this would a' happen."

"It's not John's fault."

"I know."

"I'm glad you did this," she said. "That way they can get tested without raising suspicions."

"We still have to tell them."

"I know." After a few minutes, Eunice began to cry and Alfred held her hand. "He was my brother," she said. "When we were young, he ..."

She didn't have to finish. He knew what she was talking about. "It's not your fault," he said.

"He was my brother an' I hated him. Maybe that's why I never felt anything for their kids 'til they came back."

"His kids, all of them, don't have to carry his shame for what he did."

She wiped her tears. "Now all we have to do is wait," she said. "If ..."

"What?"

"I was thinking bad thoughts."

"What?" he asked again.

"I was gonna say, what if John or Eva are ..."

"Compatible?"

"Yes, what if they're compatible. Then we have to tell them, but ..."

"But only if she lives."

"Yes, that's what I was thinking."

"And if she doesn't?"

"Then we don't have to say anything."

Chapter Thirty-one

It had been an anxious week for John. He had called his parents to give them an update on Tina, and they'd driven up to be with him and to see if there was anything they could do.

Eunice had called and told him they'd held a special prayer service for Tina at St. John's Anglican Church in the community. They had even taken up a donation so Abraham and Sarah could fly out again to be with her. John had picked them up and brought them to the hospital, where Sarah cried when she saw Tina's condition. Abraham was quieter, more sombre.

Chief Alfred and Eunice had driven down with their daughter, Sarah, and her friend Liz. Olive had decided to stay in Aberdeen and wait for their return, since someone had to look after Edward while Alfred and Eunice were gone. "How's he doing?" John asked Eunice.

"He's doin' good. All we do is check in on him once or twice a day an' see if he needs anything."

"He's fixin' up his ol' Ski-Doo," Alfred said. "It's over ten years ol', but we locked it up after he lef' an' it was still there."

They had all seen Tina and were shocked at her condition. She'd tried to put on her usual brave face, but Sarah, Eunice and

Alfred's daughter, and Liz hadn't taken it well. They'd cried and had to be led from the room.

John and Eva had introduced everyone to their adoptive parents; they seemed out of place, but had stayed and tried to be as helpful as possible.

Doctor Markham was waiting for the test results. "I'll have an answer late this afternoon," he said. "We've had to run the tests twice on each, but three times on the donors that may be more suitable, just to be sure."

It was probably the longest afternoon any of them had ever experienced. They kept looking at the clock in the hall as if willing it to speed up so they could hear good news, or willing it to slow down to keep from hearing something they didn't want to.

John sat by Tina's bed. She was getting weaker. She'd wake up occasionally and squeeze his hand. "John?" She was up again and looking at him. "What are you thinking?"

"I'm thinking of what a lucky man I am to be married to you, to have you as my wife. But more importantly ..."

"That you're my husband?"

"You got that right."

"Fuckin' A."

He smiled, and then they heard a commotion in the hall. Eva came rushing in, smiling and exuberant. "I'm compatible!" she screamed, and then burst out crying. She hugged John, and then leaned over and hugged Tina carefully. "I'm compatible," she whispered.

"Thank you," Tina whispered. "But I'm not deaf an' I'm not really that fragile."

"I'm compatible," she said again.

"So," Doctor Markham said, smiling, "when can we get down to business?"

"Any time you want," Eva said. "The sooner, the better. Me an' Tina have to get back to university."

Doctor Markham looked at Tina and smiled. "I'd say you have a good to fair chance," he said. "The boys upstairs say they've never seen such a close match except with sisters."

"She *is* my third or fourth cousin, once or twice removed," Tina said.

Alfred and Eunice later took a walk. "What if we tell them not to have kids?" Eunice asked.

"It would still be wrong."

"I know. I'm jus' lookin' for excuses."

"I've thought about it," Alfred said. "Edward was right an' this test with Eva proves it. There is no way out."

"I know."

"We have to tell them soon, before they …"

"Before they start havin' sex."

"They've already had sex. They've been married seven months an' seein' each other for over a year before that."

"She's so happy," Eunice said.

"I know, but it's the only way."

"What if they don't believe us?"

"I think we should get in touch with Jim."

"I think he left."

"What about that other doctor, Edward's doctor? I think we should have him there."

"I'll call him tomorrow."

"How do we do it?"

"What you mean?"

"I mean, who do we tell? Do we tell Tina firs', an' then John, or do we tell them together? An' what about Eva? Does she have to know? An' what about our kids? Do we tell them Tina is their firs' cousin? I know we agreed not to tell Abraham an' Sarah, but is that right? To keep it from them?"

"I don't know," Eunice said. "I think we tell Tina firs', an' then John." She took a deep breath, exasperated. "I don't know. I'm tired. Let's sleep on it, think about it."

Chapter Thirty-Two

It was Thursday, October 30, four weeks since the operation, and Tina was getting her strength and colour back, and eating solid food. "I wanna get up an' walk," she said to Doctor Markham. "I'm gettin' itchy."

He laughed. "You'll get your chance, but a few more days is not gonna …"

"Not gonna kill me," she said.

"Yeah, wrong choice of words, I'm afraid. But resting a few more days, or a week, is not going to kill you."

"A week! Boredom is gonna kill me. I wanna get back to university. I wanna go for a walk. I wanna enjoy my husband."

"I'm sure you do. I'm gonna miss you when you leave. But hey, you might decide to come work for me when you're done with university."

"I've had enough of you over the last three months; I don't think I could work for you for more than a day."

He laughed. "You sound like my first ex-wife."

"How many you had?"

"I'm single again, but workin' on my third."

Tina laughed. "Me, I'm on my first, an' after what I've put

312

him through, I think I'll keep him."

"Thanks," John said. He had just returned from work and was feeling better knowing she was getting well.

"I mean it."

"I know."

She took his hand. "I love the hell out of you."

"Me too," he said and kissed her hand.

"Hey, doc. When can I … you know."

"Enjoy your husband?"

"Yeah."

"Well, at least let me get out of the room first." They laughed. "I'd like to tell you right now," he said, "but I'm afraid not for another week or two. You are still very weak." He looked at his watch. "Well, Mrs. Daniel, I've got to make some other patients happy."

"Thanks."

"You're welcome."

"I mean it," she said, tears forming in her eyes.

"I know, Tina. It has been a pleasure. Seeing you get better almost makes up for those who didn't."

"I owe you my life."

"You owe Eva."

"I know, but I also owe you, an' I'll never, ever forget you."

"Mussi cho," he said.

They smiled. "You know that sentence Sarah an' Liz were teaching you?"

"Yes?"

"I wouldn't say that to any woman."

"Why? What's it mean?"

She grinned. "It's not something any women would find appealing. It has to do with your ... you know, your manhood and its size, or lack thereof."

"They told me it was a greeting for a woman you had high hopes of marrying."

Tina laughed. "They're the female Mutt an' Jeff of Aberdeen."

"Who's Mutt an' Jeff?"

"The Cheech an' Chong of Aberdeen."

"Oh. Anyhow, you'd better get some rest. Chief Alfred and Eunice and Olive should be here tomorrow."

"I hope Eunice brings some bannock an' dryfish."

Alfred, Eunice and Olive arrived the next day and were amazed at Tina's recovery. And Eunice *did* bring some of her bannock and other goodies. Tina was in very high spirits and couldn't wait to get back to university and married life. "Geez, you guys," she said, "I'm getting better, you know. I've beaten the big C. You should be happy."

"We are," Eunice said.

"You sure don't look it. You look like you're goin' to a funeral."

"We had a long drive," Alfred said. "We're tired."

They left soon after and went to Doctor Stilman's office. "How is Edward?" he asked.

"He's doin' fine," Eunice said. "He's doin' everything by himself. He'll not need us soon."

"Good. It must be winter up there."

"It is," Alfred said. "Him an' I went huntin' last week."

"Caribou?"

"Yes, we got fifteen. He did good."

"I never knew him before he came here, so I don't know how he was."

"He's back to his old self," Eunice said. "So? How do we tell John and Tina?"

"Well," Doctor Stilman said, "I've talked to Jim, since he had it all down to an art at one time. He says we should tell them exactly as he told you."

"He told me in a boat," Alfred said. "An' I sorta read between the lines an' I think I might 'a dragged it outta him."

"I think we tell John what happened to Edward when he went up to the cabin," Olive said.

"That means he's gonna have to know the details."

"Does he have to know?" Doctor Stilman asked. "I mean, does he have to know that his dad killed his mom, and that Edward killed his dad?"

"I see what you mean," Alfred said. "We can jus' say that his dad, before he died, tol' Edward about Margaret an' Tina."

"Then we tell him," Olive said.

"Then we tell Tina," Eunice said.

"That sounds like a plan," Doctor Stilman said.

John had to admit that Tina had been getting more amorous over the last few days, and had even suggested she give him some head while he did likewise to her. Even if they had wanted to, they could never find the time to be alone. "I guess we'll just have to wait 'til we get to our apartment," she said. "An' then you can jus' cancel all your plans for a whole week 'cause you an' me are gonna reinvent sex."

He looked at the time and got up. "Well, I'd better see what they want. You, in the meantime, should be sleeping, or doing your homework."

"I'd rather give you a hug, a kiss and a good feel."

"You wish."

"Up yours."

"Bite me."

"Hmmm, that sounds even better." He leaned over and kissed her and she copped a feel. "Oooh, is that for me?"

"My one an' only."

"God, I can't wait to feel you inside me." She closed her eyes. "I've missed you."

"I've missed you too, my love and wife, but we've got our whole lives ahead of us."

"Yes, we do," she said. "Yes, we do."

John felt like it was all a dream, or a nightmare. His ordeal, Tina's ordeal, had taken a lot out of him in the last three months and sometimes he lost track of time. What they were telling him was not what he had expected. What they were telling him was not real. It couldn't be. He kept waiting for them to say "April Fool's!" but they didn't.

"What we're saying, John," Doctor Stilman said, "is that your father, William, had a relationship with Margaret, Tina's mom, and they had a child."

"Tina," he said.

"Yes."

He didn't want to believe it; he couldn't. He felt the walls closing in on him; he was hyperventilating.

"Surely you've noticed the resemblance between Eva and Tina. And Eva, her blood being compatible with Tina's, that's what finally gave us the confirmation we needed. We sincerely hoped Edward was wrong, but as we've learned, he is not capable of lying, and there is no other explanation. Believe you me, we have gone through this a hundred times and we cannot find another explanation. Even the dates of the birth and ... well, they match what Edward's told us."

John thought about the many times he and Tina had made love, kissed, held each other, fondled each other, felt each other, given each other pleasure in ways that only lovers could. He loved her like a man loves a woman. He'd married her. They were man and wife, so how could this be? "She's my wife," he said, hoping they'd accept that as proof that this couldn't be true.

"She's your sister," Eunice said. "She's my niece. You're my nephew."

"Half-sister," Alfred said.

"She's your father's daughter," Olive said. "And it's not your fault; it's not her fault; it's nobody's."

"Maybe Edward's wrong," John said, but the more he thought about it, the more it made sense. And he didn't want it to make sense. Yes, Eva did look like Tina. And Tina did look like Eunice and her daughter Sarah. And yes, Eva was the only one whose blood had been compatible with Tina's. "Is that why you asked Eva an' I to get tested?"

"Yes," Eunice said. "We had to."

"Maybe Tina knows who her father is?" But as soon as he said it, John knew she didn't. She'd said so. She'd said she didn't know and that if her father came waltzing back into her life, she wouldn't care.

"John," Alfred said, "we went through everything. We thought of everything, but we didn't find nothing."

"I can't believe this," John said. "I don't believe it. There has to be a mistake. Edward was in here for how long?"

"He's not capable of lying," Doctor Stilman said.

"How do we know?"

"Because we've talked to him over the last year and he isn't. If he doesn't want to tell the truth, he goes inside his head, which is what he did for almost ten years. For ten years, he had to hold this in, until he couldn't do it any longer. He had to talk about it, to tell what he knew."

"John," Eunice said, "I wish this never happened, but it did. An' we have to deal with it."

"Who else knows?"

"Just the four of us, an' Edward an' Jim."

"I love her."

"She's your sister, your half-sister."

"We're married."

"John," Doctor Stilman said. "As much as we didn't want to, we had to tell you. And now that you know as much as we do, do you think you can carry on a relationship knowing what you know?"

John wanted to leave. He wanted to take Tina and leave. He wanted to get out of there and never return. Go someplace where no one knew them. But he'd know. He'd always know. "Why'd you have to tell me?"

"You had to know," Olive said. "You had to."

"She know?"

"No, we haven't told her yet."

"What do we do?"

"You can't … You can't be with her any more," Eunice said. "You can't be married."

"I gotta go," John said, getting up. "I gotta ..." He wanted to say he had to take Tina back to Calgary so she could get back to university. He wanted to say he had to go get his wife so they could spend the rest of their lives together, have kids, have grandkids, have great-grandkids and have a life. He wanted to tell them they were full of shit and nothing but a bunch of fucking liars like his dad. "How do we know he was telling the truth?"

"I've already said that Edward is ..."

"Not him."

"Who?" Alfred asked. John didn't answer. He was glaring at him, and Alfred got the picture. "Oh."

"He was a fuckin' drunk, an' an abuser, an' an asshole, so how do we know he wasn't a fuckin' liar too?"

"Because of Edward," Doctor Stilman said. "Because of the blood tests, because of the resemblance and because of the dates."

"I gotta go."

"Where are you going?" Olive asked. "What you're gonna do?"

"I don't know," John said. "I don't know. I just gotta go."

"John," Alfred said.

John looked at Alfred and truth and dignity came to mind. This man was the Chief of the Blue People, a trusted leader and an honest one.

"I'm sorry," Alfred said. "I'm real sorry, but we got to tell Tina."

"I'll leave."

"What?"

"I'll leave. You don't have to tell her. She doesn't have to know. I'll leave an' never come back."

"She has to know," Olive said. "She has to."

"You can tell her ..."

"Tell her what? Lie to her?"

"She doesn't have to know. She doesn't have to find out."

"She has to."

Finally, it happened. John stood his ground and cursed the gods who spared Tina's life. He screamed at the Old People, who had listened to his prayer and given him back his life. "Why the fuck is this happening to me?"

No one answered. No one had an answer.

"We called your friend," Alfred said.

"Who?"

"Elmer. He's gonna drive you home."

Home, he thought. Home was their apartment. Home was their future. But they didn't have a future. Not any more. No future, no home.

The drive to Calgary was the longest drive John had ever taken. Many times he wanted Elmer to turn around so he could see Tina just one more time, so he could hold her one last time, so he could kiss her, make love ... She was his sister, his half-sister. Even when the fucker that spawned him had died a deserving death, he'd still managed to fuck up his life. John wished William was still alive so that he could kill the fucker over and over again.

"Are you okay?" Elmer asked.

"I'll never be okay."

"Wanna talk?"

"My life is over," John said. "My marriage is a farce, a fuckin' abortion, an abomination."

"What happened?"

"A sick joke."

Elmer drove and remained silent. He knew John well enough to know when to talk and when to shut up. And this was a time to shut up.

"Someday I'll tell you, an' you an' me will laugh. But right now it's no laughing matter. It's a sick world, Elmer. A sick fuckin' world."

They arrived at the apartment late that night, packed up everything Tina owned and put it in Elmer's truck. "What you want me to do with it?" Elmer asked.

"Drive it up to Aberdeen for me. I'll cover gas an' whatnot."

"Not a prob."

"I'm never going back."

"Where? Aberdeen?"

"Yeah, I'm a fuckin' joke, an' a sick one at that."

"What are you going to do right now?"

John shrugged. "I've no idea. Any bars open?"

Elmer checked the time. "Still ten. Lots of time."

"Let's get drunk."

Elmer laughed. "You sure?"

"Fuckin' A."

"Okay. But only to watch you get drunk 'cause I've never seen it before. Gonna be lotsa witches an' goblins out tonight."

"What?"

"It's Halloween. But to me, they all look like witches an' goblin's 'til closin' time."

Tina looked out at the street lights and wondered where John was. He hadn't returned and that was strange. Usually he spent the night holding her hand and sleeping in the chair, unless she felt safe, and then she'd send him over to the apartment hotel where he stayed when he wasn't working. She was tired: tired of the hospital and tired of being sick. She wanted to get back to university. She wanted to get back to their apartment and their lives. These last few months were the hardest on her, ever: physically and mentally. Now, according to Doctor Markham, she was making remarkable progress. But she still didn't believe him when he told her she'd be leaving in another week or two. Somehow, she felt she was in for more bad news, a longer stay. She sighed. That she would accept: a longer stay. She had been lucky, luckier than most. And she hated to admit it, but she was scared; she was still scared. But now she had something to live for and she planned to start living her life right: eating, exercising and *living*. And even though she'd continued with her studies from the hospital bed, she knew she was so far behind that she'd have to drop out and start again next semester. *But what's five months out of my life*, she thought. It would give her time to recuperate and to study on her own so that the semester she'd missed wouldn't be as difficult as the last one. She thought about looking for a part-time job, but she'd have to talk to Doctor Markham and John first.

"Tina?"

She turned to see Chief Alfred and Eunice with Olive and Doctor Stilman. Doctor Markham stood behind them. She smiled, and then frowned; they weren't smiling. Something was wrong. "Yes?" They walked in, and she realized John wasn't with them. "Where's John?"

"We've come to talk to you," Chief Alfred said.

A million things ran through her mind: He was dead; he was in the hospital; he was missing; he'd run off; the cancer was back; she was dying. "About what?"

"I think you should sit," Olive said.

Tina sat in the armchair while Olive, Eunice and Doctor Stilman sat in the other three chairs. Chief Alfred and Doctor Markham leaned on her bed. "What's wrong?" she asked. "Is it my grandparents?"

"Your grandparents are fine," Doctor Stilman said.

"Is it John?" No one said anything. "What happened to him? Is he hurt?"

"No," Olive said. "He's fine."

"Where is he?"

"He's gone back to Calgary."

"Why? For what?"

Doctor Stilman took a deep breath. "Tina, do you know who your father is?"

"What?"

"Do you know who your father is?"

"No." Something told her *they* knew and it wasn't good. "Why?"

"Do you know why Edward was in the institution?"

Edward was there because he found John's parents frozen upriver. So what, she thought. "Yeah."

"John's parents were still alive when Edward found them."

She didn't understand. What did it mean? They were alive when he found them. So how did they die? Did he kill them? And what the hell did this have to do with her and her father? Was Edward her father? Her grandfather had told her that Edward was sweet on her mom. "Edward?"

"What?" Doctor Stilman asked.

"Is Edward my father?" If Edward was her father, then John was her first cousin, and first cousins in Aberdeen was a no-no, but not really. She knew of two couples that were first cousins and living together. They were not married, but they were living together. No one in the community, except their parents, was concerned. It was not as if they were going to have any kids: They were middle aged and had kids from other relationships.

"He's not your father," Alfred said.

Then who? What the hell were they talking about? Who was her father, if not Edward?

"Tina," said Doctor Stilman. "Edward … William, John's father, told Edward something before he died."

What? Did he tell Edward who her father was? That's it. William told Edward who her father was. "What?"

She could tell Doctor Stilman was searching for words. "William told Edward … He told Edward that he'd had a relationship with your mom."

William had had a relationship with her mom? What kind of relationship? Tina thought about it, but she didn't want to. There was only one kind of relationship he could mean: sexual. If William and her mom had a relationship, then that meant … "No. I don't wanna hear this."

"You have to," Olive said. "We already told John."

She looked at the door. "John!" she screamed.

"He's gone."

"Why are you telling me this?" she screamed. "Why?"

"Because you have to know."

"I don't wanna know. I want John. John!"

Olive and Eunice both held her, as if their hugs would draw the pain from her; it didn't. She started crying, sobbing. She felt the needle go into her arm and looked up at Doctor Markham. "I'm sorry," he said.

Chapter Thirty-three

John looked at the almost empty apartment. He had spent the better part of the night packing, cleaning and taking his belongings out to his truck. He had gone out with Elmer, but after an hour had decided to leave. The bar, despite it being a Friday night, was dismal. He kept thinking of Tina, wondering what she was doing. How was she taking it? Did she want to come to him as much as he wanted to go to her? Did she want to leave and never come back? Live a lie? And what would they do? How would they act, knowing what they knew? Could they still continue a relationship like before? Not likely. No matter how much he thought they could, he knew they couldn't. He wanted to do something, anything, but he didn't know what. He didn't have to return to work for another week and he was tired. He had been tired for the last three months, working and taking care of Tina. And he had been looking forward to returning to their apartment and getting on with their lives and ... He couldn't think about it, but he did. He now knew he could never return to her, ever.

He leaned his head back against the sofa and closed his eyes. What would he tell Eva? And his parents. They had to know sooner or later. And what about the divorce? Could they get an annulment eleven months after they had been married?

It was six in the morning. He wanted a cup of coffee, but he had packed their coffee maker and it was in the back of Elmer's truck. Elmer said he'd start out for Aberdeen first thing this morning.

John wondered how much he had in his bank account. He had enough to get down to Nashville, cut a demo, hang out for a few months trying his luck on Music Row and then ... And then what? There were thousands of singers on Music Row, each waiting for their big break into the big time. His chances were one in a million, if at all. But if he didn't at least give it a try, he'd be wondering *what if* for the rest of his life. After a few minutes, he stood, looked around and then left.

The ceiling was white, but out of focus. It was blurry, like a snow-storm. Or like the fog on the highway in the hills outside Aberdeen. It took Tina a few seconds to realize where she was: in the hospital, getting better and getting ready to leave. She couldn't wait to get to their apartment and start their lives again. She had beaten the big C and a healthy lifestyle was all she needed to keep the sucker at bay. And what had they told her last night? Who had been there? Alfred and Eunice and Olive and two doctors. One was Doctor Stilman; the other was Doctor Markham. What was it they'd told her? Something about her and John. About Edward and ... What was it?

"William told Edward ... He told Edward that he'd had a rela-tionship with your mom."

Then it all came back: the discussion, the crying, looking for John to take her out of there and then the needle and peace.

Maybe it hadn't happened. Maybe it had been a dream. She looked around the room, but there was no one there. Where was John? He was usually there. Maybe he was at the apartment hotel. Maybe he was going to come over soon. Maybe they'd release her today and she and John would go home. Home to their apartment in Calgary.

"Tina?"

It was Sheila. "Sheila?"

"Yes."

"Where's everyone?"

"They went home late last night."

"Where's …"

"I've called Doctor Markham. He should be here in a few minutes."

Doctor Markham had been there last night. He and Doctor Stilman and Alfred and Eunice and Olive. It had been like a conspiracy, as if they had been deliberately trying to hurt her. Why? Didn't they like John? Wasn't he one of them? A Blue Indian? He was. His father was William. His mother was Elizabeth. Edward was his uncle. Olive was his aunt. Eunice was his aunt. Alfred was his uncle, by marriage.

"William told Edward … He told Edward that he'd had a relationship with your mom."

"Tina?" Sheila asked. "Are you okay?"

She looked at Sheila. Where had she come from? What was she doing here? "I think I'm …" She slowly started crying. Great big sobs of grief oozed from her body onto the sheets, and then onto the floor. It took a long time for Sheila to wade through that crap. Sheila lifted the needle and slowly stuck it in her arm. The ceiling lowered and the walls closed in on her.

Tina woke up later that afternoon to find ghosts circling her bed. They moved in and out of focus and disappeared into the walls. They talked and looked at her, and sometimes they held her arms so hard that it hurt. She found that if she hid her arms beneath the covers and held them close to her sides, and then closed her eyes, the ghosts would disappear. If she didn't move, they'd be quiet and leave her alone. If she sat and stared into oblivion, they'd sit and look at her and smile. If she did nothing, they were harmless. If she cried, they held her and hit her on the back. If she screamed, they poked her with a needle until she could scream no more.

When John arrived at the ranch, his parents and Eva could see that he was deeply troubled about something. It took him a while to work up the courage to say it, but after a few days he finally told them what he knew.

Eva said nothing. She no longer had a sister-in-law; she had a sister, and she knew her relationship with Tina, if they still had one, would never be the same.

Their mom asked John how he felt now. He shrugged and said he'd live. Then he told them his plans. He was going to drive to Nashville, cut a demo and send it to every radio station that he could. He was also going to sing wherever he could and do whatever it took to get on the Grand Ole Opry. He was going to stay until he made it to the big time, or until he knew he couldn't do it, whichever came first. Given his situation, they didn't discourage him. Perhaps Nashville would be far enough away that he'd have time to think and get Tina out of his system. And who knows, maybe he just might make it. No pain, no gain.

A few days later, John stopped for coffee and gas in Great Falls, Montana, and then continued on to Helena: Helena, Montana. He thought about the first time he'd seen Tina and how he had fallen in love with her from the get-go. She was so beautiful, he'd have done anything to be with her, and he did. Even after only a few days, he knew she was the one he'd spend the rest of his life with. He remembered it was Elmer who had convinced him to spend a few days in Helena. He hadn't wanted to, but some strange, perverted twist of fate had forced him to. He remembered the good times they'd had. They had not been together long enough to have had any bad times, but they'd had them anyway: her illness. That was the bad times, but it had not been of their doing. It had been fate again.

John was tired, but the further he drove, the further away his problems seemed to be, or so he thought. Now that he was alone, he hoped he would have the time to concentrate on making it in Nashville, on making it to the Grand Ole Opry. And if he made it, it was fate. If he didn't, that's just the way it was meant to be. What was fate? Fate was his destiny. It was his providence. It was just the way things were. It was neither good nor particularly bad. It just was.

But still, no matter how far or how fast he drove, he thought of Tina and the great love he had for her. And again he thought about turning around, picking her up and going somewhere, anywhere, where no one knew who they were, what they were … But he, they, knew. She was his sister; his half-sister, but his sister nonetheless. And the love they'd once enjoyed could never be the same.

On a dark stretch of highway somewhere in South Dakota, a truck came to a slow stop and a man stepped out into the cool night air. He walked to the edge of the highway and looked west towards the Black Hills, the home of the Lakota for generations. It was the centre of their world, where creation had begun and where they'd come to converse with their Creator.

And so, in this place sacred to the Lakota, a lone man sank slowly to his knees. No one heard his prayer, and no one heard a response, if there was one. Only he heard his cries, and only he felt his anguish.

Chapter Thirty-four

The building was new. It appeared to be an institution, like a hospital. From the outside, the lights within appeared to be a brilliant white. Inside was a long hall with doors on either side. The doors, like the ceiling and the walls, were white. Behind each door was a room that contained one bed, a dresser, a night table and two chairs.

In one of the rooms, the bed contained a woman in a white smock. At first glance, she appeared to be white; she wasn't. She was an Indian: a pale Indian. Hers was a paleness that could come only from a prolonged lack of exposure to the sun. Her age was indeterminate; the lack of light, her benign expression and the paleness of her skin made it difficult to tell.

She was looking at the city lights through the wire mesh that covered the windows. She also looked at the reflection of the room in the window; it was distorted, bent and twisted out of shape. Occasionally, without moving her head, she would look at the door as if she expected someone to walk in.

An old Indian couple sat in the chairs. They were quiet. The man was dark, solemn, dignified. He was dressed in a flannel shirt, work pants and moose skin slippers. The woman, his wife, looked tired, ancient. She wore a black handkerchief with bright flowers around its edges, and she had on a blue windbreaker and a homemade dress. The woman in the bed could have been their daughter, or granddaughter.

After a few minutes, the old woman began humming, and then singing in her own language, a language as old as time itself. She sang a song written by a former captain of a slave ship more than two hundred years ago.

Amazing grace, how sweet the sound ...

EPILOGUE

✧

The Indian sat alone on the weathered bench atop the riverbank in front of the small northern community and stared at the river and the hills and mountains to the west. He could have been any age between forty and sixty: His hair was completely white; his face, devoid of wrinkles, was dark from the summer sun.

The river spewed forth from the dark and ominous mountains like the tongue of an ancient serpent about to devour everything in its path. Its clear, cold water surged silently past the community on its never-ending journey to the Arctic Ocean. Winter was coming and soon the river would freeze. Even then, the river would run under the ice; nothing could stop it. It provided his people with a means to travel and with the fish they ate during the summer. But it also took from them. How many had they lost? And why? Had they done something wrong?

The hills and mountains were ablaze with colour: reds, oranges and yellows. It was as if the Old People had set fire to the land in anger. Or was it sorrow? Maybe it was shame. Maybe they set fire to the land to hide the secrets and lies their People carried. He had carried one for so long it hurt his head whenever he thought about it. *Why did he give it to me? I didn't want it. Did I do something wrong?*

The Indian looked up and was surprised to see the sun had set and darkness now enveloped the hills and mountains. He wondered how long he had been sitting there. Hours? Days? Years? Forever? He shivered in the coolness of the evening, then took a few steps into the river. He dipped his hand and drank as the water soaked his shoes. He peered into the night, then stepped further into the river.

This was where Margaret used to walk. It was also where she met William: where he took her innocence, and ultimately her life. It was also where he gave her Tina. It was also where she left this world for the Old People.

The Indian was sad and alone. He was always sad and alone. More so now than ever before. He had kept himself in the Dream World for so long he didn't know right from wrong, good from evil. All he knew was truth and honesty.

He shivered in the coolness of the evening. He remembered when he was young, two people had drowned right here in the river. Later, more people fell in; they too had died. Margaret fell in and they buried her and froze her. She had William's baby. She didn't want to, but he gave her one anyways.

He looked for the sun, but it had disappeared over the Blue Mountains hours ago. Where did it go? Did it go to the Gwich'in? Did it go to the Yukon? Maybe it went to Alaska.

He looked at the river and felt its clear, cold water. His father had told him it came from ice in the mountains, where the Old People still lived, and it went into the land of the Slavey, and then into the land of the Gwich'in, and then into the land of the Eskimo. It came from ice, he'd said. And it turned back to ice.

The Indian stepped further into the river and the cold rushed through his groin and into his chest. He took another step and was up to his neck. When he was in the army, they'd had to swim across this creek with all their clothes on. It was hard, but they'd done it. He'd almost drowned, but Floyd had held him up. Maybe if he'd been there, he could have held Margaret up.

He lay back and floated in the water, looking up at the sky. He felt the current turn around and around him. He was tired. Tired of being slow and stupid. Tired of having people look after him. Tired of having people look at him. Tired of being tired. Tired of secrets, lies, truth and honesty.

He felt cold, and then he felt warm, and then cold, and then warm. He wondered if he could swim to the land of the Slavey. Could he make it to the Gwich'in? Maybe he could even swim to the Eskimo. Maybe he could go whaling with them. He had seen shows where they harpooned whales from boats and then pulled them up on shore. Then they skinned the whale and had a big feast and a drum dance. Maybe he could drum dance. He pictured himself dancing while they drummed for him, like he'd seen those Indians at the powwow drumming and dancing. He'd danced at the powwow. That is what Jim had called it: a powwow. He'd gone to the other side where only Indians were and danced. And nobody had looked at him, nobody had laughed at him, nobody had looked at him funny. He'd moved his feet like he had seen others do and still no one had looked at him.

He remembered once, a long time ago, his father and him had looked at the northern lights dancing across the sky. "That's the Old People," his father had said.

"Who are they?" he'd asked in the language. He'd spoken the language then.

"They live up in the mountains."

"What do they do?"

"They look after us."

"Why?"

"They are our People, the People who have gone on before us."

"What are they doing?"

His father had looked up and smiled. "They're dancing, and those are their fires."

He remembered he'd held his hand up to the sky to see if he could feel their warmth, but all he'd felt was cold. "Why is it cold?"

His father had laughed. "They are far away."

"How far?"

"Far."

"Can we go to them?"

"Someday."

"When?"

"Someday, when we have to leave."

"Can we go together?"

"No, your mom and I will go first. We'll make a place for you near the fire."

"Can you make some donuts?"

His father had laughed. "Yes, my son. We'll make donuts. I'll even dance for you."

He looked up at the Old People's fire and smiled. He pictured his father dancing and his mother laughing. He was tired. He closed his eyes.

And still the river flowed as it had since the last ice age. It was alive, but it had no conscience. It was merciless, but never malicious. It was just a river on a never-ending journey.